Death and Tides

It's bloody murder up North! - Book 3

JD Benn

Copyright © 2024 JD Benn

All rights reserved.

ISBN: 9798875562013

This is a work of fiction. Unless otherwise indicated all names, characters, businesses and events portrayed in this book are either the product of the author's imagination or are used in a fictitious manner. Any similarity to real persons, living or dead, or actual events is coincidental and is not intended by the author.

Books by JD Benn:

It's bloody murder up North!

    #1   Touch of the Winer Beast

    #2   Tears of the Falcon

    #3   Death and Tides

For Yvonne, the love of my life

There is a destiny which makes us brothers; none goes his way alone. All that we send into the lives of others comes back into our own.

Edwin Markham

PROLOGUE

8th April - Easter Saturday

The rolling thunder of the cannonade had been magnificent, but it was the massed volleys of musket fire, orchestrated with clockwork precision, that had scythed down the poorly disciplined forces drafted in by supporters of the King. Peering through the lingering smoke, the tang of black powder harsh at the back of his throat, Sir Thomas Fairfax, Captain-General of the New Model Army, gazed out across the battlefield. Fallen bodies clad in the finery of Royalist dandies lay still alongside those in the drab of the infantry, the field dotted with the occasional red coat of a fallen Parliamentarian. It wasn't the end of the war, far from it, but the Battle of Naseby would be forever remembered as a pivotal moment in history, one which would shape the future of England for years to come. After carefully surveying the field, Sir Thomas decided the time had come to claim his victory. It had been a good day and, apart from a few idiots taking selfies amid the carnage, reasonably authentic. He took his mobile phone from the inside pocket of an expensively tailored uniform and rang his opposite number, King Charles the First.

"Hiya Gary, that's another one to me mate!" The triumphant greeting made as soon as his call was answered. Over recent years, and always on opposite sides, the two had waged war on many occasions. From the Battle of Edgehill in 1642, right up until the Battle of Worcester in 1651, they had researched and restaged all of the major conflicts of the English Civil War. As widowers, and neither being in any hurry to go home to an empty house, they'd got into the habit of going out for a meal and a couple of drinks after a re-enactment. This time it was retired Detective Chief Inspector Andy Bithell's turn to pick the pub and King Charles' turn to drive. "Are you ready to make your escape yet?"

"Hello Andy, did you see Prince bloody Rupert of the Rhine flashing his new i-phone around out there on the field? Honestly, some of these arseholes just don't, or won't, take it seriously!"

"Never mind, you know you wouldn't enjoy it half as much if there was nothing to moan about afterwards." Since taking early retirement from the police force almost ten years earlier, researching, organising and taking part in Civil War re-enactments had become a big part of Andy Bithell's life, even more so since his wife had passed away. As an ex senior officer, he liked to be in charge, always had, and his team, his wife and the boy had all learned to live with that. Nowadays though, if he wanted to be in control of anything more exciting than choosing what to have for dinner, it meant that he needed to be around other people. Gary was one of the few men whose company he actually valued, the grumpy old sod was very nearly as critical of historical inaccuracy, particularly by people who should know better, as he was himself.

"True enough. I'll give the order to sound the retreat. Just give me ten minutes or so and I'll meet you back at the tent."

"Cheers mate, see you shortly." Andy ended the call and slipped the phone back into his pocket. A quick change in the Chorley and Euxton Civil War Society marquee, hopefully before the masses made their way back from the battlefield, and they'd be ready to go. The society were doing the Battle of Preston on the Bank Holiday so there was no need to pack everything away. He was aware that quite a few of the re-enactors, or living historians as they now preferred to call themselves, were camping on site for the weekend. As such, he reckoned that the barbeques would be lit and the place awash with beer in next to no time. Slipping off his heavily embroidered topcoat he stepped through the flapping canvas door of the marquee and, once his eyes had adjusted to the gloom of the interior, saw that someone was already inside. Andy nodded a greeting to the redcoat who was walking towards the door, lobster tail helmet in one hand, weapon in the other. He was about to explain that it was too late to rejoin the action on the battlefield when his words were quite literally cut off as the redcoat's sword flicked up to waist height and the long blade was plunged deep into his stomach. The force behind the blow was sufficient to cause the pointed tip to make a tent of the rapidly expanding red patch at the back of his long linen shirt. Sinking to his knees, shock protected him for a brief moment, then pain flared with a searing vengeance as the cold steel was roughly tugged and dragged from his body, opening up the already huge gash in his belly. While his hands worked in vain to try and hold the gaping wound closed, Andy's brain struggled to comprehend what had just happened. Through the tears that sprang from his eyes, he could do little more than take in the finer details of the weapon that was now being raised high above his right shoulder, poised to strike a killing blow. As the blade descended in a powerful arc, Andy Bithell's final, puzzled thought was that this just wasn't right at all, the Cuirassier trooper's sword was completely the wrong weapon for a 17th century English redcoat to be carrying.

Chapter One

"Welcome back lass, so how was the honeymoon then?" Detective Inspector Joe Penswick asked as his newly married colleague, Detective Sergeant Cathy Bell, got into the car. Strictly speaking she wasn't due back at work until the following morning but, when the late summons had come through from the Chief Super's office, Joe had decided to give her a quick call and pick her up on the way to the scene. Having worked together for several years he knew that she'd want to be in at the start of a new investigation. "You and Augusta still speaking?"

"Ah Joe, Iceland was amazing, you and Val have got to go, you'd both love it, you too Autumn." Cathy twisted in her seat to face the third member of their small team, Detective Constable Autumn Jackson. "It turns out that Gus is a bit of an adventure nut with a thing for volcanoes, she'd kept that quiet! Anyway, she'd gone and booked for us to be lowered 400 feet down into an empty magma chamber. I mean, how cool is that? We went hiking on the Vatnajokull glacier, crampons, ice axes, the works! We even went snowmobiling on the same volcano that stopped all the flights back in 2010. It's an awesome place, we're already planning our next trip."

"Sounds amazing, you must be exhausted," Autumn smiled at her friend. "When did you get back?"

"We finally arrived home about three or four hours ago, we were stuck in queues at Manchester for ages. I've had to leave

Gus unpacking and sorting out the laundry, so it's not all bad. Anyway, enough about me, how are things going with you and the lovely Tom, anything to report?" Cathy was referring to Detective Inspector Tom Barron who'd been attached to the team for two recent investigations and had been badly injured in the last one, less than six months ago. Although he and Autumn had grown closer during his recuperation and now spent a lot of their free time together, at the very beginning he'd confided to her that the loss of his wife and children had left him unsure that he would ever be ready to fully commit to another relationship.

"Let's just say that we're working on it," Autumn giggled and blushed.

"Okay, that's enough, man present, time to change the subject!" Joe blustered loudly from the driver's seat. "Can we focus on work, that is why we're here after all?"

"Sorry Boss," Autumn replied, laughing again as Cathy raised a quizzical eyebrow before turning back in her seat to face forwards.

"Okay DI Spoilsport, what've we got?"

"Well, I'm glad you asked me that DS Bell, now that I've finally got your full attention. It's a bit of an odd one, and it's fallen to us courtesy of Iron Annie." Joe and the two female officers had been retained by Chief Superintendent 'Iron Annie' Atkinson as an independent investigative unit. For reasons known only to herself, and presumably the Chief Constable, she had what she referred to as a 'special remit' within the Lancashire Constabulary.

Although never fully explained, it was apparently something that allowed her to cherry pick any cases that she deemed to have a special significance or be outside the usual range of insult and injury that people managed to inflict on one another.

"They always seem to be 'odd ones' when we get brought in. What do we know?"

"Not a huge amount," Joe said as he accelerated to join the M6 at the Tickled Trout roundabout, "but it seems that King Charles the First went arse over tit in a pool of blood and gore when he went to pick up the top man in Cromwell's army, just after the Battle of Naseby."

"We're good," Cathy offered after taking a moment to work through what she'd just been told, "but there's a chance that even we may struggle a little with this one. I was never big on history but that must be what, six or seven hundred years ago?"

"Middle of the 17th century," Autumn corrected, "so nearer to four hundred. Still not great for gathering any forensics though."

"Actually, you're both wrong. It was about an hour and a half ago!" As a man who rarely had the pleasure of the last word, at work or at home, Joe took his opportunities where he found them. His usually chatty colleagues' puzzled silence making it all the sweeter.

Not much more than ten minutes later they had left the motorway behind and were being directed on to Worden Lane by one of the many officers clad in Lancashire Constabulary hi-vis jackets. The majority of her colleagues were busy marshalling traffic on the approach road to Worden Park, which mostly seemed to involve turning round the various media vehicles that were attempting to either gain access or park up. Other officers were doing their best to disperse a growing crowd of gawpers, ghouls and smartphone heroes, redirecting them away from the park entrance. All in all, it was pretty clear that word of 'an incident' had travelled fast, hopefully the grisly details had not. Joe slowed the car to a crawl as they approached a temporary barrier that had been erected across the road, then stopped and opened the driver's window, holding up his warrant card for inspection.

"Ah'reet cock?" The uniformed constable in charge of managing access to the park smiled a greeting and waved away Joe's proffered ID as he retracted the tape barrier from across the pillared gateway. "There ain't a copper for miles who dunt know who you three are. Must be a bad 'un if you lot 'ave bin brought in!" It was fair to say that the team had unfortunately gained a certain notoriety since the bloody conclusion to their most recent major case, one that could have so easily have ended very differently. The media coverage, no doubt ably assisted by the HQ rumour mill, had elevated them from reluctant participants who were simply getting on with the job in hand, to heroes touted as Lancashire's answer to the Marvel Avengers. They were all hoping things would quieten down and get back to normal but, as yet, there was little sign of that happening.

"Which way?" Joe asked as he slipped the car into gear, ready to move forwards.

"Keep left squire, top car park's still bein' cleared," the beaming officer bent lower to have one last look at the three detectives, definitely something to tell his mates about. "Forensics van an' t' Chief Super are already up there."

Joe thanked the man and raised his window as they drove slowly into the park, conscious of the first faint prickings of concern. While it was by no means unusual for the Chief Super to visit a potential crime scene, for her to drop everything and rush straight there ahead of her own team was pretty much unheard of. Something about this one was clearly different, and anything capable of unsettling Iron Annie….

After a couple of hundred yards the long, log-barriered car park came into view, a solitary and harassed looking PC controlling entry and ensuring that none of the parked vehicles could leave until the occupants' identities and contact details had been confirmed. The Chief Super's Jaguar was parked at the top end next to a liveried transit van belonging to the Forensic Investigation Team. Beyond the car park, blue and white 'Police' barrier tape had been erected around a medium sized marquee leaving a wide perimeter around each side. Further off to the left, close to where at least thirty smaller tents and several gazebos had been erected, a handful of officers in hi-vis were attempting to corral a group of maybe sixty individuals. Everyone appeared to be fairly amenable and prepared to cooperate, which was fortunate as they also appeared to be wearing fancy dress and carrying a fearsome array of weapons. It was still quite pleasant in the last of the afternoon sunshine, but this early in the year it could change quickly and Joe wondered just how long the good mood of the re-enactors would last.

"Oh my God," Cathy commented, "what the hell is going on here?"

"Well, either we've slipped back in time by several hundred years," Autumn replied, "or this is a Civil War re-enactment. I'm not sure which is worse."

"People actually do this for fun?" Joe was eyeing up what was, even at a distance, an impressive selection of weaponry. "They've got muskets, swords, pikes and, unless I'm very much mistaken, they've got two cannons. I mean…. what could possibly go wrong?"

"I thought pikes were fish." Cathy commented. "What do they do, fire them out of the cannons or something?"

"How did you ever get to be a sergeant?" Autumn chided her colleague. "Pikes are the really long spears that were used to stab people, hopefully before they could get close enough to chop bits off you with their sword."

"I know this may be difficult to believe, Constable Jackson," Cathy made a point of emphasising her friend's lower rank, "particularly for one so young, but medieval warfare, with or without the fish, didn't come up in the sergeant's exam. Anyway, I still think my way's more fun, although maybe not so much if you happen to be a pike!"

Joe ignored the banter, knowing it was just a way of preparing for whatever lay in wait for them. He parked in the nearest available space then they walked across to where the Chief Super was stood at the rear of the Forensics vehicle, removing the disposable coveralls and overshoes that she'd been wearing, presumably while being shown inside the marquee.

"Good afternoon, Ma'am," Joe announced their presence while they were still several yards away, not wishing to startle his boss while her back was turned.

"Afternoon Joe, Cathy, Autumn." Never one to worry unduly about rank, Iron Annie greeted her team as friends, not just fellow officers. As far as she was concerned, coppers were coppers and titles were only important for pay scales and disciplinaries. However, despite the genuine warmth of her greeting, Joe couldn't fail to notice that she seemed distracted, disturbed even, which was totally out of character. The faint prickings of concern he'd experienced a few minutes earlier were now ramping up several notches at a time.

"Ma'am, is there something….?" Unsure of quite what it was that he was asking, Joe let the question hang, unfinished. The Chief Super was first to break eye contact, then they both looked across to where a white clad figure had just emerged from the marquee and was walking towards them.

"I'll let John fill you in on all the details but, in a nutshell, the victim is retired Detective Chief Inspector Andy Bithell. He has sustained a huge wound to the abdomen, most likely from a long and pointed blade, and then his head was roughly hacked off." Iron Annie paused for a moment and took in a deep breath before continuing. "And yes Joe, there is…. something. I will explain, but first I need to give this some serious thought. Shall we say my office, tomorrow morning, eight o'clock?"

"Yes Ma'am, of course." Joe nodded, noticing the slight hesitation before she continued.

"I never liked Andy Bithell, Joe. He and his crew were 'old school' in the worst possible way. There were lots of rumours about them but nothing was ever proven. After he retired, which must be at least eight or ten years ago, he wrote a book about his experiences, or more likely someone wrote it for him. They peddled it as an insider 'true crime story', it was supposed to be a factual account of his most famous case." The expression on her face made her opinion only too clear. "But, whatever else he did, and by all accounts he didn't have many boundaries, he didn't deserve what happened in there." After a final glance at the marquee, and a nod to Cathy and Autumn, the Chief Super went back to her car, reversed out of the parking space and was gone in a matter of moments.

"Is it just me, or was that really odd?" Cathy asked.

"No, it weren't just you lass, she was rattled. She said the victim was a retired DCI, and she clearly knew him well enough to take a dislike to him, but her reaction was more like she was suddenly carrying all the worries of the world." Joe's thoughts were interrupted by the approaching figure who, now that the hood and face mask had been removed, they could see was John, the new Head of the Forensic Investigation Team.

"Afternoon Joe, ladies. Happy Easter!" he grinned, "Not quite as enjoyable an occasion as last time we met up I'm afraid." John and his wife, along with Helen the previous Head of FIT, had been guests at Cathy and Augusta's wedding two weeks previously. "I'm surprised to see you back at work so soon Cathy, I thought you'd still be honeymooning."

"Flew back this morning, and you know what a hard-arse my boss is. Came round to the house, banging on the front door, then dragged me straight out here. Bank Holiday weekend and all!"

"I'm choosing to ignore that slanderous and somewhat insubordinate comment on the assumption that you must be suffering from jetlag." Joe was smiling broadly as John passed him an extra-large Tyvek suit and a set of overshoes from the storage boxes in the back of the van.

"If you think that was insubordinate, just wait 'til we start talking about your antics on the dance floor. Poor Gus is still limping!" Cathy joked. Having lost both parents in her early twenties, and with no other close family, she had rather nervously asked Joe if he'd be prepared to give her away. They'd been friends for several years and it was something he was only too happy to do, every bit as proud as if she'd been one of his own daughters. "Helen didn't change her mind at the last minute then?"

"No, once she'd made her mind up, that was it. She said she might take on some occasional consultancy work but...," John shook his head, "I don't know. I think she'd just had enough. I know she wanted to spend some time travelling, and to see more of her grandchildren, she certainly earned it."

Cathy, Joe and Autumn all nodded their agreement. The banter, the brief moments of laughter between friends, helped to take the edge off the darker aspects of the professions they had chosen. Dealing with the bloody aftermath, when rage, love, hate or simple greed spiralled out of control, was not work for the fainthearted. Even those who believed themselves to be strong enough still paid a price, and each had to find a way of coping with the thoughts and memories that came unbidden and without warning. While the three of them donned their protective clothing, John quickly outlined what they should expect to find when they entered the marquee and warned that the body was still in place as they were waiting for the Coroner's Officer to arrive. Once they were fully suited, booted, gloved and masked, they crossed to an access point in the tape barrier where another uniformed officer made a note of their names and time of entry. They waited while John checked with his team to ensure that they'd finished photographing and documenting the scene then, after issuing a final warning to closely follow his steps and tread only on the transparent stepping plates, he pulled back the canvas door and they went inside.

The rusty, metallic smell of blood was almost overwhelming from the second they entered the marquee. It took a moment or two for their eyes to adjust to the harsh brightness of the scene of crime lighting, but it soon became abundantly clear where the smell was emanating from. A large patch of the grassy floor was awash with pooled blood and there were splashes of darkening red high on the canvas walls and across the stacked storage boxes.

"He must still have been alive when he was decapitated," Autumn commented, "for the blood to spurt like that, I mean."

"Yeah, the post-mortem examination will confirm it, but I think you're right." John led the way along one side wall of the marquee which gave them an unobstructed view of the body, which appeared to have fallen onto one side and, a couple of feet away, the severed head.

"Did you find anything that could have been the murder weapon?" Joe asked.

"No, there's nothing in here that could have inflicted those wounds. The killer must have taken it, although with so many replica weapons on show it's unlikely that anyone would have noticed."

"Whoever killed him must have been covered in blood," Cathy added.

"Sorry, I should have mentioned that we found a bloodstained uniform coat, breeches and a helmet over by the storage boxes, they've already been bagged up for testing back in the lab. There are still some spare costumes, uniforms, I don't really know what to call them, in the storage boxes."

"So, it's likely that the killer changed his clothes, or her clothes, but there's no way they could have got properly cleaned up." Joe looked thoughtful for a moment. "Could a woman have done this, I wouldn't have thought a sword was a woman's weapon?"

"We can't rule it out," Autumn said, "didn't you and Val watch Game of Thrones?"

"I may have caught the odd episode," Joe replied. "Unfortunately, much like on the telly, there's so much fake blood sloshing about on the battlefield here that it's unlikely anyone would have noticed, even if someone was covered in the stuff." He took a last look around the marquee, if there was anything to be found here he was confident that John and the Forensics technicians would find it. "Come on then you two, it's time we went and had a word with King Charles the First."

Gary Cookson couldn't have looked less regal if he'd tried. A big, balding man in his early sixties, he was sat in the back of an ambulance, draped in a blanket and wearing nothing but his underpants, everything else had been bagged up for testing. His hands had been cleaned, but there were still traces of blood evident on the back of his head and neck. Someone had managed to find a cup of tea for him and, to his credit, he was trying hard to put on a brave front, something that Joe knew wouldn't last when the bravado faded and he was faced by the stark reality of the situation. Not wishing to overwhelm the man with their presence, Joe and Cathy had left Autumn to liaise with the uniformed officers who had already begun to take the names and contact details of the still 'in-character' re-enactors, most of whom had no idea what had happened in the tent, other than there had been an incident of some kind or other. They'd agreed that after Joe made the introductions, Cathy would lead the questions. The softer approach being more appropriate at this stage as they didn't know how long the man would hold up for.

"To start off with Gary, could you just... lead us through events immediately prior to you entering the marquee?" Cathy had been on the verge of saying 'run us through' but stopped herself just in time. Given that his friend had just been 'run through' with a sword, it would have been a rather unfortunate turn of phrase.

"Sure, but it's only going to be the same as I told the other officers. A large brandy might help steady the nerves though." He looked round hopefully, but the gesture was clearly more for effect than anything else. "We'd had the battle, everything went as planned, apart from Prince bloody Rupert, that is."

"Sorry, what happened with Prince Rupert?" Cathy asked.

"Flashing a sodding great mobile phone around on a seventeenth century battlefield, I ask you, really? I'm sure he was taking selfies, what an arse!"

"Okay, maybe that's something we'll come back to. What happened after that?"

"Andy rang me, I agreed to sound the retreat and wrap things up. We usually have a couple of pints and a bite to eat afterwards so we wanted to get a flier, before the marquee filled up. I dashed over there, opened the flap and stepped inside. At first I thought..." Gary paused, his shoulders sagged, and the remaining colour left his face.

"What was it that you thought Gary?" Cathy spoke softly, knowing that she was asking the man before her to relive a nightmare.

"As soon as I stepped inside my feet slipped out from under me and I went skidding across the floor on my arse. Everything was wet, then I saw it was red." Gary paused again, his eyes now blurry with tears. "I thought, I clearly remember thinking, that some daft sod had spilled the canisters of fake blood. But there was so much, and then the smell…"

"When did you realise what had…" Cathy's final question was cut short as the man began to speak.

"Where I was lying, there was something under my right arm," his words were coming slowly now, tears were tracing lines down his cheeks, "and when I looked, it was Andy. No, no, that's wrong, it wasn't Andy, it was just his head."

Chapter Two

Sophie: 1996

Since dropping out of sixth form college part way through her final year, leaving her home and friends behind, Sophie had been a mess. What's more, she'd be the first to admit it, to herself and to anyone else who may care to listen. In fact, if she was completely honest about it, she'd been going downhill ever since everything that she'd once taken for granted had been snatched away, the day her mum died. The brain haemorrhage that claimed her mother, without warning or time to prepare her only child, had occurred while she was at work and Sophie was at school. She remembered being sent to the Headteacher's office and being surprised to see her father waiting for her there, the sight of his tears, his utter desolation, making any further explanation unnecessary. They'd always been happy, Sophie had always known that her mother was the stronger of her parents, her dad was more of a follower, but that was okay. It had worked just fine for them, no major upsets or problems to mar her childhood, just as things should be, right up until the day the backbone had been torn from their little family.

By the time Sophie was fifteen, the 'go with the flow' attitude to life that her father still somehow maintained was getting her down. What she'd once thought of as an easy-going charm, she now saw as weakness. That she loved him dearly was never in question, he was in so many ways a perfect father, but being the focus of his growing neediness was beginning to stifle her. She didn't want to be his only friend and confidant, she didn't want to be his rock, dry his tears and share his pain, she had enough of her own, thank you very much! Above all, she just wanted him to stand on his own two feet and be her dad.

The big surprise came one Friday evening, she remembered that it had been around three months after her sixteenth birthday and, as had become her habit, she'd stayed on late at college, chatting with friends and delaying the time when she'd have to go back to the house. If she stayed out too late he'd start calling her mobile, 'just making sure you're okay luv', or, 'do you need a lift? I can come and pick you up if you want'. She hated him for it and at the same time she loved him for it, and felt guilty about both. When Sophie had arrived home that particular evening, curious as to why she hadn't yet received 'the call', all became clear when she walked into the lounge. There was a woman sat on the settee next to her father, and two small children, a boy and a girl, maybe five or six years old, watching cartoons on television.

"Hello luv." Her father jumped to his feet, she could tell immediately that he was nervous, guilty almost. "We've been waiting for you, there's someone, well, some people, that I'd like you to meet. They're going to be staying with us." As she turned to face the three strangers who had just been thrust into her life, the introductions that her father was attempting to make were drowned out by a flood of competing emotions. Taken completely by surprise, her dad had never mentioned a single word about meeting someone else, let alone moving them in, Sophie was completely and utterly overwhelmed. An unexpectedly fierce loyalty to her dead mother rose up, momentarily pushed back by the thought that her father deserved to be happy, then reignited by the knowledge that it had only been eighteen months, how long was too soon, when had he first betrayed her memory? An initial relief that she would no longer have to be strong for him, clashed with how easily he'd moved on from that part of their relationship, what was coming next? Love it or hate it, as a single child she'd always been the focus of her father's attention, would she now be pushed out by his newly acquired ready-made family, had he made a choice? It was simply too much to deal with, she turned and fled but still noticed that it was the first time she'd heard a faint trace of anger, or was it regret, in her father's voice as he shouted after her. That night, staying over at a friend's house, was the first time Sophie had ever been drunk. Never having liked the taste of her father's beer or whisky, the vodka and white wine sneaked from her friend's parents' well-stocked kitchen cabinet had come as a revelation. She hadn't been falling about or sickly drunk, just tipsy enough to take the edge off her worries and paint the world in brighter colours. The drinking became a regular thing, but she was always careful that it was never too much, and 'never on a school night'. She'd never been a smoker, hated the smell of it but, as she began to mix with a different crowd of people, soon found that she enjoyed the happy, silly, smiley atmosphere of smoking weed with her new friends. She reassured herself that so long as she kept it light, and didn't stray onto anything harder, she'd be fine.

A year passed, life went on, Teresa and her two children had all but taken over the house and, even though her dad no longer seemed smitten, she knew that he'd never do anything about it. Sophie did her best to avoid any contact with Teresa, but the woman went out of her way to find fault and cause arguments, constantly picking and criticising, trying to drive a wedge between Sophie and her father.

The final straw came when 'the woman', by this time Sophie wouldn't use her name on principle, announced that her son and daughter were too old to be sleeping in the same bedroom and that Natalie would have to move into Sophie's room, which was big enough for the two girls to share. She didn't particularly mind the kids, it wasn't their fault that their mother was a manipulative bitch, and she knew it was just another power play by the woman who she was convinced had deliberately targeted her father and now dominated their lives. But this was a step too far, her bedroom was her refuge, it was where she listened to music, watched TV, studied for her A levels, kept in touch with friends and events on social media, day-dreamed, in fact spent almost all of her time when she was at home. She couldn't imagine having her life turned upside down by having to share with a seven-year-old child. Waiting until 'the woman' had gone shopping, so she could speak to her father without the bitch queen from hell being present, Sophie drew a shaky line in the sand.

"Dad, I'm not sharing a room, okay? In another six months I'll be off to uni and Natalie can have the room, I don't care, but right now it's not happening. I'll move out if I have to, I mean it."

"It's okay luv, I get it, I understand." He leaned in and gave her a cuddle, something he'd not done for a while. "I'll have a word with Teresa, don't worry, it'll be fine, I promise." And it was fine, for three whole days. Sophie returned home from college the following Thursday evening, went straight up to her room in order to avoid any contact with 'the woman', and found all her belongings in a heap at one side of the room. Another bed, complete with a unicorn duvet cover and a legion of cuddly animals, was now taking pride of place beneath the window. She turned to see that her father had followed her up the stairs.

"I'm sorry luv," he said quietly, "we talked about it and Teresa thought, we agreed, that it's for the best, now that Natalie and Tim are getting a bit older. Like you said, it's only a few months before you'll be off to uni." Sophie didn't speak right away, not trusting herself to hold in check words that she would never be able to take back. When he put a hand on her shoulder she turned to face him and forced a smile.

"It's okay dad, I get it, I understand." She leaned in and gave him a cuddle as she echoed his words from a few days earlier. "It'll be fine, I promise." Later, when he'd gone back downstairs, Sophie sorted through her clothes and put everything she thought she might need into the big rucksack that had been purchased for a school camping trip when she was thirteen. She added her i-pad, chargers, some make-up and a few pieces of jewellery. The final, and most treasured, item to be packed was a framed photograph of her mother, taken on her wedding day.

With almost £150 in cash, and just over £3,000 in her 'uni fund', the savings account her parents had set up for her years ago, she was confident that she would manage just fine until such time as she could find a job. With no real plan in mind as to where she would go, or even where she would sleep that night, Sophie slipped silently out of the house. Ducking down low to avoid being silhouetted against the lounge window, she could hear the family she had once been a part of shouting out answers and laughing together as they watched Richard Osman's House of Games on television.

Chapter Three

It was a few minutes before seven-thirty when Joe pulled into the car park of the Lancashire Constabulary HQ in Hutton. He wasn't at all surprised to see that the Chief Super's Jaguar was already there and, parked next to it, the dark blue BMW X5 belonging to DCI Yvie Gray. Despite their late finish the previous evening, and after dropping Autumn back in Clitheroe to collect her car, Joe and Cathy had called in at Yvie's house in Chipping. They'd been regular visitors during her maternity leave and only a couple of months earlier both had attended the christening of Yvie and James' son, but this wasn't a social visit. While James put young Conor to bed, Joe had spoken of his concerns over Iron Annie's reaction to the murder of retired DCI Andy Bithell. Cathy had voiced the same concerns, adding that she'd never seen the Chief Super preoccupied, or troubled, to such an extent.

When James came back downstairs, Conor's gentle snoring reassuringly loud and clear on the baby monitor, Joe and Cathy had already left. He went into the kitchen and poured them both a glass of Malbec, since Conor had been born they only allowed themselves a single glass each evening, something to be savoured.

"So, when are you going back?" he asked, watching as she took a sip of the dark red wine.

"Would you mind if I did? Just for a few days, until we're sure that Anne is okay."

"Yvie, I'm amazed that you've stayed off work as long as you have, I was fully expecting you to go back months ago."

"Are you sure, really?"

"Really. I can work round His Nibs, it won't be a problem, in fact I quite like the idea of being a 'stay at home' dad. We'll be fine."

"Thank you. I knew there was a reason I liked you, apart from the cooking that is!"

Joe signed in at Reception, noting that for once there was no sign of Bill the seemingly ever-present desk sergeant, then took the stairs up to the Chief Super's floor. The previous evening they'd been unable to track down Bithell's nominated next-of-kin, his son and only surviving family member, so this morning he'd left Cathy and Autumn in the Clitheroe office with the task of finding the young man. Although it was still early, there were already a few staff in on the top floor corridor and somehow he managed to ignore the now annoyingly predictable 'Rambo' comments without losing his temper. He was about to knock on her office door when he heard the Chief Super raise her voice and say, 'No Yvie. You've got a child, you take your full entitlement.' He knocked and entered without waiting for a reply, finding both women stood up, facing each other across the small coffee table. The Chief Super turned and launched straight into him.

"I suppose you've got something to do with this?"

"Sorry Ma'am, I don't know what you're talking about."

"I think you bloody well do Joe Penswick! DCI Gray back here five minutes after giving birth."

"It's actually closer to seven and a half months." Yvie corrected her boss, quietly.

"No, sorry Ma'am, I'm here because you said there was, 'something'," Joe fashioned air quotes with his fingers, "and that you would explain this morning."

"You're a terrible liar, you know that?"

"Yes Ma'am." Joe was staring through the window at a point on the far horizon.

"Good, I'm glad that somebody can finally agree with something that I've said this morning!" The Chief Super slowly shook her head before raising both arms in a gesture of defeat. "Okay, I think you should know that Yvie has already thrown you under the bus and told me that you and Cathy had, and I quote, 'some concerns over my reaction', yesterday."

"Yes Ma'am." As far as Joe was concerned, the point on the far horizon had just become even more interesting.

"I will admit to being a little distracted, maybe not my usual sunny and cheerful self. I first met Bithell not long after I was promoted to DI, and the manner of his death dredged up some pretty dark memories that go back over twenty years. Memories of events that I thought, hoped, were well and truly buried in the past. Joe, the reason that I asked you to take on the case, rather than let the Chorley CID team pick it up, is that I've a very strong feeling that this one might be personal."

"Personal to who, Ma'am?

"Me, and a few others. It's a long story, so I suggest we all get a coffee before I start. If I'm right, if it is what I think, then a ghost from the past has returned, and with a vengeance." As suggested, and without any further questions, Yvie poured coffee from the catering size pot her boss had prepared earlier. Joe ferried cups across to the small coffee table and then they both sat, notebooks at the ready, waiting for Iron Annie to begin.

"Although I was brought up not too far from here, I began my police career with the Devon and Cornwall force. I'd been at university in Plymouth, had a decent but boring job, and had already met the man who I thought I'd be spending the rest of my life with. As it happened, the romance fizzled out not much more than six months after we'd moved in together. By which time I'd decided that I wanted to change career paths and become a police officer. I was accepted onto a fast-track scheme for graduates and, when I took up my first post in St. Austell, I knew that I'd made the right decision. For the next year or two I moved around the area quite a lot, kept my head down and worked hard, passed all the exams and eventually got a promotion to Detective Inspector, working out of Exmouth." She paused for a moment and looked at both of her colleagues. "Look, I'm sorry to bore you with all the details but I want you to understand how and why certain things happened."

"Not at all, Ma'am," Yvie was fascinated. Outside work she knew the Chief Super as Anne, a friend, while at work she would always be Ma'am or Boss, anything else was unthinkable. To the best of her knowledge, no one had ever called her Iron Annie to her face, although Yvie suspected that she quite enjoyed the well-deserved nickname. "Any attempt I've ever made to get personal information out of you has been like trying to draw blood from a stone. You carry on!"

"So, one day, out of the blue, I was called into the Assistant Chief Constable's Office. He had another chap in there with him who he didn't introduce by name but I later found out was Head of Internal Affairs, although they didn't call it that back then, for West Midlands. The two of them grilled me on my training, my work experience, all sorts of things, for the best part of an hour. I honestly thought that I was under investigation for something."

"Why West Midlands IA when you were Devon and Cornwall?" Joe asked.

"That's where it became interesting. They told me that for some time there had been concerns about one particular CID team, but they didn't tell me where, at least not right away. The team apparently got great results, a high collar rate and convictions to match. If anything, they were possibly too successful, and the rumours about how they managed it included the use of some highly questionable methods and cooperation with known criminals. They asked me what I thought should be done."

"I would have thought that if there were any concerns over criminal activity it would have been a job for the relevant force's Internal Affairs or Internal Investigation team, possibly an initial covert investigation." Yvie offered, although as they were now talking of events that had taken place long before she'd joined the police herself, she wasn't entirely sure of procedure at that time.

"That's pretty much what I said. Then they told me that it was a team working out of West Lancashire, headed up by Detective Chief Inspector Andy Bithell."

"Yesterday's victim. I still don't understand, why were West Midlands IA, and an ACC from Devon and Cornwall, asking you about potentially bent coppers in Lancashire?"

"I asked the exact same question Joe. All the West Midlands chap would say was that they had reason to believe that due to some very high-level contacts, and not just in the police, the team were virtually untouchable by any investigation that Lancashire had an involvement in."

"They wanted you to go undercover and investigate a DCI from another Force?" Yvie guessed, intrigued.

"Yes. One of Bithell's DIs had just gone off on long term sick, he was having treatment for colon cancer. West Midlands IA must have been in touch with someone at Lancashire, though I've no idea who, because strings were pulled in HR and I was drafted in as temporary cover before Bithell could object."

"You went undercover, with no immediate back-up or support, to investigate a well-connected and possibly dangerous gang of bent coppers?" Joe was amazed at the woman he thought he knew. She'd already earned his respect many times over, but this was on another level altogether.

"I didn't view it quite like that, and all I was supposed to do was try and be around whatever they had going on, no questions, no pushing my luck, no heroics, observation only. Believe it or not, back then I looked quite young for my age, so they decided it would be best if I went in as a green as grass fast-track candidate, one who'd just been given a promotion she didn't deserve?"

"Did it work?" Observation only or not, Joe was still trying to get his head round the sheer courage it must have required for a young woman, effectively alone, to take on such a role.

"In a way it did, but not in the way anyone was expecting. No one wanted me in the team, which was made very clear from the off. However, by the time a couple of weeks had gone by, they must have decided that I was too green and dumb to be a threat. They would often talk in front of me, just coding the odd word which, in itself, was enough to draw attention. I began to catch occasional references to a place they called 'the puppy farm' and to someone called Gryce. I had no idea what the puppy farm was, I wrongly assumed that maybe someone was breeding American pit bulls or another banned breed, possibly even dog fighting, which was still going on in some parts."

"It still is in a few places. It never ceases to amaze me what some sick bastards will resort to in the name of entertainment." As a farmer's son Joe had been brought up with intelligent, well-trained, working dogs from long before he was old enough to walk. He found any form of cruelty to animals abhorrent and unfathomable.

"As I said, I was wrong about that part, fortunately. Gryce was a lot simpler though, it's such an unusual name that he was fairly easy to track down." Despite the years that had passed, the Chief Super recalled the details and events as if they'd occurred only yesterday. "Eric Gryce was a successful, well-liked consultant paediatrician when he was struck off in 1995. He'd been challenged about helping himself to the drugs cabinet in order to self-medicate a mental health condition that he'd previously failed to disclose. The people who worked with him at the hospital were stunned when the accusation was first made, even more so when he immediately admitted everything. He was described as the nicest, kindest man you could ever wish to meet, dedicated to his work and his young patients. This had happened six years before I was sent to join Bithell's team, so by then he was in his mid-forties. I also found out, although not until much later, that Gryce had been unofficially diagnosed with Episodic Dyscontrol Syndrome, otherwise known as Intermittent Explosive Disorder, while he was at med school. He'd suffered from anxiety and bouts of depression since his younger sister, Amy, discovered she was pregnant and took her own life. She was just fifteen years old and, in the note she left for her brothers, she claimed that their father, Victor Gryce, had been abusing her for almost two years. She also claimed that he was the father of her never to be born child. Growing up in a household with an abusive father, it's not difficult to understand why Gryce may have developed anger management issues. He was in his second year of medical school in Manchester when she died, the sister and her twin brother Edwin being almost five years younger."

"So the abuse started as soon as the older brother left home." Joe was still appalled, but no longer surprised, at the misery some people were prepared to inflict on others. "What happened to the father?"

"Don't know, according to the old reports he just disappeared, no trace of him was ever found. The thinking at that time, and it would have been back in the late 70's, was that he'd possibly done a runner rather than go to prison. His passport and credit cards were gone, clothes too, and his car was never found. However, his bank accounts were never accessed, which gave rise to speculation that something may have happened to him. That was countered to some extent by the fact he was a very wealthy man so it was considered possible that he had assets squirreled away somewhere."

"So what was Eric Gryce's link to Bithell?" Yvie had doodled her usual Venn diagram and a timeline that was now stretching well into the past, but she couldn't yet see how all the players would interact.

"Patience Yvie," the Chief Super smiled at her protégé, despite her earlier protests she was pleased and relieved to have her back for this case. "I'm getting there, but again I need to jump backwards and forward in time a little. You've got to remember that I only found out about most of this as a result of the subsequent investigation."

"Sorry Ma'am!"

"Seven years after their father had gone missing, Eric and Edwin Gryce applied for a Declaration of Presumed Death, which was eventually granted. They sold what had been the family home and split the proceeds of what turned out to be a very sizeable estate, certainly enough that neither would ever need to work for a living, although Eric Gryce chose to continue working at the hospital. There was some talk of a rift between the brothers who, up until that time, had shared a house with Eric's partner Anthony Daniels. He was a male nurse and had also trained as a midwife, which was pretty unusual back then. The rumour was possibly borne out by the fact that Eric Gryce bought himself and Daniels a restoration project, an old vicarage over towards Becconsall, while his brother dropped out of medical school, where he'd followed in his brother's footsteps, and moved away. For a good few years after the split it appears that everyone just got on with their lives, nothing out of the ordinary was reported right up until the time Eric was struck off. That's when he and his partner opened what Bithell had christened the 'puppy farm' at the old vicarage. Only they weren't selling puppies, they were selling babies."

Chapter Four

"I'm starting to get the impression that this kid just doesn't want to be found." Cathy had spent the past two hours trying to trace Andy Bithell's son, Oliver Stephen Bithell. When they'd called at the empty house the previous evening, the next door neighbours from one side had confirmed that the son hadn't lived at home since starting university in Cardiff, which was shortly before his mother died. Neither set of neighbours recalled seeing him at the house for the last week or so, although the elderly couple living on the other side had speculated about a possible falling-out. Apparently they'd both overheard raised voices one morning around shortly after Oliver had returned home for the Easter break. Although Bithell senior was deceased, there was no automatic power of entry to what had once been the family home. It was still too soon to expect a warrant to search the house or to obtain phone and bank information, any of which may have helped to find the young man. The university hadn't been much help either, other than to confirm that Oliver hadn't attended any classes since the last week of March. His name wasn't coming up on any of Cathy's usual searches and he hadn't posted anything on his preferred social media platforms since he left Cardiff. The last posting simply said, *'going back up north for a couple of weeks to get my laundry done'*, presumably a reference to the end of term trip back to his father's house. The friends she'd managed to contact had neither seen nor heard from Oliver in over a week. The simple conclusion was that he was either deliberately 'off grid', for reasons unknown, or something much worse.

"Perhaps he doesn't?" Autumn switched off her terminal and was heading for the coat rack in the corner of the office. They'd grown used to their regular base out at the old police station in Clitheroe and had long since given up wondering why the Chief Super was reluctant to have them working from Hutton. Whatever the reason, it suited them and Joe just fine, although sometimes they had to allow for a little extra travel time. "Are you nearly ready, we don't want to be late?"

"You might not want to be late, but we don't all share your unnatural keenness to attend post-mortem examinations." Cathy had guessed what was coming when Joe rang to let them know that he was going to be tied up in Hutton for longer than he'd been expecting, and she was right. It was a part of the job that, no matter how hard she tried, she had never been comfortable with. It wasn't any particular aspect of the process, it wasn't to do with the opening up of the body, or the associated sights and sounds. It wasn't even the smells, as bad as they may sometimes be, it just felt wrong, and it always took a couple of hours for her to shake the feeling.

"I can't help it if I find them fascinating. This one should be a cracker though, the guy was virtually disembowelled and then decapitated."

"Yeah, thanks for that, you're really selling it to me Autumn!" Resigned to her fate, Cathy reluctantly closed her lap-top and placed it in a padded backpack before putting on a lightweight jacket and sighing deeply. "Okay, let's go then. Death and tides wait for no man, or something like that."

"I'm pretty sure that it's 'time and tide' actually, or maybe you're thinking of 'death and taxes'. You know, Benjamin Franklin, 'nothing can be said to be certain, except death and…'" Autumn's correction was cut short by the withering look she received before her friend turned and headed for the door.

"Whatever!"

The mood in the car was certainly much lighter on the return journey than it had been on the way to Chorley. Autumn was buzzing, and Cathy was forced to admit that the post-mortem examination hadn't been quite as much of an ordeal as she'd been dreading. It wasn't so much that she'd hung back, leastways not enough for anyone to notice, it was more that eager beaver Autumn had been right up there, front and centre. She'd been firing questions at the Home Office Pathologist, asking to be shown everything he referred to, and generally hanging on to his every word. Unused to anyone taking such a direct interest in the mechanics of his work, the man had responded in kind, to the extent that Cathy had almost begun to feel left out. Before they left, the pathologist, who insisted that they call him Stuart, had promised that his full report would be with them by lunchtime of the following day. Expecting to brief Yvie and Joe on their return, Cathy asked Autumn to run through the key points and findings while she drove them back to Clitheroe.

"Will do sarge, just the highlights or do you want more detail?" Autumn was a prolific note taker and when Cathy glanced across at her young colleague she saw her thumbing through several pages of her notebook, filled with small, neat handwriting and some alarming sketches.

"Just the hi…," she stopped herself, "key points, if you don't mind."

"Sure. Cause of death was interesting in that Stuart said the initial penetrating wound to the abdomen would almost certainly have been fatal by itself, and quite quickly, due to massive blood loss from what he said were catastrophic internal injuries. These were made significantly worse when further damage was sustained as the blade was pulled out. He said that the sucking action on the blade means that it takes much more strength than people realise, and the light bruising to the middle of the chest was most likely where a boot had been placed to help the attacker pull the full length of the blade out from the wound."

"I thought we said just the key points?" Cathy chided her colleague. She remembered the overly enthusiastic pathologist getting down on his knees and telling Autumn to pull hard on a plastic ruler he was holding in front of his stomach. All to demonstrate, to a dubious Autumn, his reasoning behind the significance of the chest bruising.

"Sorry, the actual cause of death was the loss of blood pressure, anoxia and shock as a result of decapitation. There were seven clearly defined blows to the neck with an edged weapon, the first of which was the deepest and was conducted while the victim was still alive and in an upright, probably kneeling, position. Subsequent chopping wounds were inflicted while the body lay on the ground, on its right-hand side." Cathy recalled that this had also involved the pathologist getting back on his knees to prove his point about the difference between the first and subsequent blows to the neck. She'd been fairly sure that Autumn was simply playing with him by that point.

"Okay, and the murder weapon?"

"The initial wound to the abdomen was made by a pointed, single-edged blade at least thirty inches long, probably longer, and it was razor sharp. Stuart thought that the most likely weapon would be something akin to a cavalry sabre. He also said that both sets of wounds would almost certainly have been inflicted by the same weapon."

"Okay, so what have we learned from the post-mortem?" Cathy asked as they turned off Whalley Road, now only a couple of minutes away from the old police station.

"We've confirmed the type of weapon used, and the actual cause of death, but not much more than that really."

"I disagree," Cathy said, trying her best to banish the images that Autumn's somewhat broad understanding of a key-point update had conjured. "You said the weapon was razor sharp, so it's most definitely not a prop or a re-enactment sword, it's a serious weapon. Which means what?"

"Someone went there with the intention of committing murder, and fully equipped to do so." Autumn nodded her understanding as she answered the question.

"Not just to commit murder, the first stab wound, or the first blow to the neck, would have done that." Cathy turned to her colleague while they waited for the traffic lights to change. "If you think about it, a gun or a knife would have been a much simpler weapon to use but, for some reason, it was important to the killer to cut off Andy Bithell's head!"

As the old station was now only open to the public on much reduced hours, Cathy managed to park directly outside, which was fortunate as the first few fat drops of rain began to pepper the windscreen as she was getting out of the car. It was less fortunate for Autumn who, having been dropped off at the bakery with their lunch order, was already walking back in what had rapidly become a torrential downpour. By the time Cathy had reached the shelter of the front door, the rain was drumming on the cars and pavements or, as Joe would have put it, 'it wer' rainin' pikels', which she was pretty sure had something obscure to do with pitchforks. After a quick 'Hello' to the uniformed constable manning the front desk, Cathy went up to the first floor and unlocked what had once been a staff canteen. When it became clear that the Chief Super intended to keep them at arm's length from HQ, they had set about making the space their own. The large room now contained four well equipped workstations, all of which faced towards the long, unbroken, rear wall - the 'murder wall', as they'd christened it. At one end of the room there was a medium sized conference table that also served as a dining table, surrounded by half a dozen mismatched chairs. At the other end was a small but functional kitchen area, complete with sink, hob, oven, microwave and a fridge-freezer. Mugs of Earl Grey were waiting on the table by the time Autumn had squelched her way up the stairs, doing a very passable impression of the proverbial drowned rat, but still managing a smile as she produced a package from beneath her hi-vis jacket.

"There we go, dry as a bone." She said, handing over the bag containing their lunches, steak pie, mushy peas and gravy for herself and, as usual after a post-mortem, a plain salad roll for Cathy. "Just give me a minute sarge and I'll be with you."

"I thought we'd eat first and then make a start on the wall afterwards." Cathy suggested, watching Autumn towel off her hair, empty the water out of her shoes, take off her sodden socks and suit trousers, and then sit down at the table in her underwear and a t-shirt – completely unperturbed by her damp ordeal.

"Yeah, sounds good to me, I'm ready for something to eat." As Autumn opened her polystyrene container the rich aromas of beef gravy and hot pastry filled the room, banishing any lingering trace of the mortuary from Cathy's memory. A salad sandwich just wasn't going to do it!

Chapter Five

Sophie: 1998

By comparison with many teenage runaways, Sophie did well to last as long as she did. Nevertheless, by her nineteenth birthday she was penniless and an addict, pimped out on the streets of Manchester by her friendly neighbourhood dealer. Passed around between men to whom her only value was how much they could make from her body before punters tired of her and she had to be moved on again. One morning, while still only twenty years old, Sophie was awakened by someone gently stroking her arm. She managed to open her eyes, and then immediately closed them as bright lights drilled into her skull. The woman stroking her arm began to speak softly to her, but the words didn't register immediately, she eventually realised that it was her name. Opening her eyes again, this time with more success, she found herself in a clean bed, connected to a host of tubes and cables. The woman who kept repeating her name was smiling at her, but it was only when she noticed the nurse's uniform that she fully understood where she was. Why she was waking up in hospital was a lot harder to make sense of. The nurse, who said her name was Dorothy, told her that she was in the Intensive Care Unit and had been in a medically induced coma for nine days. Her first thoughts were that she must have overdosed but, when told the actual reason why she was in ICU, the memories came flooding back. She began to shake as she recalled the beginnings of the assault she had suffered at the hands of a mean, petty little man. Her savagely beaten body had been dumped outside A&E, presumably by a pimp who didn't need damaged goods or the hassle of getting rid of a body. The majority of her injuries were from the neck down, but the doctors also believed she had been struck on the side of the head, probably with a bottle. The resulting injury caused the swelling inside her skull that had necessitated the induced coma. As her thoughts slowly became clearer, cutting through the lingering aftereffects of the anaesthetic, she remembered how the man she'd been delivered to had started to slap her around almost as soon as she'd been dropped off at his house. He was a small, slightly built man, with a funny little Hitler moustache, but there was nothing humorous about the anger that he'd vented on her. She was every woman who'd ever turned him down, belittled him, or simply failed to notice him, and he was going to show them all who was the boss. It was nothing new, the guy who was pimping her out knew his client's tastes well and prided himself on meeting any of their needs. If it was a punter who wanted rough sex, she was always given a small amount of heroin beforehand, enough to dull the pain, but not enough that she'd be unresponsive. This one had tired of knocking her about when she no longer cried out at his blows. Instead, he'd straddled her on the carpet and put his hands around her throat. It would have been easy to do nothing and allow herself to drift into darkness but, somewhere deep inside, there was a little bit of the old Sophie that wanted to live. As he lowered his head to peer more closely into her face, wanting to see her cowed submission, her acceptance of his total dominance, she brought her right hand around and drove a thumbnail deep into his eye. He rolled off her, bellowing in pain as blood and tears seeped from beneath the fingers he was pressing over the wound. Sophie rolled over and managed to get to her knees, one hand gently massaging her throat as she struggled to get her breathing under control. She made the mistake of turning her back towards the sobbing, mewling punter and never saw him pick up the wine bottle from the table or swing it in a wide arc before smashing it across her skull. Fortunately, nor did she feel the kicks and punches that he rained down on her defenceless body long after she had ceased moving.

Two days after regaining consciousness, it was the same nurse who had asked her if she was aware that she was pregnant, somewhere in the region of four months gone. When she'd admitted that she had no idea, it was put to her tactfully, but firmly, that a decision needed to be made, and quickly. It was, by any definition, a no-brainer. Sophie hadn't got the faintest clue who the father may be, she was an addict, penniless, a prostitute and homeless without her pimp. There could only be one answer but, with a rush of overwhelming certainty, Sophie knew that without this child she would die.

Following a move from ICU to a female surgical ward a couple of days later, Sophie was interviewed by two female police officers. Although initially wary, it soon became clear that they weren't interested in her prostitution or past drug use, nor was there even the slightest inference that she was in any way responsible for what had happened to her. For the first time in a long while she was treated with respect, as an equal, as someone who mattered. After identifying her pimp, and providing a description of the punter who'd assaulted her, she had been considered to be 'at risk'. A fortnight later, when she was due to be discharged from hospital, she was offered temporary accommodation in a women's refuge operated by a social housing association in Leyland – a new start.

By some miracle or other, her baby survived not only the beating, but also the rigours of her young mother's previously calamitous lifestyle. Five months later, having stayed clean for the sake of the child growing inside her, Sophie named her daughter Lucy, after her mum.

As he looked up and down the roadway outside the airport, waiting impatiently for his lift, there was only a single thought in the mind of the tall, tanned young man shivering in a T-shirt and shorts, 'Why is it always fucking raining in Manchester'? Adz Wilkinson considered himself to be a street-smart entrepreneur, though he could never have spelled the word in a million years. In truth, he was a spotty twenty-two-year-old thug, but quick fists and a complete lack of conscience had allowed him to make a living dealing drugs and whoring out any of the girls foolish enough to depend on him for their supply. This was his first time back on home turf since the night, almost twelve months earlier, when he'd been called back to a punter's house in Salford. He remembered that the guy who answered the door, he never asked their names and they never volunteered them, had been holding a wet. bloody towel to his face and hadn't spoken a word, just led him through to the lounge. When he saw the state of Sophie's body, lying battered on the floor, he'd been convinced she was either dead or very close to it. Either way, she was no longer of any use to him. Thinking on his feet, he decided that the only way to turn a final profit was to milk the punter for every penny he could, maybe a couple of grand to keep his mouth shut. He rang Gaz, his younger brother, and half an hour later they carried her body out to the street and loaded it into the back of a stolen Ford Focus. It was Gaz who noticed that she was still breathing so, in a quick change of plan, they pulled up outside A&E and pushed her body out of the car and onto the tarmac. Fifteen minutes later the car was ablaze. Their initial intention had been to leave the body inside when they torched it, and the pair of them were still laughing and joking about it as they legged it back to Adz's flat. It had taken several hours for doubt to penetrate his cock-sure confidence but, by the following morning, he'd decided that it would be a good idea to make himself scarce for a few months. Gaz could look after the business while he met up with some mates who ran a bar in Magaluf, he'd tell them he was thinking of moving over, maybe even do a bit of business. A few months had quickly stretched to a year, but now he was back. So where the fuck was Gaz? Adz's arms were pinned high up behind his back and the handcuffs were on his wrists before he knew what was going on. That became apparent when the plain-clothes female police officer moved to face him and identified herself as Detective Inspector Sharon Green.

"Adrian Wilkinson, you are under arrest for the offence of Causing, Inciting or Controlling Prostitution for Gain. You do not have to say anything but, it may harm your defence if you do not mention when questioned something which you later rely on in court. Anything you do say may be given in evidence." Smiling as she put her warrant card back in her jacket pocket, she added, in a much softer voice intended for his ears only, "and that's just for starters you nasty little piece of shit!" As a police car pulled up to the kerb alongside the three burly coppers who were holding him, a new thought occurred to Adz, the fucking bitch had stitched him up.

It took several months for Gaz to track down the dozy cow who'd got his brother arrested. Fortunately, the people he was dealing to would have grassed up their own grannies for a freebie, unfortunately they would also make up any story that they thought he may want to hear. After following up several false leads, always taking the time to ensure that appropriate punishment was swift for anyone who had wasted his time, he was eventually given the address of a flat above an empty shop just off Leyland town centre. Gaz had no problem with taking advantage of the vulnerabilities of anyone he considered to be lower down the food chain than himself, as he liked to point out at any given opportunity, 'Law of the fuckin' jungle man, innit?'. He'd taunted the pathetically desperate couple who'd told him where Sophie was living, only handing over two small paper wraps instead of the promised five, then an extra one when the man had said she had a sprog with her. Reporting back to Adz, who was still being held on remand awaiting trial, he was surprised when his offer to snatch the kid was turned down.

"Too obvious bro, we've gotta be clever. That's too risky."

"So fuckin' what? We've gotta stop her testifyin' against you and it's either get the kid or torch the place." Gaz said, not seeing any downside to burning down the property with Sophie and her baby still inside.

"No, I've had time to think about it, and this is what I want you to do." Adz quickly gave his brother instructions before his time was up on the mobile phone that was rented out by the minute.

Early the following morning, having been woken by her daughter demanding attention, a bleary-eyed Sophie found a tiny, self-seal bag of white powder lying on the mat by the front door. Rushing straight to the bathroom she flushed the unmistakeable package away, not daring to give herself time to think about what she was doing. It was only after flushing the toilet for a second time, just to be sure, that she allowed herself to ponder who, or why, the drugs had been posted through her letterbox. The only logical explanation was that somehow Adz had found her, it was how he lured in and controlled all of the girls whose bodies he rented out by the hour, herself included. The next morning, having hardly slept and sick with worry at what he might do next, she flushed away another unopened package, and again the day after, and the day after that. She lasted almost a full week before the stress and worry, the sleepless nights, and above all the temptation and her growing need for peace, outweighed her will to stay clean. The little packages of powder continued to arrive, the only difference was that now she would be waiting for the rattle of the letterbox, anxious that it might not come. It was two weeks later on an overcast Wednesday morning when her fears were finally realised, by lunchtime she was jittery, needing something, anything. By late afternoon she was hurting, but afraid to leave the flat in case she missed a delivery. On Friday morning there was a knock at the door, she ran to open it, hoping it was one of Adz's crew, she would promise to withdraw her statement, she'd promise to do anything they asked, if only.....

The social worker, accompanied by two uniformed police officers, introduced herself and the officers before explaining that they were responding to a potential safeguarding issue. A telephone call from a concerned individual had been received, stating that a young child at this address was being severely neglected and was considered to be at risk.

"We'd like to come inside and see for ourselves, if that's okay." The woman, who said her name was Gillian, was taking note of Sophie's dishevelled appearance and agitated state. She took a step backwards and, as the two police officers stepped forward, Sophie understood that it wasn't a request. It was little more than a couple of minutes later when Gillian excused herself and said she was stepping outside to make a phone call. The male officer accompanied her outside while the female officer stayed in the single bedroom. Despite her current state, Sophie could sense the anger that the woman was silently projecting towards her. It was all so unfair, she'd been meaning to give Lucy a bath and get her out of that dirty nappy, just as soon as...., or was that yesterday, she couldn't be sure. And she'd meant to feed her, she just needed to get her head together first, it was all so difficult. Hurting as she was, for once without drugs clouding her perception, Sophie managed a moment of clarity. The realisation hit her like a punch in the stomach. Lucy lay on the urine soaked and badly soiled sheet, painfully thin, sores on her legs and buttocks, breathing fitfully. Her beautiful baby daughter, what had she done, how had she allowed this to happen? Even when the tears came, as she sank to the grubby carpet sobbing uncontrollably, the expression of distaste on the female officer's face never faltered for a second.

"Your child will be removed under the protective powers available to the police." Gillian was speaking but the words were meaningless to Sophie. "These powers apply for a maximum of seventy-two hours but, during this time, an application for an Emergency Protection Order will be made to the court. The Emergency Protection Order allows for a further period of up to eight days, and all subsequent decisions with regard to your child's care will then be made by the court. Do you understand?"

Sophie didn't understand, but nodded her head anyway. She had failed her little girl, the one good thing in her life and she'd let her down so badly. Her only thought was that Lucy should have a better mother, a real mother who would care for her in the way she deserved. Gillian and the two officers stood in silence and waited, not looking at the weeping, grief-stricken woman who was breaking her heart on the floor. A few minutes later, two paramedics announced their arrival and entered the now crowded bedroom. Sophie couldn't bring herself to look up as they first checked, and then removed, her baby daughter.

Sophie was still sat on the floor, gazing at the soiled cot where her daughter had slept, thirty minutes after everyone else had left her home. The rattle of the letterbox prompted a Pavlovian response that she couldn't have denied, even if she'd wanted to.

Chapter Six

"What do you mean selling babies?" As a fairly new mother herself, only recently beginning to enjoy the luxury of an occasional good night's sleep, Yvie was outraged. "Don't tell me they were the ones buying them in from orphanages in Eastern Europe, that was still going on back then wasn't it?"

"It was, but no. The set up was nothing like that, quite the opposite in fact. Girls and young women who were pregnant but, for whatever reason, had nowhere to go, or didn't want to keep their babies, were taken in towards the end of their term. They had their own rooms and facilities; were well treated and received a high standard of care. Before and after giving birth they were encouraged to keep their child, which some did, but if they still chose not to they received an agreed payment in full. Even afterwards, when we interviewed seventeen different women who had given birth there, not one would say a word against Gryce or his partner Daniels. Quite a few of them had been in the care system themselves, one or two admitted to being sex workers, and a number had been homeless. Every single one of them said that they never felt they'd been judged in any way, most also agreed that during their time at the vicarage they received better care and treatment than they'd ever experienced before."

"That doesn't sound like any criminal enterprise that I've ever heard of." Joe said. "If anything, it's more like a charity, or a public service." Yvie was nodding her head in agreement.

"Do you think that it was perhaps his way of making good for not being able to protect his sister?"

"I honestly don't know Yvie. Possibly, it would explain certain things, but we'll never know for sure." Iron Annie paused for a moment. "One thing we do know is that it was a very well run, very discrete operation. It had to be in order to operate for as long as they did, and it would most likely have needed some form of protection. With the benefit of hindsight, I think Bithell had known what was going on for some time and had managed to insert himself as a middleman, maybe introducing potential clients who had the money and were desperate for a child. Something that may well have given him access to the secrets of some very influential people."

"Which is what made them untouchable." Yvie added. "But if that was the case, what happened to warrant an investigation?"

"I was in the office one morning when it all kicked off. Bithell came in just before lunch and he was spitting feathers, I'd never seen him so angry. He shouted to his three closest buddies to grab their coats, saying that he'd just received an anonymous tip-off about two guys who were offering a baby for sale, and he intended to raid the place before the sellers had chance to move the kid on. I tried to go with them but he wouldn't let me, said four was enough."

"Surely they couldn't just go off and do something like that without clearance, planning, risk assessments, back-up, the whole shebang?" Joe thought back to the recent suspension that he and

Cathy had endured following their showdown with the Lees brothers.

"Bithell was a law unto himself, a combination of excellent, if dubious, results and a weak chain of command meant that he could do whatever he wanted. He wouldn't get away with it today, but back then….?" Iron Annie shook her head sadly and left the sentence unfinished. "No babies were found on the premises, which turned out to be the old vicarage that Gryce and Daniels had restored, but two pregnant young women, and one who had not long since given birth, were brought in for questioning."

"What about Gryce and Daniels?" Joe asked.

"According to Bithell's report, Anthony Daniels, Eric Gryce's partner of many years, jumped from a second-floor window while trying to evade capture. There was some speculation by Bithell and Williams that he'd been hoping to land on the ridge of the conservatory and slide down to a point from where he could jump safely to the lawn. Instead, his feet went straight through the old-fashioned single glazing and he fell forwards, until being caught by the neck on shards of broken glass lodged in an angle formed by two of the glazing bars." The Chief Super paused, grimacing as she recalled the grisly outcome. "Later, when giving evidence at the Coroner's Inquest, Bithell and DI Paul Williams both said they saw Daniels hanging momentarily, his head trapped beneath the chin in a 'V' shaped section of the frame. They said there was a lot of blood and he was kicking and struggling violently until his headless body fell through to the conservatory floor."

"My God, that's awful!" Yvie exclaimed.

" Yes, it is. The Home Office Pathologist's report indicated that severe lacerations to the neck from the broken glass and metal glazing bars, combined with body weight and movement as he struggled, would have been sufficient to cause his subsequent decapitation. His head was later recovered from where it remained wedged in an angle of the conservatory roof."

"Where was Gryce when this happened?" Joe asked. "Did he see his partner die?"

"Again, according to the report, he was in the conservatory when Daniels' body came through the roof. Bithell said that they heard him howl with rage, but he was gone before any of the team could get to him." The Chief Super went on to describe how, in the press conference that had followed the raid, a buoyant Bithell claimed that his team had, 'uncovered, and put an end to, the exploitation of desperate young women by a ruthless criminal gang'. She recalled that he'd also made a statement to the effect that his team would not rest until they had reunited the missing child with his grieving mother, something that never happened.

"So, a man dies, a baby goes missing, and Bithell and his team come out of it smelling of roses?" Joe asked.

"Not entirely, no. It was only a couple of days later when we heard from Gryce, he copied the same letter to the Police Complaints Authority, half a dozen newspapers and several radio and television news-desks. He claimed that he hadn't taken the child, that Bithell wanted the baby for himself and had raided the house solely in order to steal the boy after his demand had been refused. He also said that Daniels was terrified of heights and would never have climbed out of a window."

"That must have at least prompted an independent investigation?" Yvie commented.

"No, if he'd left it at that, it may have done. Unfortunately, he went on to swear vengeance against the four officers he claimed had murdered Daniels. Again, with hindsight, he was clearly off his meds by that point and the trauma of witnessing the horrific death of his partner may well have triggered his underlying mental health condition. Whatever the reason, the letter also included a statement that he wouldn't rest until each and every one of them had paid for what happened to his partner. The implied threat made it easier for the whole thing to be dismissed as the ravings of a madman. Even more so when information about his past mental health issues and drug use was leaked to the press. Despite that, it must still have taken a huge amount of high-level interference to ensure that any thoughts of investigating Gryce's claims were crushed, but they were. At the same time, there was a noticeable change in Bithell. I think someone must have made it clear to him that he'd used up the last of his goodwill."

"I've just realised where this is going," Joe said, "it's the Headhunter case isn't it? I think I was only late teens or maybe early twenties, but I remember some of it being on the news. Didn't he go on to kill two police officers?"

"Three. DI Paul Williams and DC Bernie Stansfield were part of the team that he held responsible for Daniels' death. WPC Julie Edwards was just doing her job, in the wrong place at the wrong time. The press nick-named him 'The Headhunter' after what he did to Williams and Stansfield."

"You'll have to bring me up to speed on that," Yvie said, "I was still at school back then."

"It's strange, it was all so long ago, but Bithell's death has brought it all back." The Chief Super sat back in her chair and gazed out of the window, the memories from twenty years ago weighing heavily on her. "When I got back to the office yesterday afternoon I had a look at the old case files. Everything relating to what happened after the raid on Gryce's house is still there, and it looks to be complete. The 'Headhunter', a man with severe mental health problems, the deaths of three serving police officers, Arnside, that's all in place. But, whoever Bithell's protectors were back then, at some point they've managed to remove almost every reference to the sale of babies. The interviews with the girls who gave birth there have gone, statements from each of Bithell's team have gone, and that takes some real clout."

"We could check the archive for hard copy records Ma'am." Joe suggested.

"If they've been able to access and amend digital records, and to cover their tracks, then I very much doubt that they'll have had any trouble making the paperwork disappear. I'll check that myself though, I've a better idea of what I'm looking for."

"You mentioned Arnside Ma'am, is that something we should know about?" Yvie asked.

"It is, it's where the Eric Gryce case ended, or where we thought it had ended." Iron Annie checked the time and stood up. "I'm sorry but that will have to wait. I've got a planning meeting with the Chief Constable and the rest of the Senior Management Team and if I don't turn up I'll lose a chunk of my budget. Just to make it interesting though, I thought that while I'm there, I might add 'unauthorised access to classified materials' to the agenda, just to see if anyone start to look uncomfortable."

Chapter Seven

The Old Vicarage: 2002

"We're so pleased that you changed your mind and decided to keep him Sophie, really we are." Anthony Daniels smiled as he watched the young woman nurse her baby, knowing how hard she'd worked to give her son a better start in life, steering clear of the drugs that had blighted her teenage years. "Eric and I have been talking and, now that you're healthy again, perhaps we can help the two of you to get settled somewhere, maybe even help you work on getting Lucy back?"

"Thank you!" Sophie couldn't say any more, the tears came, happy tears, the wave of emotion provoked by these two men was overwhelming. Such genuine and generous people, they cared enough to help her turn her life around, to keep her son, even to get her daughter back, things she'd never dreamed possible. A new start made possible by the selfless kindness of strangers. No, not strangers, she thought, Anthony and Eric were angels, her very own guardian angels.

Anthony left her to enjoy her son, still smiling as he closed the bedroom door behind him and went down the stairs in search of his partner. He found him in the huge conservatory, their favourite space in the Old Vicarage, a home that they had restored together over several years. Eric Gryce was pacing the stone flagged floor, mobile phone to his ear, and clearly not happy.

"I'm sorry but, as I said, she's changed her mind. You know how we operate, the mother always has the final say." He grimaced and held the phone away from his ear. Anthony could hear the angry shouting from across the conservatory, he mouthed the word 'Bithell' and Eric nodded sadly and ended the call, cutting off the rant in mid flow.

"Was that wise?" Anthony asked.

"Probably not! I imagine he'll be round here shouting the odds before too long. He's insisting that we give up the child."

"We should never have let his wife hold the boy, that was a mistake."

"Yes, but even so, they're not taking him, I won't allow it. We made a promise to Sophie and I'm not going back on it."

Until recently, their forced relationship with Bithell had been surprisingly straightforward. It had begun the day he'd confronted them both with the story he'd been given by a sex worker, one who was hoping to avoid being charged with possession of stolen goods. He had threatened the pair with criminal charges, then proposed an alternative arrangement that they had little choice other than to accept. Over the last four years he had occasionally steered a pregnant young woman in their direction, but his primary involvement had been in finding wealthy childless couples who were prepared to pay whatever he asked for a healthy new-born child. What made the service he offered so attractive, at least to the types of client he favoured, was that a 'genuine' entry would be made on the NHS Numbers for Babies database. In addition, an appointment would be made with a particular Registrar, a married man who hadn't been able to believe his luck when he'd been seduced by a much younger woman after a chance meeting in a hotel bar. He'd still had a spring in his step the following day, right up until the time Bithell had shown him the high definition video of his sordid brief encounter. The subsequent new working arrangement enabled clients to register the child's birth with themselves named as the parents, all they had to do was devise a way to introduce a new baby into their lives without raising too much suspicion. For his part in the arrangement, Bithell took fifty percent of the price paid by the client, he called it his 'arrangement fee'. Eric and Anthony were fairly sure that he also charged prospective parents a similar 'finder's fee', but that was his business, for them it had never been about the money. They had gained a measure of protection, the knowledge that the young women were well cared for and that their children, should they choose to give them up, were going to homes where they were truly wanted and would be part of a loving family. That was their entire motivation, a shared desire to keep the young mothers safe and give their children, who may have otherwise been at risk, a better start in life. The uneasy relationship only really changed when Bithell and his wife completed their third round of IVF and Sheryl Bithell, now in her mid-forties, finally conceded that it was unlikely she would ever become pregnant. More than anything else in life, Sheryl wanted a child, a baby, and despite his faults and dubious morals Andy Bithell was determined that she would have one.

The anticipated hammering on the door by an enraged Bithell never occurred, at least not in the way they were expecting.

Anthony was upstairs keeping an eye on Sophie's son while she had lunch with Jo and Shaz, two girls who were both approaching full term in their pregnancies. Meanwhile, having needed to regain a sense of calm following the angry telephone call with Bithell, Gryce was in the conservatory, happily tending some new additions to their collection of exotic plants. His head bobbed and swayed as he worked, unconsciously following every rise and fall of Samuel Barber's Adagio for Strings, currently playing in his Apple AirPods. It was a piece of music he had always found to be incredibly soothing, unlike Anthony who said it was funereal, but then his partner had never really moved on from disco. At the rear of the property, and with his music on, Eric Gryce didn't hear the three cars that pulled up outside the house. As soon as it came to a halt, the driver of the first vehicle got out and waited for the three occupants of the second car to join him, the driver of the final vehicle executed an untidy three-point turn then remained in the car with the engine running. The four men grouped together and, if anyone had been watching, it would have been clear that three of them were being given some very specific instructions. Revelling in the skill of the Vienna Philharmonic, Eric Gryce also failed to hear the front door burst open when it was impacted by a 16kg hardened steel Enforcer ram, in fact he remained completely unaware that Bithell and three of his close confederates were already rushing into the home that he and Anthony had built together.

Following the earlier telephone call, and knowing it was unlikely that Gryce would back down and hand over the child voluntarily, Andy Bithell had decided that his only remaining option was a show of force, something that had always served him well in the past. Given more time he would have been able to distance himself entirely from the events he was about to initiate but, for all he knew, he might only have a matter of hours. Once the mother and baby left the old vicarage it would be too late, he had to act now. The three police officers he chose to accompany him had all benefitted significantly by pledging their allegiance to him, rather than the law. After years of carefully squirreling away their substantial additional incomes, each man had too much to lose to refuse any request that 'the Guv'nor' might make. They were his men, bought and paid for. He called his wife, the plans they had made for the time when Sophie's son was supposed to have been handed over would need to be brought forward a little, but that was okay, they were ready. An hour and a half later, Sheryl's car tucked in behind the two unmarked police cars as they turned off the lane and into the driveway of the old vicarage.

"We go in fast and hard." Bithell was used to thinking on his feet, while the plan he'd devised on the drive over was simple in the extreme, he needed to conduct his part without any witnesses. "Get the women together in a room at the back of the house. Don't take any shit, they do as they're told. Okay?" He made eye contact with each of his men. "Keep them there until I say otherwise. Mark, you stay with them."

"Got it Guv."

"Paul, Bernie, I want Gryce and Daniels in cuffs and shittin' themselves, I want the pair of them in fear of their lives. Gryce is a gobby bastard, but there's no fight in either of 'em so I'm not expecting any aggro, but by all means give 'em a slap if you need to. Put them in the kitchen, away from the women, tie them to a couple of chairs, put tape across their mouths and then and hood 'em with these." He handed two black cloth bags and a roll of parcel tape to the oldest member of the group, Detective Inspector Paul Williams.

"Jesus, Guv! What are we planning to do to them?" Bithell noted that the DI seemed more than a little excited at the prospect of imminent action, maybe too much so. In the past, Williams had quite often displayed a tendency to get a carried away when throwing his weight around, usually with women. On some occasions that had been a useful trait to exploit, maybe when a certain point had needed to be made, but not today. He'd need to quash that before they went in.

"You got shit for brains Paul? You really think I'm stupid enough to spoil a nice little earner like this?" Bithell spat angrily and stepped forward into the man's space, forcing him to back up. "I said a slap if you need to, and that's it. Got it?"

"Got it, yeah, sorry Guv. I wasn't thinking."

"Well think on this. It's not what we do, it's what they think we might do, that's important." Bithell tapped two fingers against his temple, then softened his voice. "Okay?"

"Yeah, sorry Guv, okay."

"Bernie, you ready with the ram?" Bithell asked the largest member of the group. DC Bernie Stansfield was well over six feet tall and weighed in at seventeen stone, he smiled broadly as he held up the 'big black key' in his left hand and nodded.

"Yeah, ready when you are Guv. Just say the word."

Bithell took a moment. He didn't need to steady his nerves, but being a part of the action rather than orchestrating events from a position of deniability was making him extra cautious. He nodded once then pointed towards the front door.

"Okay, let's go!"

Chapter Eight

I have always believed, mistakenly as it turns out, that the death by decapitation of the corrupt policeman Andy Bithell, would make me feel, I don't know, lighter, somehow. In the small hours when sleep won't come, which is happening more frequently as I grow older, I've long imagined that his death would be like laying to rest a ghost from the past, almost bringing an element of peace, the relief of finally scratching a chronic itch, but it has provided none of those things. Instead, it still burns inside me, it rankles that the man responsible for bringing so much misery into our lives was allowed to walk away, and then to profit from writing a book about it. Never mind profit, he shouldn't have been allowed to draw breath for as long as he did. The problem, the reason why I know I won't sleep tonight, is that his long overdue death, just isn't enough, there needs to be greater recompense. I can't escape the thought that the whole sorry episode is unfinished, that it remains a job half done. What about the others, the fourth man, what was his name? I think hard for a minute, then it comes to me, Brandwood, Detective Constable Mark Brandwood, that was it. I wonder where he is now, perhaps I should pay him a visit, perhaps that would bring me the closure I've waited so long for. Or the two who were in the river at Arnside, they must also take a share of responsibility. I can't remember their names, I don't think I ever knew them, but I know where I can find out. Hah! Finally, a purpose for Bithell's sorry excuse for a book.

As I sit, looking out into the night, I can feel the blood pounding in my ears, a deep bass rhythm all of my own. I can sense my heart rate quickening and the heat of anger blooming in my cheeks. Over the years I have become used to these feelings, coming as they do whenever I think too long about the past. I know that the adrenaline surging through my body is nothing more than the result of a chemical reaction inside my brain, an out of proportion response to particular stimuli. I have learned to be patient, to wait until the rage passes, until my mind clears and what passes for peace returns. It has been a long while since I last allowed myself to explore the full depth and darkness of my thoughts, but for some reason I am finding that rather than quenching the fires that once raged inside me, Bithell's death has reignited them.

Chapter Nine

The Old Vicarage: 2002

A single strike of the battering ram was sufficient to splinter the timbers of the front door, the sole of a heavy boot completed the job by pushing aside the lacquered hardwood that would never again fit into its frame. With a bellowing shout of, 'Police, stay where you are with your hands raised', Stansfield was first in, revelling in the shock and awe of his entry, closely followed by Brandwood as they began to search the ground floor. Hearing the commotion, the three women who had been having lunch got as far as the door to the hallway before being held back by the impassable barrier of Bernie Stansfield. The room was at the rear of the house so Brandwood decided there was no need to move the women or unsettle them further. While Stansfield went off to continue the search for Gryce and Daniels, Brandwood stayed with them and did his best to reassure them that everything was okay. The two heavily pregnant girls both looked to be in their late teens and, apart from a few worried glances, were easily persuaded to go back to their meal. The slightly older woman was becoming upset and was insisting that she be allowed to go to her baby. As per his instructions, Brandwood told her that they'd received information that Gryce had arranged to sell the child to a known paedophile who may already be on the premises. Dismissing her protests and arguments to the contrary, he said that they believed the transfer was imminent and that they were there to prevent it from happening. As such, it wasn't safe for anyone to moving around the house until they'd secured the child and the traffickers. He was a good liar, and with fear blocking out logic and experience Sophie told him that Daniels was keeping an eye on her son while she had lunch. She even appeared to calm a little when he promised that they'd be reunited in just a matter of minutes.

Once through the front door, Williams had gone straight for the stairs and was busily searching the bedrooms and en-suites for any sign of Gryce or Daniels. Bithell had followed him up the stairs but continued on to the upper floor where, as he knew from recent visits, Gryce had converted the attic rooms into a fully kitted out delivery suite and bedrooms for mothers and their newly born children to spend quiet time away from the noise of the rest of the house. Leaving the stairs he could immediately feel a cool breeze from the large open window at the opposite end of the landing, the ex-doctor was clearly a believer in the value of lots of fresh air. Checking his phone, he was pleased to see a message from Brandwood that simply read 'women secure, Daniels upstairs', one potential problem removed, and one that he'd need to deal with right away. As Bithell continued towards the first of the bedrooms, Daniels stepped out of the room carrying a tea tray. On seeing the policeman he quickly put it down and closed the door behind himself.

"You're not taking him, we won't let you." Anthony Daniels' voice was cracking with apprehension as he spoke. He was maybe six inches shorter and three stone lighter than Bithell, never in a million years would he be a match for the policeman if it came to a struggle. He was fidgety, clearly nervous and, to his credit, bravely standing his ground.

"Don't be stupid, this is going to happen, and there's not a damn thing you can do about it." Bithell didn't want to waste any more time than he had to on pointless melodrama. "Now get out of the fuckin' way before you get hurt." He lunged for the door but halted instantly when he saw the flash of a knife in Daniels hand. Then very nearly burst out laughing, the fool was brandishing a butter knife he'd held on to from the tea tray. As far as offensive weapons were concerned, this one was about as threatening as a ripe banana. "Really?"

"I mean it, get back." Daniels raised the useless piece of metal in a shaky hand, his voice now raised in pitch in his near panic. The next second he found himself rapidly moving backwards as Bithell charged and lifted him off his feet, propelling them both down the short landing until Daniels was forced back against the sill of the window, trapped by the body weight of the bigger, stronger man. His flailing arm caught the side of Bithell's head and, by sheer chance, the blunt butter knife poked him in the eye. Eraged at the combination of the sudden sharp pain and his own stupidity in letting it happen, Bithell reached round Daniels' squirming body and unlatched the partially open window, then took a half step backwards and pushed with both arms.

Despite the noise and the shouting elsewhere in the house, Eric Gryce's first inkling that anything was wrong came a few seconds later when he was showered with broken glass as something heavy shattered the conservatory roof just ahead of where he was standing. He staggered backwards, shocked and wondering what the hell was going on, his first thought was that a ridge tile, or something similar, must have come loose and fallen from the main roof. Only when the glass had stopped falling did he dare to look up, to be met by the sight of his life partner trapped by the neck and swinging from a triangular section of the ornamental frame. Eric could only stare, unable to fully comprehend just what he was seeing, as Anthony's body came free and dropped to the tiled floor, blood gushing from the ragged stump of his neck. Gryce threw back his head and cried out in anguish, the cry changing to a primal howl of rage when he saw, through the broken conservatory roof, Andy Bithell looking down from the second-floor window.

As he looked down on the shattered glass below him, with Daniels' head still wedged in the corner of the broken frame and Eric Gryce's scream of pain and anger ringing in his ears, Andy Bithell experienced an uncharacteristic moment of self-doubt. After the best part of twenty highly successful, and undeniably lucrative, years on the force, was this where it would all come to an end? From day one on the job he'd always been careful, one step removed and never getting his own hands dirty. He'd only ever being in the pay of a single dominant career criminal at any one time, although there had been a number of them over the years. His 'loyalty' could always be relied upon, right up until such time as his paymaster was taken out by a more powerful opponent, something that he often likened to a prospective new employer taking on a greater share of the market. In return, as well as regular cash payments, he received tip-offs and information about other, lesser gangs that enabled his small, hand-picked squad to put away more dealers, pimps and wannabe gangsters than any other team in Lancashire. He'd often joked with the guys that what they did in order to keep the streets free of lower-level crime was a public service, one they could be proud of. Looking down at the severed head he wondered if today was the day that he'd finally overreached, overestimated his own ability to always come out on top. With a much more characteristic exclamation of, 'No fuckin' chance!', the moment passed and his usual confidence flooded back. He reasoned that nothing of significance had happened, at least nothing that would necessitate changing his simple plan. As for Daniels, something along the lines of 'fell to his death while attempting to evade arrest after attacking an officer with a bladed weapon', should suffice and, just to make sure, 'witnessed by several serving police officers'. Bithell turned from the window and walked quickly back to the bedroom where the boy was still fast asleep, snuggled down on a fleecy blanket in a high-sided blue cot decorated with hand-painted butterflies. He very gently picked up the baby, wrapped another blanket around him, then made his way down the stairs and straight out of the front door to where his wife was waiting in the car. With the women secure at the back of the house he only had Gryce to look out for, he wasn't bothered if his own guys saw him with the child. Not wanting to share any personal matters, he'd told them that the baby was for a relative of MDM, their current source of additional funding, and no-one in their right mind was going to ask questions of Mad Dog McCabe. He'd embellished the lie further, saying he was pissed off that after a last-minute call he'd had to involve his wife. Explaining how she was supposed to be driving up to Scotland that morning, her mother wasn't well and she was going to stay with her for week or two.

He opened the back door of his wife's Lexus SUV and placed the baby carefully in the brand new child seat, then moved out of the way so that Sheryl could check he was strapped in properly.

"Congratulations Mrs. Bithell, you have a beautiful baby boy."

"Thank you, Mister Bithell," she raised a sleeve to wipe tears from her eyes, "thank you." She got back into the driver's seat and put her own seat belt on. "Love you, Andy."

"Drive carefully love, I'll come up and see you both at the weekend. Love you too." He stepped back and waved as she set off very cautiously down the drive. Okay, he thought to himself, just got to deal with Gryce and we can start wrapping things up.

Over the next hour, the two pregnant teenagers, who had both been planning to part with their babies for cash, came to a joint conclusion that it would be in their own best interests to play dumb and say nothing. Bithell was insistent that all three women should be taken to hospital to be checked over but, when they tried to get her into one of the ambulances, Sophie was ready to fight, insisting that she wouldn't leave without her son. The fight went out of her the moment Detective Chief Inspector Andrew Bithell, a long serving member of the Lancashire Constabulary, looked her in the eye and told her that there was no trace of her baby.

The media conference took place in time for the early evening news. The headline stories that followed were all was based around three women having been 'rescued' without harm from a vicious gang who had been trafficking in new-born babies, and how the gang had been taken down due to the heroic actions of a small team of Lancashire detectives. Much was made of the fact that DCI Andy Bithell, who had led the operation, refused to take any credit for the outcome. He stated that he deeply regretted arriving a matter of minutes too late to prevent a newborn baby being abducted by one of the ringleaders, a doctor who had been struck off for drug abuse. On the television news there was a particularly poignant moment when Bithell looked directly into the camera and promised the unnamed mother that his team would not rest until they had reunited her with her son.

Chapter Ten

"Are you ready to make a start?" Cathy asked as she took a stack of A4 colour photos from the printer.

"Yeah, I just need another minute to get my head around this timeline the boss sent through. It goes back nearly fifty years, but the guy who it's mostly about hasn't been seen for the last twenty." Autumn was stood on a three-tread stepladder at the far end of the room, now wearing a spare pair of trousers that she'd retrieved from her locker. She had a large roll of black electrical insulation tape in her hand and was trying to work out how to run a straight line of tape along the top of the off-white painted murder wall without a repeat of all the peaks and troughs that had resulted from her first attempt. She was still pondering when Joe and Yvie arrived back in the office, the smell of hot vinegar from the plastic carrier bag in Joe's hand making Cathy's nose twitch and even overpowering the lingering aroma of pie and gravy.

"Detective Inspector Penswick, excellent timing sir!" Autumn greeted him loudly. "We urgently need your input and expertise on establishing this timeline, sir."

"Certainly," Joe replied, feigning interest in what he knew for an absolute fact was going to be a wind up, "and is it any particular aspect of advanced detection technique that you're struggling with?"

"Nah," Autumn slapped the roll of tape into his hand, "we just need someone tall."

"And I don't mind looking after your bag while you help." Cathy added, very nearly drooling at the prospect.

"Funny you should say that, because a certain Detective Constable messaged me and said that her DS was in need of hot and fatty sustenance, either that or we'd be dealing with, and I quote, 'a right narky cow', for the rest of the afternoon." He handed the bag over.

"Seems about right," Cathy agreed, nodding her head happily, "get the brews on DC Jackson and the 'narky cow' might just forgive you." While Autumn did as she was told and went off to busy herself with the kettle, and Cathy did the same with the chips. Yvie and Joe were looking through the items that had been printed off and were laid out across two desks, ready to be attached to the wall once the big black timeline had been put in place.

"I know I suggested that we should run the timeline from the first significant event, which would be when Gryce's sister committed suicide, but I'd like to go back a little further." Yvie paused for a moment to clarify her thoughts. "Maybe to when he started med school?"

"You think him leaving home gave the father an opportunity to start abusing his daughter?" Joe was reluctantly following her thinking. Despite his years in the job he'd never come to terms with how some parents could behave towards their own children.

"I don't know, it's possible. Either that or when the one he'd been abusing moved out, he started on the next in line," she said sadly. "We'll probably never know." Yvie watched as Joe reached up and fixed one end of the sticky black tape towards the top of the wall. Seeing his intention, she climbed on the stepladder and made sure the tape didn't come adrift while he walked almost to the other end of the room, letting the roll unwind as he went. With a final pull to tighten up the slack he fixed the long line of tape to the wall.

"Not perfect," he said looking back at his handiwork, and the noticeable bowing towards the centre of the line, "but not too bad." Cathy raised her head to glance at the tape then made a muffled comment through a mouthful of food. All Joe caught was her final few words, which he decided to ignore, considering that, '…as bent as a dog's hind leg', was a tad harsh. With fresh mugs of tea now ready, three Earl Greys and a pint pot of treacly brown builders, the four of them gathered around the dining table for their first proper catch up. Yvie was about to speak when the office door opened and a familiar figure walked in, raising his walking stick by way of greeting.

"So, what's a man got to do to get a brew around here, then?" DI Tom Barron asked. "Afternoon Boss, Joe, Cathy, Autumn."

"Why didn't you say you were coming in?" A surprised Autumn blurted out, fortunately managing to stop herself from adding, 'while we were having breakfast'. She could feel the colour rising to her cheeks and from the smirk Cathy was giving her it hadn't gone unnoticed.

"Hello Tom, we weren't expecting you today." Yvie was genuinely pleased to see the young DI. At Cathy's wedding, he'd seemed quite down when he'd told her that his doctor was urging him to take a further month off work.

"To be honest, I wasn't expecting to be here either. The Chief Super rang a couple of hours ago and asked if I was up to manning a desk. Which I thought was a little bit odd as when we were at the wedding she expressly forbade any attempt to return to work until the doctors said it was okay. I'm assuming it must be a new case?"

"Yes, and no," Yvie replied. "I can't argue that we don't need the help, but I don't want you overdoing things. It's strictly desk work until the doctors say otherwise. Okay?"

"Got it Boss."

"Good to have you back mate." Joe said.

"Agreed," Cathy added, getting to her feet. "I'll make you a cuppa, you need to keep your strength up." Only Autumn saw the outrageous wink that was aimed in her direction.

With an eye on the time, and wanting to make best use of the afternoon, Yvie asked Cathy to start things off with a quick summary of the murder scene. As the murder wall wasn't yet up and running, Cathy passed round printouts of the photos sent through by FIT. Explaining that the victim had been identified by the Chief Super, who was already at the scene when they arrived, she paused when she saw the DCI raise a finger.

"The Chief Super provided a lot of information about the victim," Yvie said, "but it's going to throw up more questions than answers. I'd like to leave that until the end."

"Is that why we've got a timeline going back for yonks Boss?" Autumn asked, "I've never seen anything like that before."

"It is, and all will become clear, hopefully. Cathy?"

Consulting her notebook occasionally, Cathy concisely described their findings inside the marquee, the layout of the surrounding area and the nature of the event. The fine detail would come later.

"Who found the body? Tom asked.

"King Charles the First," Joe said, unable to resist, "but most of the time he's a retired accountant by the name of Gary Cookson. We'll stop in and see him again later this afternoon. He tried his best yesterday, but the shock kicked in and he could barely get his words out."

"Hardly surprising," Cathy added, "he walked into the tent, fell flat on his back in a pool of blood and found his friend's headless body. Not really something that your average accountant would have much experience of."

"Forensics?" Yvie asked.

"We should have the initial FIT report through by end of play today. Unfortunately, so many people had been in and out of the marquee that John wasn't hopeful about being able to identify or isolate anything significant."

"Uniform stayed on and spoke to the re-enactors who were camping there for the weekend." Joe took over from his colleague. "Apparently the murder didn't do anything to dull the party atmosphere. The ones who knew Bithell didn't have much to say about him, other than that he never stayed for the post battle piss-ups. No one reported seeing anything untoward, but there were so many people sporting fake wounds and bloodstains that it doesn't really count for much. A good number had already gone off to their hotels and others may not have stayed over. The organisers are sending through copies of all the confirmations they received, so we should be able to trace everyone who took part. I'm not sure it will be much help though."

"The park staff reckon that on a Bank Holiday weekend there could easily have been at least four or five thousand people either watching the event or using the park throughout the day." Cathy added. "We can do an appeal but, same as Joe said, I don't think we'll get a lot from it."

"Before we left, I spoke to the Gun Captain. He's the guy in charge of the muskets and rabinets, small-bore cannons," Joe said, pre-empting the obvious question. "Apparently, Bithell was a stickler for the rules, he described him as being 'overly officious'. He wouldn't let anyone near the muskets, let alone the cannons, until he'd personally checked their shotgun certificates, black powder licences and training records."

"Even someone with his reputation, you can take the man out of the police," Yvie nodded, "but….."

"Yeah. I got the distinct impression that he liked throwing his weight about, he certainly wasn't overly popular. We might get a bit more from Cookson, if he's recovered, that is."

When Yvie paused proceedings for a quick comfort break, Joe took the opportunity to have a private word with Tom. The DI had been badly injured in their encounter with the Lees brothers, the men responsible for the murder of his wife and two young children. His most serious wound had been a gunshot to the leg, but he'd also been shot in the chest and was only alive because he'd had the sense to put on a lightweight ballistic vest beforehand. Joe knew that the broken bones would knit together, the wounds would heal, but it was whatever may be going on in his friend's head that was the cause of his concern.

"You okay?"

"I'm glad to be back at work, if that's what you mean. Daytime television was driving me spare. Do you know what they…."

"That's not what I mean, and you know it." Joe interrupted and held eye contact with the younger man. "I'm asking if you're really okay?"

"I'm better than I was before, honestly mate. It was hard, constantly reliving what happened to Fern, Emily and Thomas. If I'm honest, I think it very nearly broke me." Tom paused for a moment. "But what happened in Woodplumpton, and since, has made me realise that I do want to go on. I want to work, I want a life, and I want people to share it with."

"That's all very well mate, but I was only asking if you were okay for a brew." Joe smiled, pleased to see Tom laugh, and then nod to acknowledge what had just passed between them. They returned to the table with fresh mugs of tea for everyone, this time accompanied by a packet of shortbreads from the pocket of Joe's ancient Barbour jacket.

"Okay, who's reporting back on the post-mortem?" Yvie asked.

"I'll do it Boss," Autumn offered. "Sarge's PPMT was playing her up again."

"Ha, ha, very funny!" Cathy replied when she'd had a moment to work out the 'pre post-mortem tension' jibe. "Go ahead smart-arse, it's all yours. Just remember that we'd like to get home before midnight."

"Okay." Autumn stood up and opened her notebook. "Sorry, I can't do this sitting down. The actual cause of death was the immediate loss of blood pressure and anoxia due to decapitation. However, Stuart said the initial wound to the abdomen would have been fatal, and quite quickly, due to catastrophic internal injuries."

"Stuart?" Yvie queried.

"He's her pet pathologist Boss," Cathy replied. "She played him like an old violin."

"Initial wound to the abdomen was made by a pointed blade at least thirty inches long, and razor sharp." Autumn stated, ignoring the comment. "The decapitation was as a result of seven blows to the neck, most likely with the same weapon."

"Do we have the murder weapon?" Tom asked.

"Unfortunately, there was nothing at the scene. But, as Sarge pointed out," Autumn gave a nod towards Cathy, "the weapon was razor sharp. It can't have been a prop or a re-enactment sword, which means that someone took it there with the intention of committing murder." She paused, confirmation of premeditation was highly significant. "Not only that, as she also pointed out, the stomach wound alone would have been fatal, so why did the killer risk taking the time to cut off Andy Bithell's head?"

Chapter Eleven

2002

Detective Inspector Paul Williams sat completely still, hardly daring to move a muscle, knowing that the slightest movement could mean it was all over. He was totally engrossed in the tiny movements of the swing-tip attached to one of the carbon-fibre fishing rods sat on a pair of rests to the right-hand side of his folding chair, silently willing the bite indicator to give him a more positive sign. He'd ground-baited this particular swim, one where he'd previously landed a couple of beauties, for several days in preparation for his 48 hour week-end fishing marathon. His baits, home-made chicken skin boilies prepared to his own secret recipe, had only been in the water for not much more than twenty minutes before there had been the first stirrings of interest. There were a number of huge common carp and mirror carp in the well-stocked private lake and he was hoping to break his own personal record, maybe even his first forty pounder. Membership of the exclusive fishing syndicate that controlled several similar waters was ridiculously expensive but, although his wife wouldn't have agreed, if she were ever to find out, was worth every penny. It wasn't as though he couldn't afford it either, the bonus that Andy had paid him after the puppy farm job more than covered it. With his share of the monthly take now significantly exceeding his police salary, his only financial concern was what to do with all the cash.

His fingers hovered over the soft grip handle of the rod closest to him, poised to strike if the fish decided to take the bait rather than just play with it. He was so focussed on the rise and fall of the swing-tip that he failed to notice the shadow that fell across the grass at his side. The blow across the back of his neck came without warning, either in the moment or in the days before, or at least no warning that that Paul Williams had considered credible or taken seriously. The sharpened felling axe dug deeply, separating his spinal vertebrae below C3 and severing the phrenic nerve, exactly as intended. His assailant knew that the wound would cause immediate paralysis and, in the absence of nerve impulses to the diaphragm, would cause death as his victim was no longer able to draw breath. But that wasn't enough. Williams' dying body was roughly dragged backwards from the folding chair so that he was lying on the muddy bank. A moment later the axe rose and fell, then again, and again, until the last sinews were severed and his head finally came free, staining the earth red as it rolled towards the water's edge. Standing back from the headless corpse, the gore spattered figure looked on with a sense of satisfaction, watching as clouds of blood slowly dispersed like ink into the shallow fringes of the lake. 'One down, three to go', the killer said softly, then took a single photo of the murdered policeman before turning to follow the path back across the fields towards the waiting car.

When the call came in, Andy and Sheryl Bithell were still getting to know their newly acquired son. Having told anyone who mattered that Sheryl was going to take care of her ailing mother up in Scotland, which was unlikely as her mother had died years ago, they had instead set up a second home in a cottage just outside Rothbury. Andy had leased the place for a full year and, in a month or two, was planning to break the news that Sheryl must have been pregnant when she went up north. By the time she returned home with their baby son, everyone would be more or less used to the idea. To say that the panicked phone call from Mark Brandwood gave him cause for concern would have been a huge understatement. As a serving police officer had been brutally murdered, beheaded by the side of a quiet lake, there was no way to suppress the story or stop it from being all over the press and every television and radio news broadcast. The immediate danger, at least as far as the Bithells were concerned, was that the media wouldn't stop digging until they'd extracted every last ounce from every available source, something that could put their new family under scrutiny. As yet, there was no evidence to suggest Gryce had been responsible for the murder of the Detective Inspector, so there was currently no link to the puppy farm, but for how long? There was little doubt in Andy's mind that the situation could, and almost certainly would, change at any moment. Leaving Sheryl and the baby at the cottage, he reversed the big Volvo out onto the lane that ran down by the golf course, crossed the bridge into town, then set off back towards Blackpool. Assuming that the link would inevitably be made, he had to switch the main focus away from the old vicarage story, and quickly, but how? By the time he'd driven as far as Sycamore Gap the decision was made, he had to give them something else to think about, and it had to be more than just an anonymous tip-off pointing the finger at Gryce. Pulling off the road into a layby, he called a journalist that he'd done business with for several years. Two hours later, when he parked up near the Bonny Street station to meet with Brandwood and Stansfield, the story from 'a reliable source' had already broken. The 'Headhunter', a former doctor who'd been struck off for drug abuse and who suffered from a severe mental health condition, was on the rampage, no one was safe.

At the hurriedly arranged press conference Bithell reluctantly confirmed that certain aspects of the 'leaked' story were correct, although he made it very clear that media speculation about Gryce being a violent psychopath who had links to a known paedophile ring had not yet been substantiated. He went on to say that while members of the public should remain alert at all times, and under no circumstances approach the suspect, there was no need for widespread panic. He remained confident that the killer would soon be apprehended.

Detective Constable Bernie Stansfield wasn't just a big man, despite the belly that he'd put on over recent times he still had the strength and power from years of hard physical training. He no longer played rugby, his knees couldn't take the strain, but he still liked to attend matches and to spend several hours afterwards in the club bar. When he left the Bonny Street station after his brief meeting with Mark and the Guv'nor, annoyed that he'd missed most of the first half of a home match, he failed to notice the faded green Nissan Micra that tucked into the traffic behind him. Nor did he notice when the same car followed him all the way to the rugby club, only dropping back when he turned off into the car park. After a home win, half a dozen pints, and an argument over the selection of a new fly half, Bernie was in a good mood. He ambled back across the now much depleted car park, unconcerned that he was well over the drink-drive limit but thinking that perhaps he should have gone for a pee before leaving the bar. He had a quick look around and, after satisfying himself that there was no one else about, he unzipped and began to urinate against a nearly new BMW, smiling contentedly to himself as leant with one hand on the car roof. The sudden, sharp stinging pain in the side of his neck was enough to jolt him upright, spraying urine over his trousers and shoes. If his reactions hadn't been slowed by beer, he might just have got a hand to the figure who quickly danced out of reach, brandishing an empty syringe. He turned to face his attacker, unsteady, but ready to beat the shit out of anyone stupid enough to tangle with him. When he tried to take a step forwards his legs felt unbelievably heavy, as though he was trying to pull his feet out from deep, sticky mud. He was puzzled as to why his arms hung limply by his sides, then found that he couldn't even make a fist. Leaning heavily against the BMW, and suddenly feeling desperately tired, he watched as someone dressed in a long dark coat retrieved a walking stick from the boot of a tiny green car. A moment or two later, when his legs gave way beneath him, he slid slowly down to the tarmac, unable to lift a hand to save himself. Lying in a puddle of his own urine, Detective Constable Bernie Stansfield had a final, albeit short-lived, moment of clarity. It wasn't a walking stick after all, the person approaching him was carrying was an axe.

Chapter Twelve

"Okay," Yvie said. "I think it's time Joe and I brought you up to speed on what the Chief Super told us this morning. She's convinced that Bithell's death is linked to the killing of three police officers twenty years ago." She saw Tom, Cathy and Autumn stiffen in their seats at the possibility. What had been an unusual case had suddenly become even darker.

"The so-called Headhunter case." Joe added.

"Oh My Days!" Cathy exclaimed. "I hope the press don't make the same connection. Any inklings that they might have done?"

"Nothing yet, but too many people know how Bithell died for it to stay that way. It's only a matter of time, so we've got to be ready for it." Yvie didn't like holding things back from her team, but she couldn't reveal details of a very private conversation she'd had with her boss before they'd returned from Hutton. Knowing that they couldn't keep a lid on the story, they'd discussed the possibility of controlling the narrative, at least in some small part. Yvonne Southern was a part-time 'general interest' journalist working for the Bowland Courier, she was also a lifelong friend of Iron Annie and, more recently, a trusted friend of Yvie herself. Whilst the paper had a limited circulation the contacts that Southern had made, both during and after the Winter Beast case, virtually guaranteed that they could put their own spin on the breaking story, but only if they were the ones to break it.

Yvie and Joe spent the next hour recapping the main points from their earlier meeting. Cathy and Autumn were just as surprised as they had been to learn that the Chief Super had gone undercover to investigate a potentially corrupt DCI. Tom had worked directly for Iron Annie for several years, often undercover himself, before joining Yvie's small team. He was less surprised, but equally impressed. Joe's description of the 'puppy farm', particularly given the comments of many of the women who had given birth there, caused some genuinely mixed feelings. Whilst the idea of anyone selling children was abhorrent, the treatment of the mothers and the fact that they were being given choices and second chances, was hard to criticise. Nor did Gryce and Daniels profit from it, in fact Gryce subsidised it from his own personal wealth. Doing the job that they did, everyone sat around the table knew only too well what could, and all too often did, happen to vulnerable young women. The runaways, the homeless, the addicts and the troubled could so easily sink below the awareness level of everyday, ordinary people. Once out of sight, cut off from the herd, they became easy prey for the predators.

"Is anyone else struggling to believe how anyone, let alone someone afraid of heights, would even consider jumping down onto a glass roof?" Cathy queried. "Whether there's a ridge there or not."

"I agree," Joe said, "but two serving officers claim that's exactly what he did."

"I'm just glad that I didn't have to attend that PM, it must have been horrendous. Bithell's was bad enough." Cathy turned towards Autumn when the expected comment didn't arise. "You okay?"

"Yes, erm. So," Autumn paused, working hard not to dive straight in before she'd got her thoughts in order. "Are we really saying that our prime suspect in the murder of Andy Bithell is Eric Gryce, a.k.a 'The Headhunter'?" The air-quotes she made with her fingers hung in the air while she looked down at her notebook, thinking through what she was about to say next. "A serial cop-killer, who was nonetheless described as being a thoroughly dedicated and decent man, who no one had a bad word for. What was it one of his work colleagues said, 'the nicest, kindest man you could ever wish to meet'? A man who, despite intensive searches, hasn't been seen or heard of since not long after I was born."

"Pretty much," Joe grinned at her. "Funny old world, isn't it?"

"You haven't said how the case was wound up Boss. Did Gryce just disappear after the killings of, give me a minute," Cathy checked her notes, "Williams, Stansfield and Edwards?"

"Not sure yet, Joe and I are back with the Chief Super first thing tomorrow morning. Her main concern is, if it is Gryce," Yvie looked at each member of her team, "and she admits that is a very big if, he might be picking up where he left off twenty years ago." Noticing that the light was fading as they moved from late afternoon into early evening, Yvie decided that it was time to get back to the job in hand before they wrapped things up. "Okay, let's get back to the Bithell case. "Any luck tracing Oliver Bithell?"

"Not yet Boss, sorry. I was saying to Autumn that it looks like this kid doesn't want to be found. His bank cards have previously been used fairly regularly for cash withdrawals and shopping, but nothing since towards the end of March in Cardiff, where he was at uni. There was a cash withdrawal on Friday 31st March in Preston town centre, and a pub lunch at a place in between Euxton and Croston on April Fool's Day. I've asked for a flag to be put on the card, but you know how long it takes for an alert to come through."

"Good work Cathy. So, all we know for sure is that he came back up here shortly before his father was murdered, and hasn't yet returned to university. Where was his money coming from, do we know?"

"Monthly transfers from his father's account, plus there was a hefty lump sum paid in from his mother's account several months before she died."

"Okay. Order of play for tomorrow then." Yvie checked the notes she'd made since arriving back in the office. "Joe, you're with me at Hutton and we'll stop in at Bithell's house on the way back. Can you put whatshisname, the locksmith, on standby?

"Will do, it was young Raj. Big gold key stuck on top of his van."

"That's the one, he was like lightning over at Kitson's place." Yvie thought back to how a few pages of ancient handwritten text, found in a locked desk drawer, had been enough to tip the balance and bring her to accept what was, even after the event, a scarcely credible theory about the Winter Beast. She gave herself a shake, time to move things on. "Cathy, carry on trying to track down Oliver Bithell and, if you get a chance, see if you can find a copy of his father's book. If possible, try to set up a meeting with whoever was the ghostwriter on it, I'm assuming that he didn't actually write it himself."

"Got it Boss, will do." Cathy replied, already keying in a broad search for the book.

"Autumn, first job is to get the murder wall up and running. After that, see what you can find out about Edwin Gryce, the younger brother. See if he's still living up at, where was it, Arnside?"

"Yes Boss, I'll get the wall done tonight."

"No you won't. We're all going home in the next ten minutes."

"Tom, a bit of digging for you." Yvie unfolded a piece of paper that contained a handwritten list of names. "The Chief Super gave me this, to the best of her memory, it's all the members of Bithell's old team. She's put a star next to the ones she remembers as being part of his inner circle. Find out what you can about any of them that are still alive. Start with Brandwood, now that Bithell's dead he's the only one left out of the four people Gryce swore vengeance against."

"Yeah, if Autumn can locate him, do you want me to have a look at Edwin Gryce as well Boss? If Eric Gryce is back, there's a chance he may have been in contact with his brother."

"Which part of 'strictly desk work only' are you struggling with Tom?"

"All of it if I'm honest, Boss. I've still got a bit of a limp but I'm up to driving and interviewing, and I promise not to overdo things."

"Let's find him first, but I don't want you going off to see him by yourself or taking any chances."

"No worries, Boss." He knew exactly what she was referring to. When he and Yvie had been taken in by a faked cry for help coming from a workshop over at Woodplumpton, they'd been lured into a trap. One that had very nearly cost them both their lives. "Once bitten, and all that!"

"Right." Yvie stood up and raised her voice. "That's it, everybody out. Go home to your loved ones, come back fresh in the morning." No sooner had Yvie spoken the words than she regretted them. Although it was over four years since Tom's loved ones had been murdered, the previous case they'd worked together had raked up some raw and painful memories for the young DI. She was relieved when she saw Tom and Autumn leaving together, glad that he had someone to confide in. Cathy caught her eye and nodded knowingly towards the couple, then made the most outrageously obscene gesture Yvie had ever witnessed.

Chapter Thirteen

It was almost six-thirty when Yvie pulled up outside the house that had now become her home. At this time of an evening the lane that ran just off the centre of Chipping village was almost free of traffic, the legions of ramblers and cyclists now gone for the day. As she got out of the car and walked towards her front door, she could see a faint glow through the curtains of what had been, until less than a year ago, her spare room. Now it was a nursery, and in it were the two most important people in her life. When she'd first accepted the short-term secondment, which had been almost three years ago but now seemed like a lifetime, it had been at a point in her life when she was in serious need of a break from the rut she'd allowed herself to settle into back in London. Considering herself to be a career police officer, something she'd wanted to do from being a little girl, and having enjoyed a rapid rise through the ranks of the Metropolitan Police, the job had always come first. It was only the breakdown of what she now recognised to have been a convenient but empty relationship, that had made her think about what she truly wanted from life. The secondment was supposed to have been a breather, a time to reflect, she had never dreamed it would be the first step into a new and fuller life. She hadn't been expecting to stay up north, nor had she been expecting the warm and genuine welcome of people who would soon become close friends, or to find the old stone house that she'd loved from the moment she first stepped inside. But most of all, she hadn't been expecting to meet the love of her life and then to have their child, something she had all but given up hope of ever happening. Even thinking the words felt strange, never mind saying them out loud, but for the first time in her life she felt truly blessed. She took a moment to fully embrace the feeling before opening the door and stepping inside to rejoin her family.

"I'm home," she shouted, finding a space her jacket on the overcrowded brass hooks in the hallway before making her way upstairs.

"We're in here, and you're just in time, I was about to give Sir his bath." James said as he handed over their baby son. Yvie's heart flipped every time she saw the broad smile break out on the perfect little face, legs kicking, tiny hands reaching out, excited to see his mother. James gave them a moment and then stepped in for his kiss and a hug. "How was your first day back?"

"It's just got a lot better, but it was okay. I'm a little concerned about Anne, there's something not right. I'll tell you about it later."

"Sounds intriguing. Do you need a few minutes or are you okay to carry on here while I get dinner ready?"

"No, we're fine, aren't we stinky bum? Did daddy really think I wouldn't notice?"

"To be fair, it's pretty hard to miss. I was about to clean him up just before you came home."

"It's okay, you go. I'll give him his bath and then settle him down."

When Yvie came downstairs forty minutes later, hair still damp from the shower, she'd changed into an ancient rugby shirt and a pair of faded jogging bottoms.

"Why can't I smell food? I know we agreed to start eating more healthily, but I'm starving. I hope you're not going to let me down Mister Costello?"

"No, we're having tuna steak with a blob of basil pesto, cucumber, apple and cherry tomato salad with some thinly sliced shallots, capers, a touch of garlic, a splash of apple vinegar, and a small green leaf salad on the side. I've also made some sourdough rolls, just in case you came home hungry, which you always do. The tuna will only take a couple of minutes in the pan, and everything else is ready, do you want a glass of wine now or later?"

"Sounds great. I'll have a glass now please, while it's still nice outside." Yvie picked up the baby monitor and went through to the garden where she sat at the small bistro table, looking out over another equally unexpected joy, her garden. James came out a moment later and put two glasses of Malbec on the table.

"So, how did you get on with Conor, did you manage okay all by yourself?"

"To be honest, I wasn't all by myself. Jenn came and sat in with Conor for an hour or so this morning, while I went to do the shopping. I think she was disappointed that he didn't wake up. Then she popped round again in the afternoon with the plants that Jeff had promised you, but I think it might just have been an excuse check up on me."

"Bless her. We couldn't ask for better neighbours," Yvie said, and meant every word of it. The elderly couple next door had treated her like family, in a good way, ever since she'd first moved in. "But I think they find it a bit odd that you're staying at home looking after our son while I'm out working."

"I know it's not the norm but, as long as we're okay with it, that's all that matters."

"You will say something if you think it's not working though, won't you? I mean it James, I know I can get a little preoccupied with work sometimes, so you've got to tell me if I do."

"Listen to me," he reached across and took her hand, "I can't think of anything I'd rather be doing than caring for our son, and that's the honest truth. Anyway, tell me about Anne, I've always thought her nickname was spot on, she's as tough as old boots."

It felt wrong to speak of murder and decapitation with the gentle rhythm of their son breathing softly over the baby monitor in the background, but it needed to be done. Deeply unprofessional as it may be, Yvie had found that it helped her enormously to talk through cases with James. He made an excellent sounding board for her thoughts, and his alternative point of view had provided some telling insights in recent cases. It was against all policy and procedure to discuss highly confidential information with a member of the public, so Yvie salved her conscience by thinking of him as an unpaid, unofficial consultant. She quickly ran through the details of Bithell's death and the findings of the subsequent post-mortem, including her team's initial deliberations. James agreed with their opinion that the type of weapon used made it almost certain that the killing was planned rather than opportunistic. However, he was less sure about their thoughts on the subsequent decapitation. Whilst agreeing that it may indicate a deeply personal motive, he pointed out that throughout history beheading had always been a symbolic punishment. Yvie made a mental note to mention the possibility at the morning team brief, she wasn't entirely convinced but didn't want to rule out anything at such an early stage.

"Why was Anne so concerned about this murder in particular, was he an ex-colleague or something?"

"She knew him, although it was twenty years ago. He was suspected of being a bent copper." Yvie thought it best not to go into too much detail about the Chief Super's undercover role. "If we're going to do this before we eat, I'll just go up and check on Junior. I need the loo, and I think that just this once I'd like another glass of wine please." When she came back downstairs there were two glasses of wine sat on the patio table. James passed her the fleece jacket that normally lived on a hook behind the back door.

"Thought you might need this as well."

"Thank you." Having quickly thought it through while she was upstairs, Yvie began with a brief description of Gryce's family and professional background, his medical condition, and the abuse his younger sister had suffered before taking her own life. James listened intently while she went on to describe the horrific death of Anthony Daniels, and Bithell's claim that the man had jumped out of a window in an attempt to escape.

"To have witnessed his partner's death in such a manner must have been unbearable, and probably deeply traumatic." James commented sadly. "To experience something like that, particularly if he had some form of anger management issues, would certainly make Gryce's subsequent accusations, and even his swearing vengeance against those involved, a lot more understandable." When it came to the beheadings of Paul Williams and Bernie Stansfield, James dimly recalled hearing about the killings on the national news, but nothing of the story behind the headlines. He'd never heard of the Old Vicarage case, or what supposedly occurred at the 'Puppy Farm', and listened intently to Yvie's description of what they'd been able to piece together. When she admitted that she shared Joe's opinion, that the way the girls had been treated was more akin to an act of goodwill than a criminal enterprise, he was forced to agree.

"Yes, but the two extremes, the sinner and the saint, aren't necessarily mutually exclusive," he cautioned, "don't let it cloud your judgement."

"No, but it troubles me that such an apparently dedicated, well-thought of, well-meaning individual could suddenly have become the 'Headhunter'. A serial killer responsible for the deaths of three police officers." Yvie shook her head as she voiced her concerns. "Bithell was the third of four officers allegedly involved in the death of Anthony Daniels to be beheaded, and there's just no way that can be coincidence. I'm pretty sure Anne believes that Gryce is back and picking up where he left off all those years ago, either that or we have some sort of tribute killer doing it for him."

"What do you think?" James asked

"I honestly don't know. But with regard to Anne, I think there's more to it than she's letting on, I think she has a connection to the case she hasn't told us about yet. Whatever the reason, she wasn't for telling us this morning. Joe and I are back with her tomorrow so, hopefully, we'll know a little more."

"Okay. I'm not familiar with, what did you call it, episodic dyscontrol syndrome?" James asked, beginning to tap the words into his i-pad.

"Yes, apparently it can result in bouts of uncontrollable and often violent behaviour. So it goes some way towards a possible explanation, particularly if he was off his medication."

"Says here that it can be caused by alcohol or substance abuse, and also as a result of limbic system diseases or temporal lobe disorders. Having said that, right now it's the behaviour that's a lot more important than what's causing it. You will be careful, won't you? Promise me there'll be no heroics from Conor's mum." The unsubtle implications of his words weren't lost on Yvie, nor had he intended them to be. Although she'd played it down, he was very much aware of how close they'd come to losing her in the same incident that had almost cost Tom his life.

"Of course I will, you don't need to worry." She said it with a smile, but they both knew he'd be worried sick until the case was closed. "Oh! One last thing. Do you know anything about these mock battle societies, are they just grown men who like to dress up and play soldiers?"

"Hah! Enough to know that you should never let them hear you say anything like that." James laughed. "Then you'd have a real battle on your hands! A lot of the people who get involved take things very seriously, painstaking research into weaponry, exact recreations of uniforms, detailed studies of campaigns and the strategies adopted by both sides. Having said that, I imagine that there are also some who are in it for the dressing up, the fun of the fight and more than a few drinks afterwards. Unfortunately, the serious historians amongst them, and they really are experts in their chosen period, need the rabble in order to make it all work."

"I spoke to the chap who found Bithell's body, they were friends, and from what he said it sounds like he was one of the serious ones. An ex-senior officer, someone who was used to being in charge, so it sort of makes sense that he'd choose to be one step removed from the masses."

"Just be glad it isn't one of the Viking re-enactment groups you're dealing with," James smiled, "because those guys are real headbangers!"

Chapter Fourteen

Before eight o'clock the following morning, Yvie and Joe were sat in the Chief Super's office, watching as she filled three cups from the pot that sat on its own little trolley in the corner of the room. Yvie had already briefed her boss on the difficulty they were experiencing in locating the son, Oliver Bithell, and also given her a quick run through her intended course of action.

"Who did you put on Bithell's old team?"

"I've asked Tom to see what he can dig up," Yvie replied. "I told him to start with Mark Brandwood, the man needs to know that he could be at risk."

"Yeah, hard to believe after all these years, but it's possible. Tell Tom to use my name if anyone doesn't want to speak to him."

"Will do Ma'am." Yvie smiled, knowing that for some people the mention of Iron Annie Atkinson would provide the carrot, but for others it would be the stick - either way it would get results. Her boss placed her own cup on the table and sat down, ready to begin.

"Immediately following on from the deaths of Williams and Stansfield, we must have had every copper in Lancashire out looking for Gryce, but there was no sign of him anywhere." The Chief Super gazed out of her office window as she spoke, she'd thought of virtually nothing else since Bithell's body had been found. As hard as it was to accept that Eric Gryce had returned, with the possible exception of some form of bizarre copycat killing, there was no other logical explanation. "Things went quiet for several days, then we had our one and only stroke of luck, if you can call it that, a chance sighting of Gryce entering a fast-food shop in Morecambe. A young WPC, although I probably shouldn't refer to her like that these days, spotted him and radioed it in. She was a bright kid, as soon as she saw him she'd got rid of her hi-vis and her hat, and bundled her equipment up inside her fleece. Her orders were simple, keep Gryce under observation while a pick-up was arranged, but not to approach the man under any circumstances. Bithell's DI was already in Lancaster, she was co-ordinating one of the search teams, and was dispatched immediately to provide a non-uniform replacement for the WPC. Other cars and officers were diverted towards the general area but everyone was told to keep well back, no one was to risk alerting him."

"You said Bithell's DI was dispatched, with Williams dead, you were...." Yvie's point was cut short as the Chief Super continued as though she hadn't heard her.

"When he left the takeaway with his food, he made his way to the promenade and sat on a bench overlooking the bay. At first, the WPC was able to keep an eye on him from a distance, but there was a delay, Bithell had insisted on an armed support unit being part of the lift. The WPC's name was Julie Edwards, she was twenty-four years old and engaged to be married to a sergeant working from the same station. Sergeant Bill Thomlinson."

"You mean our Bill, Old Bill, from downstairs?" Yvie asked, watching as her boss, her friend, nodded sadly in reply.

"By the time Gryce had finished his meal, the DI had arrived in Morecambe and made contact, they agreed to keep their distance unless there was any danger of losing him. When he first got up from the bench, Gryce began walking along the promenade towards the West End, which was okay, but then he joined a small queue at a bus stop. It was nearly four o'clock, the schools were out for the day, and they knew the buses would be packed with kids. When a double-decker came down the road towards them, the DI gave the signal to move in." The Chief Super reached for her coffee and, finding the cup empty, got up and walked over to the trolley to replenish it.

"Ma'am, you were the only other DI in Bithell's team. It was you?" Yvie was insistent, needing to know. What had begun as a case conference had turned into something much more personal.

"Yes." Iron Annie still had her back to Yvie and Joe as she spoke, taking an age to stir a tiny splash of milk into her coffee. "I've only discussed this with one other person since the inquest and internal investigation were concluded, and that was nineteen years ago. However, that doesn't mean I haven't endlessly examined and re-examined what happened, what I could, and should, have done differently." Yvie was stunned at her boss's admission, and at the slight crackle in her voice. She knew from experience that behind the 'Iron Annie' nickname, was a deeply compassionate and caring woman. From what they were being told, it sounded very much like she blamed herself for the death of

Bill's fiancé. "I thought that perhaps I could give you a more accurate and objective description of what happened as a third party account rather than as a participant. I was wrong, I'm sorry."

"Anne," Yvie had never used her boss's given name at work before, "you don't need to do this. Honestly, you really don't."

"Excuse me a minute." The Chief Super placed her coffee cup on the table and left the room. Yvie and Joe exchanged concerned glances, neither had seen her like this before.

"She really doesn't need to do this, we…." Yvie stopped speaking when Joe interrupted her.

"Yes she does, and you'd do the same." Joe spoke softly but the emotion in his words was clear. "She's sending us out to catch a killer, one who targets police officers. You, me, Tom and the lasses, she'll give us every bit of information she can, she won't hold anything back, whatever it costs her." They sat in silence until the door opened and a much more recognisable Chief Super re-entered the room and took her seat.

"Sorry about that, it took me by surprise for a moment."

"Ma'am," Yvie began, but whatever she was about to say was waved away by a raised hand from her boss.

"So, I was only a couple of yards away from Gryce when he looked directly at me. Whether it was the expression on my face, or whatever, he knew immediately that I was coming for him. Up until then he'd seemed quite calm, just another guy in the street, I even thought for a moment that maybe we didn't have the right man. Then his head came up and I saw his whole face change, I saw the panic flash in his eyes. His movements became jerky, as though his arms and legs were hard to control, I remember the change in him being quite unnerving. I was already reaching for him and Julie was coming in from the other side when he pulled an old long-barrelled revolver out of the inside pocket of his coat. He struck me across the side of the head with the gun held in his fist, but even in his rage I noticed that he was careful to keep the barrel pointed upwards, away from anybody. I went down, dazed but still conscious, and saw him grab Julie and place the gun next to her head but, again, not pointing it directly at her. He half dragged her into the road; gesticulating with the pistol he forced a woman in an old Fiesta to stop and get out of her car. He bundled Julie in and before I could even get to my feet they were gone." The Chief Super shook her head and smiled, but there was no joy in it. "I was so close, I was sure I had him, but I messed it up. I let Gryce escape, but even worse than that, I let him take Bill's fiancé with him."

"Boss…, Anne…." Yvie struggled to find the right words, imagining the weight of her friend's self-inflicted but wholly misplaced guilt. It was Joe who calmed the moment.

"No lass, you didn't mess up, and you didn't 'let him' do anything." Despite being at least ten years her junior, not to mention several ranks lower down the ladder, Joe spoke with all the calm and reassurance of an older brother. Yvie had never heard anyone call Iron Annie Atkinson 'lass' before, it was akin to addressing the Pope as 'mate'. Having once queried his use of the term herself she'd been laughed at by Cathy who had told her it was a term of endearment and respect that Joe reserved for a very select few, and it had to be earned. "There's no way on earth you could have let him get on a bus full of kids. Instead, you put yourself in harm's way. You did the right thing, for all the right reasons, and I'm willing to bet my pension that in the same circumstances you'd do exactly the same again." Joe held her gaze until the Chief Super acknowledged his words with a nod of her head, before sitting up straighter in her chair.

"Yes, faced with the same choices I would. I've always known that I would, but sometimes that's just not enough." The Chief Super took a brief moment before continuing. Yvie and Joe could both sense the change in her, it was back to business. "Right, I've had my wobble, which I trust will stay between these four walls. Now let's crack on or we'll never get to the end of this."

It took the remainder of the morning for the full horror of that day, twenty years earlier, to be recounted in full. Despite the objective manner in which the Chief Super went on to describe the events, it was an uncomfortable experience for all of them. Somehow, knowing the outcome in advance made it even more difficult to listen to, anticipating the death of a fellow officer, the loved one of a colleague.

"The duty officer in the station had made sure that Bill, who wasn't on duty that morning, was informed that his fiancé had spotted Gryce. As soon as he was told, he'd immediately jumped in his car and made his way towards her location. He later told me that the moment he turned on to the promenade and saw people helping a young woman to her feet, he'd known that something was badly wrong. When he pulled up beside us and said he was a police officer I jumped into the passenger seat and shouted at him to drive. He didn't know me from Adam, but I managed to convince him." Yvie and Joe shared a knowing glance, both could imagine how that exchange would have gone. "We set off after the Fiesta which was heading north on Marine Drive. As I understand it, there were another half dozen cars taking positions around the promenade, but we never saw any back-up, at least not until it was too late."

"Why was that Ma'am?" Joe asked.

"Everything happened so fast that there was no effective co-ordination. Apparently, someone radioed in that they'd spotted a red Fiesta being driven at speed back towards Lancaster, so all available units went chasing after it. When they eventually managed to stop him, it turned out to be a boy racer in an XR2. Bill and I were pretty sure that we'd caught sight of Gryce once, up by Hest Bank, but we lost him again somewhere in the lanes by Bolton-le-Sands. As we were in Bill's own car, we didn't have a police radio, he had an old Nokia and I had a Blackberry but coverage was patchy at best. I spent ages with my arm stuck out of the window, just trying to get a signal so I could speak to Control. We couldn't get a helicopter, apparently Bithell tried but it wasn't available. Even twenty years ago, we didn't have the technology that's available now. Drones hadn't been invented; smart phones were only just being introduced, maps were all on paper…"

"You're not going to give us the old, 'You kids don't know how lucky you are speech', are you Ma'am?" Yvie had been in need of the bathroom for quite a while and had decided that a forced interruption was called for. "Back in a minute."

"Cheeky sod!" The Chief Super waited until the door had closed then turned to Joe. "How is she Joe, is she ready to come back?"

"She is Ma'am. James is great with little Conor, and they're making it work."

"Good. I know you'll look out for her Joe but, with a child and everything…." she paused, looking for the right words. "I know it's what we do, but Gryce is the only serial killer I've ever come up against who specifically targeted police officers. Promise me that you'll do your best to keep her out of harm's way."

"Always Ma'am."

Chapter Fifteen

Sophie: 2009

It had taken a superhuman effort for Sophie to stay away from drugs after her son had been stolen, but she'd managed it. Always hoping that he'd be found the next day, or the day after, had kept her clean for just over seven years. Even now, she still couldn't quite believe that Eric would have taken or sold her child, no matter what the police had said. Eric and Anthony were the kindest, most gentle people she had ever met, they'd even talked about helping her to get Lucy out of care. Strangely, it had been Bithell, the policeman she didn't believe, who'd helped her more than anyone. After the events at the Old Vicarage he'd advised her not to speak to the media, or agree to any interviews, no matter what they offered her. He cautioned that, whatever they promised, they would drag up her past and it would go against her chances of ever regaining custody of her daughter, and possibly young Anthony when they found him. Instead, he'd provided the rent deposit for a nice little terraced house in a half-decent area and fixed her up with a job in the new Asda. He'd also said that he knew people who could help her get Lucy back, but she needed to stay clean and maintain her silence. When she'd asked why he was helping her, an ex-junkie who'd sold her body for pennies in order to feed her habit, he'd simply said that he felt guilty about not preventing Gryce from taking her son.

Initially, Sophie was only allowed to meet her daughter for short, supervised visits. She remembered being so nervous that Lucy wouldn't remember her, or would want to stay with her foster family, but that very first visit had been a joy, it couldn't have gone better. It had subsequently taken almost a year of monitoring visits and inspections, not to mention endless meetings with social workers and an Independent Reviewing Officer, before Lucy was finally returned to her. It was the week before her eighth birthday and Sophie, for the very first time in her life, had been saving up to buy her daughter a present. That had been two years ago and, although she still thought constantly about her son, wondering where he was, what he was like now, she was as close to being happy as she'd been in many years. Lucy was doing well at school, she seemed popular and regularly had her friends to the house for play dates and sleepovers. Sophie often heard them talking about moving up to secondary school, giggling about the boys in their class, who they would snog and who they would marry.

Sophie hadn't seen or heard from Bithell in a very long time, in fact the last time there had been any contact between them was before Lucy had been returned to her. So, when she answered a knock at the door and found him stood there, her immediate thought was that they must have found her son. For a moment she couldn't speak, or even breathe, but her hopes were dashed almost as quickly as they had risen.

"No," Bithell was shaking his head, realising what she must be thinking. "It's not Anthony, that's not why I'm here." It took a moment or two for Sophie to regain her composure.

"Do you want to come in?"

"No. I just wanted to let you know that I've passed your name and phone number to a journalist, Philip Garmond. He's been helping me with a book about the Old Vicarage case and he wants to interview you."

"Wait, why does a journalist want to speak to me? You've always said that I should say nothing to anyone about Eric and Anthony." Sophie was adamant. "You said that the papers would drag up my past and use it against me. Why should I risk that?" Bithell was taken aback at the change in her, she wouldn't have dared to challenge him when they last spoke.

"I think that perhaps I'd better come in after all, if that's okay?" He stepped forwards leaving Sophie with little choice other than to move to one side. Once inside the house, he immediately noticed that it was spotlessly clean and tidy, windows were open and there was a freshness about the place. The modest furniture looked to be well cared for and the mirrors in the hall and lounge sparkled. Bithell hadn't been sure what to expect, it had been a couple of years since he'd last seen the woman whose child he had stolen, but he was surprised at the neat and comfortable home she had created for herself and Lucy. He followed her down a short hallway to the kitchen, where she had been chopping vegetables for soup. He sat at the small kitchen table and waited while she rinsed her hands at the sink before taking the only other chair.

"The guy helping me with the book says that an interview with you will add authenticity, particularly as you've never spoken about it before. All you'd need to do is…"

"You warned me not to talk about it," Sophie interrupted him, "and I didn't, even when they offered me money for my story. I've got a good life now, I'm not risking anything…"

"You won't be risking anything Sophie, I promise you. Doing it this way means you will have full control over the information that is included, nothing about your past will come out."

"No! You can't be sure about that. What if Lucy found out about my life back then? What would that do to her?" She was becoming increasingly anxious, Bithell decided to try a slightly different approach.

"Sophie, I've always been pleased that I was able to help you get Lucy back, and to get you started here," he raised his arms slightly in a gesture that took in the house, her life, everything. "I'd regard it as a personal favour if you would do the interview for me,"

"I know that I owe you, but you're asking me to risk everything. I can't…." she sobbed.

"Okay, don't get upset." Bithell sat back in the chair and paused, savouring the moment before delivering what he knew would be the killer punch. "I thought it would be better if you had the chance to put things in your own words, but I understand if you don't want to. Unfortunately, we can't leave you out of the book entirely, not the mother of the stolen baby. Philip will just have to do a little digging, maybe speak to a few other people who were around at the time and come up with his own version of events." He saw the fight go out of her and knew she understood exactly what he was threatening.

"Okay. I'll do it but, please," she looked up at him, tears streaming down her face, "don't let him write anything about me from before I was at the Old Vicarage."

"I think we can manage that, Sophie. In fact I'm sure of it." He nodded reassuringly. "Oh! There is one other thing though. I know you've never fully accepted what I said about Gryce having taken your son, but there really is no other possible explanation, there never was." He studied her face as he spoke. "If you could go along with what I said at the time, I would appreciate it. How do you feel about that?"

"Just tell me what you want me to say." Her head was down, for the first time in a long while she felt vulnerable again, helpless. "I don't care, so long as Lucy doesn't find out."

"No, that's the only thing I'd like us to be clear on, anything else that you tell Philip is up to you." Bithell stood up then reached into his jacket pocket and withdrew a fat black leather wallet. He counted out a number of £20 notes and placed them down on the table. "Philip has a house in Penwortham, but his wife is ill and he doesn't like to leave her on her own, so you'll need to take a taxi. This should more than cover it." After he'd gone, Sophie counted out the notes, there were ten of them. She knew, and she was in no doubt that Bithell would also know, that just one or two of the notes would have been sufficient to pay for any taxis. The message wasn't lost on her, she'd been bought and paid for, again.

When Sophie's mobile rang later that afternoon, she correctly guessed that it would be the journalist. Apart from Bithell, work, and a few of the mums at school, no one else had her number. He sounded friendly enough and was understanding about her work commitments for the next couple of days, so they agreed that she would go and see him the following Sunday morning. Lucy and two other girls were having a birthday pizza night and sleep-over at Natalie's house on Saturday, followed by a trip to Blackpool Zoo on Sunday, so she wouldn't have any explaining to do. The interrogation skills of a bright ten-year-old weren't to be underestimated.

Rather than waste money on taxis, Sophie had decided to set off early and catch the bus from Leyland town centre. Having mistakenly got off a stop too early, she had then had a lengthy walk to get to the very nice-looking detached house situated on a leafy cul-de-sac. Arriving on time, but slightly out of breath, she noticed the long access ramp leading up to a broad turning area outside the front door. A couple of minutes later, when her first ring of the doorbell had gone unanswered, she was about to give it another try when the door was pulled open.

"Hi, sorry about that, please come in." The voice was immediately recognisable as the man she's spoken to on the phone, he smiled at her then immediately turned his back and set off up the stairs. "If you could close the door, my office is on your right, make yourself comfortable, I'll be back in a minute." The words came out in a rush but Sophie got the gist of it and did as he asked. The room she found herself in, unmistakeably used as an office, was large and airy with a bay window overlooking the front garden and two walls taken up by floor to ceiling bookshelves. An untidy desk was placed to one side, and on it were piles of notebooks, newspaper cuttings, loose papers and photographs. A large screen monitor stood towards the back of the desk with a mouse and keyboard taking up the only other clear space. There was a tiny table in front of the bay window, her mother would have called it a wine table, and on it was a broad wooden bowl that had such a warmth about it that it appeared to glow. She moved closer to get a better look at the intricate inlays and, inside, a collection of highly polished apples, oranges and pears, all crafted from different types of wood. She fought the urge to reach out and touch.

"Beautiful isn't it?" Sophie started in surprise, she hadn't heard him come into the room. "Sorry, I haven't introduced myself, I'm Philip, and I'm assuming that you must be Sophie?" He smiled and gestured towards one of two chairs by a small coffee table.

"Yes, that's right. Pleased to meet you."

"Sorry about your wait, my wife had been taking a shower and I was hoisting her back into bed. She hates it when I leave her hanging in the air."

"I'm sorry, I didn't realise."

"No, that's fine." He waved away her apology. "Now, would you like a tea or a coffee before we start work?"

"Tea would be nice, if it's no trouble?"

"Excellent, I'll go and make us some." He went to the desk and picked up a stack of photographs. "In the meantime, would you mind having a look through these. There are photos of the Old Vicarage, some of the girls who stayed there, maybe even when you were there. See if anything jogs your memory, or if you think there's something that may help to paint the picture of what went on there."

"Why did you want to speak to me, what has DCI Bithell told you about me?" Sophie blurted out. She'd been determined not to ask the question but, now that it was done, she wasn't sure she wanted to hear the answer.

"Andy and I go way back, that's why he came to me. The book is his early retirement project, or at least he hopes it will be. He told me what he thought I needed to know in order to write the book but, in my opinion, it needs a level of corroboration from people who were actually there. I'm sorry to say that Mark Brandwood flatly refused to be involved and, apart from some of the girls who gave birth there, you are the only other 'involved person'," he let the air quotes hang for a moment, "who is still around. I'm aware that your son Anthony was taken by Eric Gryce, and I can't imagine what you've been through since then. Before we begin, I'll take you through the broad outline, chapter by chapter, if you decide at any stage that you don't want to continue, then that's fine, it's your choice."

"Okay, thank you. I'll be fine." Feeling reassured, Sophie picked up the pile of photographs from the table and began to flick through them while Philip went off to make the tea. There were photographs of the house from all angles, the conservatory, the delivery room, the guest bedrooms, she even recognised the room where she'd stayed for those few short weeks with Anthony. It brought back fond memories of that time, and of Eric and his partner Anthony. She regretted never having told them that she intended to name her son Anthony Eric, after the two of them. To that day, it was still the name she used whenever she thought of the son who had been so cruelly taken from her. When Philip returned with a tray holding two mugs of tea and a plate of biscuits, Sophie was sat upright in her chair, her back rigid. He could immediately sense the tension in the room.

"Who's this with Bithell?" Sophie asked, her voice cracking slightly as she struggled to control her emotions.

"Oops, sorry! They shouldn't be in that pile. The publisher requested some shots of Andy and his family for the back cover, if we ever get that far. As you can see, I'm not the tidiest worker in the world." Philip joked and was about to continue but, when he looked at Sophie, the phrase that came immediately to mind was, 'looks like she's seen a ghost'. The colour had drained from her face, he could hear her taking deep breaths while she stared at an image of three smiling people. The photograph looked like it had been taken in a professional studio; she recognised Bithell, she assumed that the woman was his wife, but the boy?

"Who are they?" She asked again, her voice barely audible.

"That's Andy's wife Sheryl, and their son Oliver."

"No it's fucking not!"

"Sorry, I don't know what you…. " Philip rocked back on his feet and looked alarmed at the unexpected outburst. Sophie could tell from his face that he clearly had no idea what she was referring to, she also knew that she had to get a grip on the rage that was coursing through her and hide her suspicions from him, or Bithell would find out. Picking up more photographs she leafed through them and allowed herself to cry, the tears coming easily when she thought of the lost years when she should have been with her child. She apologised time and again as she stood up, saying that seeing photographs of the house, as well as Eric and Anthony, had taken her by surprise, that she was being silly, but she couldn't stay.

Chapter Sixteen

When Yvie returned, fresh cups of coffee were on the table and Joe was showing the Chief Super pictures of a litter of springer spaniel puppies. His younger sister was gaining a reputation as breeder of champion gundogs, as well as running a thriving boarding kennel from the family farm.

"They'll be ready in another ten weeks or so, Ally won't let them leave their mother any younger. You'll have to let me know soon if you want to take your pick though, there's a waiting list."

"Already decided Joe, I want that one." She pointed towards a liver and white coated bundle of fur that was looking quizzically back into the camera lens. "She's a beauty."

"She is Ma'am, but I thought you said you wouldn't have a dog while you were still working." Yvie stopped, realising what she'd just said. "You're not thinking of retiring surely, you're not…"

"No, I'm not! Anyway, who said the pup was for me?" Iron Annie closed off the discussion. "Now you're back, we can carry on."

"Just a quick update before we do, if that's okay Ma'am. I've had a call from Cathy, still no trace of Oliver Bithell, but she managed to track down the guy who worked on his dad's book. He only lives a few miles away in Penwortham, so she's arranged to see him later this morning. It's a long shot, but I think it's worth looking into."

"Yeah, you never know your luck!" Joe agreed. "Does make you wonder about Bithell's son though; we should have been able to locate him by now."

"Either he doesn't want to be found, which in itself is highly suspicious, or something has happened to him. Whichever it is, he needs to remain a priority action." The Chief Super added.

"Agreed. Also, Tom's been following up the list of names you gave me and he's on his way to interview DS Mark Brandwood, as we speak. Sounds like he's not in the best of health, he told Tom that he's got chronic COPD, he's on ambulatory oxygen and lives on his own. Apparently, he jumped at the chance of being interviewed."

"Must be starved of company," Joe commented, "poor bugger!"

"No, Joe." Iron Annie was shaking her head. "I remember Mark Brandwood from years ago, he was only a DC back then, Bithell's man through and through. He was, and you can quote me on this, a right little shit. If there is any justice in this world, you reap what you sow, and in his case that would be pretty bloody awful." Yvie and Joe exchanged a glance, it was so unusual for their boss to make such a comment, or speak of anyone with such obvious distaste, that neither of them was about to contradict her.

"That's it Ma'am, nothing else to report."

"Okay kids, shall we continue with the history lesson then?" The Chief Super asked, making a point of holding eye contact with Yvie, just to let her know that her earlier comment hadn't been forgotten. "We searched the lanes for half an hour or so, nothing! Bill was beside himself with worry, desperate for news. He was fully aware of what had been done to Williams and Stansfield and, as much as I tried to reassure him that Gryce had no grudge against Julie, he was struggling to hold it together. I managed to get a signal and spoke to one of Bithell's admin support staff, I couldn't get through to Bithell himself, and asked her to check if Gryce had any links or connections to the area north of Lancaster and west of the M6. I didn't think he'd risk the motorway, or the A6, and with nothing else to go on it seemed to be the most likely option. She rang me back five minutes later, we hadn't dared to move in case I lost the signal, and said all she could find on the electoral register was an Edwin Gryce, living on Sandside Road, just outside Arnside. With it being such an uncommon surname, I thought it was definitely worth a shot and I told her to redirect a couple of cars to meet us there."

"I don't know the area," Yvie said, "is that the place you mentioned yesterday, Arnside?"

"It is, yes. We were convinced that Gryce would stick to the quieter lanes; I remember that Bill set off like a bat out of hell, terrified that we'd be too late to save Julie. Up until then, other than a quick introduction, we hadn't really spoken about anything other than finding Gryce and Julie. It was only when we'd passed by the holiday parks around Silverdale that he told me they were getting married in three weeks' time."

"Jesus Christ." Joe said softly. "It must have been hell for him."

"Oh, it was," Iron Annie sighed deeply, "and then it got worse. We caught sight of Gryce's car again just after we'd passed Arnside Knott, I remember it because Bill said that was where he'd proposed. All I could do was keep trying to reassure him that it would all be okay. We were in Bill's own car, so Gryce wouldn't have recognised it, but I still told him to hang back, not to risk spooking him, but he just couldn't do it. He was desperate to get close enough to find out if Julie was still in the car. We both knew that what he really meant was to check if she was still alive."

"Understandable Boss," Yvie commented, "the not knowing if she was okay or not, must have been tearing him apart."

"Yeah, I know, but it's something he's never forgiven himself for, and probably never will." The Chief Super gathered herself for what was to come. "We caught up with them only a couple of minutes later, Bill tucked in close behind and we could both see Julie in the front seat. Whether we were too close, or possibly he recognised me in his mirror, I don't know, but something made Gryce panic. He put his foot down hard, and Bill's reaction was to do the same, he wasn't going to risk losing them again. It was a decent enough road, but we were both rattling along at breakneck speed. Gryce reached Arnside ahead of us, there were cars parked on either side of the promenade and we were both going way too fast. A young boy on a bicycle came off the little stone pier and straight out into the road ahead of Gryce's car. I don't know how he missed him, he didn't have time to brake, he just swerved hard to the right and ran straight into the back end of a council wagon. We were only a matter of yards behind and we both saw Julie thrown clean through the windscreen, we even heard the second impact as she crashed head first into the tailgate of the wagon."

"Oh, dear God!" Yvie was horrified. "Bill saw his fiancé die, the poor man."

"He swerved hard, trying to avoid crashing into the back of Gryce's car, and next thing I knew we were rolling over. Fortunately, Bill's car had airbags and they probably saved us, but my window had been open and something caught against my shoulder. I was bleeding quite heavily and I later found out that my arm was broken but, apart from that, we had no other significant injuries. The car was on its side, I remember that it took me a minute or two to scramble up and out of the driver's door once Bill had got clear. While he was climbing out he'd asked if I could manage, as soon as I said that I could he went straight to Julie. By the time I got to my feet I could see him cradling her body." The Chief Super paused again, lost in the moment.

"Was Gryce injured," Yvie asked, in an attempt to rouse her boss from the dark thoughts that must have plagued her for twenty years.

"I don't think so, he must have been wearing a seatbelt. I was just about to ring for an ambulance when Gryce grabbed my injured arm and pulled me towards a gap in the railings. Other people were beginning to gather but once he started waving his gun around they all backed off. There were some steps leading down to the shore and he forced me to go down onto the sand. I had no idea what he was going to do next, or how he was hoping to escape by going down onto the foreshore, I thought maybe he had a boat stashed somewhere but he kept heading for the river. I could hear a siren, but it didn't sound like the emergency services."

"It was probably the tidal bore siren, they sound it twice when the tide is on the way in," Joe said. "It's possible that Gryce was intending to wade across the river, ahead of the bore."

"What's the bore?" Yvie asked, looking puzzled.

"It's the tidal bore on the River Kent. In a lot of places the water isn't very deep but as the tide rises across Morecambe Bay it's funnelled into the mouth of the estuary. It builds up even higher where the estuary narrows and forms a mini tidal wave that sweeps down over the sands, it's quite something to see on a high tide. It can be dangerous if people aren't aware of it, which is why they sound the sirens as a warning. My parents used to take us to visit an auntie who had a smallholding in Storth, a little further up the estuary, quite near to Sandside. We spent many a happy hour making rafts or treading for flounders." Joe saw that Yvie was looking even more puzzled by his reminiscences, and he'd also noticed that the Chief Super looked to be in need of a break for a moment or two longer, so he continued. "Flounders are little flatfish, like plaice but not as tasty, ask your James, he'll know. They bury themselves in the sand and we used to wade out and feel for them with our toes, then we'd try to grab 'em."

"And you think that Gryce could have been trying to get across to the far side before the tidal bore came in?" Yvie was well aware that there was often little logic in the last resort of a desperate man.

"Possibly, but there's deeper channels and quite a lot of sinking sand in places, it could have made it difficult if he was dragging an injured hostage with him." Joe glanced towards the Chief Super; she was nodding her agreement.

"I think you're probably right Joe, it sort of makes sense, but we'll never know for sure. Whatever the reason, we were soon wading into the river. I don't know if it was shock, pain or blood loss but I remember feeling that I was close to passing out. We were probably halfway across when I heard Bill shouting, raging at Gryce. He'd left Julie's body in the care of a first responder and was striding out into the river, gaining on us with every step. Gryce pointed the gun at him but he ignored it, he just kept coming. I couldn't do anything to help, by then I think I was probably dropping in and out of consciousness, struggling to stay upright. I remember hearing three gunshots but it wasn't until later that I found out the first shot had missed but the second caught Bill in the leg, and the third shattered his left elbow. I don't know exactly what happened after that, but for some reason Gryce just let go of my arm and I found myself laying on my back in the water, then I felt the wave take me."

"It's hard to believe that it's Bill we're talking about." Yvie thought back to when she'd first visited HQ with Joe and had commented on 'Old Bill', the quirky, but highly popular, desk sergeant with a fractured sense of humour. Joe had told her that as long as anyone could remember, Bill had been on the desk after some sort of incident years earlier had left him with limited use of his left arm. Another piece in the Iron Annie puzzle dropped into place.

"We didn't know it at the time, maybe Gryce did, but it was a spring tide, a high one at that. They always produce a much more powerful bore and, according to the people who were watching, when it hit Bill and Gryce they were both knocked off their feet by the sheer force of the wave. I was rolled over and over, drowning, I couldn't have saved myself for all the tea in China. I'll never know how he did it, but somehow, despite being shot twice, Bill managed to regain his footing and grab me before I was swept away. He dragged me to the shore, gave me mouth to mouth, and kept me alive until the paramedics reached us. There was a massive search operation, but Gryce was never found, alive or dead."

"That's a hell of a story lass." Joe was clearly impressed. "Sounds like you should have written the book, not Bithell."

"Not my style Joe." This time her smile held genuine warmth. "I never went back to my old post with the Devon and Cornwall force. My parents were getting on a bit, and my father had been quite ill, so I decided to stay up here, to be nearer to them."

"You stayed even though you'd been working undercover for IA?" Yvie asked.

"Yes, although I did transfer across to HQ when I returned to duty. There was never a formal case against Bithell's team, so I was never required to give evidence against other officers. Fortunately, the way the whole thing had been set up, there was no record that I'd been placed here as part of an internal investigation."

"....and Bill?" Yvie was intrigued.

"He was off work for several months getting over his injuries, but quite early on it became clear that he would never regain full use of his arm. His line manager at the time, who is now our illustrious Assistant Chief Constable Gregory Chaperon, with the backing of HR, wanted to retire him on 'ill health'. Bill didn't want to go."

"He's still here, so what happened?"

"Everybody loves a hero. The Cabinet Office Honours and Appointments Secretariat were bombarded with hundreds of nominations for him to receive an award. I believe the wording of the letters contained multiple variations on the theme of *'for saving the life of a fellow officer.... in the line of duty.... no regard for his own personal safety.... facing an armed criminal'*. There was even a public campaign that started off in several local papers and radio stations, it was soon picked up by media outlets across Lancashire." Iron Annie smiled at the memory, although Yvie wasn't sure if the smile was for the outcome or, more likely, the orchestration behind it. "He was awarded the Queen's Medal for Gallantry."

"Bloody hell! I'd no idea," Joe exclaimed.

"No, he doesn't like to talk about it. The then Chief Constable stepped in, overruled them all, and created a post for him here at HQ." There was no mistaking the genuine fondness in the Chief Super's tone. "The daft old bugger has been here ever since."

Chapter Seventeen

Sophie: 2009

When Sophie returned home from Penwortham she wasn't surprised to see Bithell's car parked outside her house. Given the state she'd been in when she'd walked out of Philip's office, what must have seemed to the journalist to be a full-on emotional breakdown, he'd probably rung Bithell as soon as she was out of the door. It had taken her nearly two and a half hours to walk home, all the time trying to tell herself that it couldn't be true, that she must be mistaken. But the mother inside her knew differently and wasn't for giving up without a fight. Ignoring the car, and Bithell, as he climbed out of the driver's door, she opened the narrow gate and set off down the path to her front door.

"Sophie, wait." he called, catching up with her in a couple of strides. "Philip said you were upset about something, that you left in a hurry."

"Yeah, I did." The one thing Sophie had known with absolute certainty from the moment she saw the photograph, was that she mustn't let Bithell know of her suspicions. She didn't know what she was going to do, or how to go about finding out the truth, let alone proving it. However, there was no doubt in her mind whatsoever that if Bithell knew what she was thinking he would find a way to crush her. Instead, she gave him the same story that she'd used with Philip. "It was the pictures of Eric and Anthony, and the room I stayed in with my Anthony for a short time after he was born. It was all just too much, I got very emotional. Please apologise to Philip for me and tell him that I'll go back and do the interview."

"Okay, if you're sure." He was studying her closely. "Philip seemed to think you were angry about something, one of the photographs."

"Not really, if anything I think it was seeing the picture of Anthony Daniels, he was so kind to me, they both were, and knowing how he died…." Sophie had to pause for a moment, there was a lot of truth in her story, and a lot of pain. "I could feel it all welling up inside me, I carried on flicking through the photos Philip gave to me, but I wasn't taking anything in. I don't think I could look at them again when I go back, that's not a problem is it?"

"No, probably best if you don't." Bithell agreed. "I just wanted to check that you'd got home safely, that you were okay." As he got back into his car ready to leave, Sophie even managed a smile, every bit as fake as his concern, when she nodded her thanks. When she closed the door behind her, the smile was gone, now she had to plan.

That evening was the first time Lucy had ever been allowed to make her own tea. She felt very grown up making herself beans on toast, it almost made up for her mum not wanting to hear about the party or the zoo. As the weeks passed by, Lucy soon found that making her own meals was no longer a novelty, and neither was finding that there was no food in the cupboards or clean clothes in the wardrobe. Sometimes her mum would be out when she came home from school, and occasionally she'd go out in the evenings, leaving her by herself. Whenever Lucy asked where her mum was going, the only reply she received was, 'I need to check something, it's important'. She didn't understand why she had to stay off school sometimes, standing outside one school while all the children arrived in a morning, a different school while they were in the playground at lunchtime, and a third school while the children left for home in the afternoon. She missed her friends; she also missed her mum.

Sophie's biggest problem, at least in her opinion, was that she didn't know where Bithell lived. Any request for information, no matter how casually it was couched, would no doubt be reported back to him, and that was something she just couldn't risk. Instead, she'd decided that, if necessary, she would stand outside every school in Lancashire until she found Anthony. Sophie's evenings were spent planning, checking locations of primary schools on a second-hand laptop that had been provided for Lucy to do her homework on. She made handwritten lists of all the schools she'd visited, the time, day and date, was there a breakfast club, or regular after school events, which school would require a second, or third visit.

A partner, or a close friend, may have spotted the change in Sophie at an early stage and offered support while urging her to 'get a grip', or words to that effect, but she had neither. An appointment with a medical practitioner, or a visit by a skilled social worker, may have identified her obsessive behaviour. They would likely have suggested counselling, or other measures to avoid a more serious intervention in the future, but she was seen by neither. Towards the end of her second month of fruitless searching for her son, Sophie lost her job. Initially, she'd been called to the manager's office to explain why she'd failed to turn up for her shift on two occasions during the previous week. Two days later, following a complaint from other members of staff, she was called in again, this time for a brief, but nonetheless embarrassing all round, word about her personal hygiene. Up until fairly recently, her manager would have named Sophie as one of her most able employees. Whilst she wasn't fully aware of Sophie's circumstances, she thought that most likely there was some sort of problem at home. When she asked if Sophie needed time off, or if the company could help in any way, Sophie merely thanked her and said that everything was fine. In reality, things couldn't have been further from fine. Her attendance continued to deteriorate and, even when she did turn up for work, she was preoccupied to the extent that she couldn't concentrate on what she was supposed to be doing. Despite repeated warnings, and even a couple of supposedly final warnings, each of which resulted in yet another offer of assistance being declined, Sophie failed to help herself and left her regretful manager no option other than to sack her. In many ways she was relieved, at least she could now devote more time to searching for her son. Money was going to be a problem, but that didn't matter, nothing was as important as Anthony.

When the breakthrough came, it was nothing to do with hard work, doggedness or planning, it was sheer fluke. Sophie was hoping to use the 'Free Ads' section of the weekly free newspaper, the one that consisted almost entirely of cut-price double glazing, 'cheap' loans, and car advertisements, to sell off a few of her meagre possessions, and maybe some of Lucy's old toys. She opened the paper on the dining table and there, looking straight into the camera, was a face she recognised immediately. One of the three she had seen in the photograph at the journalist's house, she would have recognised Sheryl Bithell anywhere. The woman pretending to be Anthony's mother, along with other Governors from a primary school in Longton, had been photographed at the opening of a new wildlife garden, designed and created by the pupils. Feeling as if a huge weight had been lifted from her shoulders, Sophie reached for the exercise book where she kept her records. It was a school she'd already been to, a lunchtime visit squeezed in between the morning drop-off and the afternoon pick-up at two larger schools. She remembered walking up and down the street, trying to appear inconspicuous, as she'd stared into the playground. It had occurred to her that maybe Anthony went home for lunch and she'd marked up the school for a further visit, but hadn't yet got around to it. Sophie checked the time on her phone, the children would have already gone home for the day, but tomorrow she was sure she would see her son. Having hardly slept, the thought that her stolen child may be only six or seven miles away had kept her awake until the early hours, she was still up and out of the house by 6am. When she'd checked the bus routes and fares on the old laptop, and then the money left in her pocket, she realised that she hadn't enough for the two buses in each direction, so she was going to walk. It would be kinder to let Lucy sleep on for an hour or two, no point in dragging her along, she reasoned as she closed the front door behind her. Maybe when she'd got Anthony back they'd have a little party, just the three of them.

In the end, it had been almost too easy. The walk had taken Sophie a little over two hours and since arriving outside the little school she'd been sat on a bench from where she had a view of the school gates. A white Range Rover Evoque pulled up no more than twenty yards away from her and, as she looked up, Anthony got out of the passenger door and started walking towards her. It was him, her boy, she would have known him anywhere. Sophie got to her feet, tears streaming down her cheeks as she called to him.

"Anthony, Anthony, it's me. I'm your mum." The horrified look on the young boy's face stopped her in her tracks. She could only watch as he turned and fled back in the direction of the car he'd just got out of. Sophie took a couple of faltering steps towards him, needing more than anything to comfort her son. "Anthony please. Honestly love, I really am your mum. Let me explain…."

"Leave my son alone." Sheryl Bithell had jumped out of the driver's door as soon as she'd seen what was happening. She positioned herself between Sophie and the boy. "I don't know who you are, or what you think you're doing but if you don't go away, right now, I'm going to call the police."

"Call them, and then they can give me back my son. Anthony, "she shouted, "it really is me, I'm your mum."

"His name is Oliver, and he is my son. Now back off or…." Sheryl didn't get to finish her threat as Sophie tried to push past her, resulting in the pair of them falling to the floor in an undignified tangle.

"Mum, Mum, no!" The fear, the urgency, in the young boy's voice was unmistakeable. Both women stopped tussling and turned towards him, then Sophie's heart broke once more when she saw that it wasn't her he was calling to. She could see the tears on Anthony's face, frightened that a mad woman was attacking his mother, the only mother he'd ever known, the only mother he'd ever loved. Sophie got to her feet and, after a last look at the boy as he rushed to embrace his mother, she turned and ran.

Retribution, although nothing was ever attributable to Andy Bithell, was swift, brutal and decisive. Later that morning, while Sophie was still walking back towards Leyland, Detective Sergeant Mark Brandwood reported receiving a tip-off from an anonymous source. After ensuring that every applicable procedure had been followed to the letter, including a fully documented risk assessment, he then led the raid on a terraced house in Leyland. In the lounge, and with a sleight of hand display that would have earned him a place in the Magic Circle, DS Brandwood himself pulled a child's pencil case from down the back of a settee. Instead of coloured crayons, it contained a number of tiny self-seal bags and paper wraps, more than enough cocaine, ecstasy, heroin and methamphetamine to be considered dealer quantity. In the kitchen, and with a further flourish, he struck lucky once more when he checked the salad drawer of an otherwise empty refrigerator and, after calling one of the uniforms over to witness his find, came out with an envelope containing just over £2,000 in cash. Before leaving the kitchen, he raised the lid of a pedal bin, reached deep inside, and came out holding several disposable gloves. With his trio of damning finds carefully sealed in separate tamper evident bags, all items duly recorded, and all relevant sections of the evidence bag labels completed, he gave himself a mental pat on the back for a job well done. Unexpectedly, the two uniformed officers he'd sent to check the upstairs rooms came back down with a bonus prize, a young girl. Tearful, and a little dishevelled, she said her name was Lucy. Yes, Mark thought to himself, this one's turned out even better than the boss ordered, a fatter than usual envelope this month was definitely on the cards.

Within a matter of hours, and for the second time in her short life, Lucy found herself the subject of an Emergency Protection Order.

Chapter Eighteen

It was mid-afternoon by the time Yvie and Joe travelled back from Hutton, although there had been a brief stop for a late lunch in the form of a tuna salad sandwich for one, and a pork pie followed by a sausage roll for the other. Unfortunately, lunch had so far been the highlight of the afternoon, Bithell's house having yielded nothing of any great significance. Raj had been waiting for them when they arrived at the nice four bedroomed detached house on a quiet lane, about half a mile off the Liverpool Road. He'd opened the front door in a matter of seconds, something that made Yvie wonder if there was any point at all in locking doors, and then worked his magic on two desk drawers and a metal storage cabinet. Apart from some basic office stationery, the drawers held nothing more than a range of domestic bills and account details, car purchase and insurance documents, bank and building society statements, all meticulously filed in date order and much the same as might be found in any family home. The only contents of the storage cabinet were two box files labelled up as 'The Old Vicarage' and a small cash box holding just over three hundred euros and two old style burgundy passports belonging to Bithell and his late wife. Leaving the cash box in the cabinet, Yvie sealed the box files into large tamper evident bags along with an older model laptop that had been sat on the desk. There was no sign whatsoever of any preparation for a new book, no notebooks, stacks of papers, photos, newspaper clippings - nothing. A quick look around the rest of the house was enough to see that only the office, dining kitchen and one bedroom appeared to be in regular use. Everywhere was clean and tidy, but Yvie couldn't shake the feeling that it was also a cold and lonely place, no longer a home and probably hadn't been for some time. Whatever it was that Bithell had been planning, if in fact he had been planning anything, they weren't going to find it here. The drive back to Clitheroe passed in silence as they both thought about the incredible story the Chief Super had related just a few hours earlier, each hoping that they'd be able to lay at least some of her ghosts to rest.

The moment they walked into the office Yvie could immediately sense the changed atmosphere in the room. It was lighter, more positive, the upshift that comes when some of the random pieces of information start to fit together and allow, what might just possibly be, the first faint glimpses of a bigger picture. Joe placed a small, white cardboard box on the table before walking over to the kitchen area to fill the kettle. He was nimbly intercepted by Autumn who took the kettle from him, not through any sense of rank or duty, but simply because he made rubbish tea. Returning to the table he noticed Cathy was intently eyeing the white box.

"Are they what I think they are?"

"Well, if you're thinking, 'are they custard slices with vanilla icing from your all-time favourite bakers', then yes, they are."

"Oh, I love you." Cathy gasped.

"It's always nice to be appreciated, but…" Joe was cut off mid-sentence.

"I was speaking to the cakes!"

When everyone was seated, all with mugs of tea and empty side plates holding only crumbs of flaky pastry and fond memories of creamy custard, Yvie asked Tom to begin the afternoon briefing.

"Okay. This morning I went to see ex Detective Sergeant Mark Brandwood at his home in Longridge; he was retired on ill-health grounds just over six years ago. He's in a really bad way, it took ages for him to answer the door even though he was expecting me. When he did manage to let me in, he had to take several breaths through an oxygen mask before he could speak, he was connected up to a portable oxygen cylinder the whole time I was there. It was odd, I think he only agreed to see me because he's housebound and, apart from a domestic care worker who visits three times a week, he doesn't get to see anybody."

"Don't go feeling sorry for him mate, the Chief Super would have something to say about that." Joe waved away Tom's puzzled glance. "I'll tell you later. Go on."

"He knew about Bithell being murdered, although only what was on the news. He seemed quite bitter about something or other but when I pushed him on it, all he had to say was, and I quote, 'The ungrateful bastard never called and never came to see me, not even once'. When I explained that he was now the last one alive of the four people Eric Gryce had sworn to take his revenge on, he just looked at me and said, 'You call this alive?'. He began to laugh but it quickly turned into a coughing fit so I went into the kitchen to get him some water. Stacks of dirty dishes were congealing in the sink, the waste bin was overflowing, it was a real mess. So, while he got himself settled, I ran some hot water and did the washing up, had a quick wipe round the worktops and emptied the bins."

"You don't even do that at home," Autumn exclaimed, and immediately realised that she may have given away more than intended.

"It was clear that he either wouldn't, or couldn't, give me anything about Bithell, probably to avoid implicating himself. However, when I was on the doorstep and about to leave, he asked me if I believed in coincidence. When I said that any good detective has a healthy mistrust of coincidence, he nodded and I thought he was agreeing with me. Then, after a good few puffs on his oxygen, he asked me this," Tom paused and checked his notebook, wanting to get the words exactly right. "What would be the odds of a baby being stolen from a crime scene, on the exact same day that the wife of the lead detective in charge of the same crime scene goes to Scotland to nurse her ailing mother? Particularly when the wife returns a full twelve months later with a child who is, as near as damn it, one year old."

"He was telling you that Bithell stole the child?" Cathy asked, then put her finger to her lips, warning Autumn not to jump in too early with their contribution.

"Yes, I'm pretty sure of it. I don't think he was helping for the sake of it, he just wanted to have a dig at Bithell, even though the man is dead."

"Interesting. Thanks Tom, good work." Yvie turned towards Cathy. "Okay Madam, you've clearly got something you're keen to divulge."

"Well, yes and no. With regard to Oliver Bithell, it's not looking good Boss. We've received the dispenser cam footage for the withdrawal from an ATM in Preston town centre, but it's not much help. Whoever it was taking the cash out was wearing a baggy hoody and kept their head well down. It's hard to say if they were deliberately trying to avoid being photographed, or not."

"Realistically though, as we're fairly sure he used his card in the pub next day, it was most likely Bithell drawing out some cash before meeting his mates." Joe added.

"Yeah," Cathy agreed, "we're not ruling anything out, but I'd been hoping for a clearer picture, just for confirmation."

"Okay," Yvie nodded, "stay on it. You never know, we might get lucky."

"Will do." Cathy jotted down a few words in her notebook, then smiled at her colleagues. "Now," she paused, hoping to hype up the drama of the moment, "this is where it all gets rather interesting. This morning, Autumn and I went to see Philip Garmond, the guy who helped Bithell with his book. He'd heard about Bithell's murder and, although they weren't close friends or anything, he said he'd like to help in any way that he could."

"We both had the impression that it was a genuine offer." Autumn added.

"Yeah, he seemed like a nice chap. He apologised for not having any of the files he was given access to when he was writing the first book, Bithell had insisted that everything was returned to him when it was completed."

"Whoa!" Yvie and Joe exclaimed together. "First book?"

"Hah! Nothing gets past you two, I told you it was interesting. Garmond said that after several years of no contact between the two of them, in fact not since shortly after the first book was published, Bithell had simply turned up on his doorstep one morning. He asked Garmond to think about putting together another book, saying that he wanted it to be a full and frank account of corruption involving the police force back when he was a serving officer."

"That's a bit rich," Joe laughed. "If he was anywhere near as bent as Iron Annie and the top brass believed him to be, he was responsible for the lion's share of any corruption himself."

"Well, he certainly had lots of inside knowledge. Bithell told Garmond that he was prepared to name names, and not just bent coppers, he said he was going to expose links to Organised Crime that started way up high. When I asked him if there was anything about Bithell that struck him as unusual, or different, he said he got the impression that Bithell was still quite bitter, possibly about the way he'd been side-lined after the Old Vicarage case."

"That ties in with what the Chief Super told us." Joe added. "How did they leave it?"

"Garmond said he'd have a think about it, and Bithell was supposed to get back to him with a basic outline of his idea and some of the main attention grabbers, but he never did."

"When was this?"

"He said it was just over three weeks ago."

"If Bithell really was going to expose some influential people, and if he had proof of any links to OC, that would certainly point towards a possible motive for his murder." Yvie had remained silent during much of the exchange but now got up from her chair and began to walk across to the tiny cubicle they had nicknamed the Quiet Room. It was nominally her office, but it was only ever used for the occasional phone call, more often than not to apologise to a long suffering partner for working late. "I need to let the Chief Super know about Bithell's intention to write a second book. If someone was concerned enough to kill him, there's no guarantee it will end there."

"Before you do Boss, there's one more thing." Cathy raised her voice to get Yvie's full attention. "Garmond said that for the first book he'd interviewed Sophie Elletson, the woman whose son was stolen by Gryce. He told us that he remembered it clearly, even though it was years ago, because she became very agitated, hysterical almost, when she was leafing through a pile of photos Bithell had provided for consideration by the publisher. He said she tried to cover it up, but he's pretty sure the photo that set her off was a studio portrait of Bithell with his wife and their son, Oliver."

"The letter Gryce sent to the Police Complaints Authority, and the newspapers, claimed that Bithell had wanted the child for himself." Joe added, then gestured to Tom to restate his earlier comment.

"On the day of the raid on the old vicarage, Sheryl Bithell disappeared up to Scotland, supposedly to nurse her mother and, according to Brandwood, came back twelve months later with a toddler."

"Bingo!" Cathy's smile was mirrored by her colleagues around the table.

Autumn got up from her chair and moved across to her workstation where she began flicking through search engines. She paused to make a brief phone call and then went back to her search, screens flashing by at dizzying speed. After not much more than a couple of minutes she was bouncing up and down in her chair, then finished with a fist pump.

"Yes! I'll need to check this out properly but, as far as I can see, Sheryl Bithell's mother died eleven years before her daughter supposedly went to Scotland to nurse her."

"Talk about 'after the horse has bolted…' seems a bit tardy by any standards," Cathy joked. "Go on, explain."

"I got lucky with the name on a Facebook search, Sheryl Bithell was a school governor. I rang the school and the secretary told me that in her application she had to state her maiden name, which was Logan-Keech. Assuming that she stayed with her mother until she died, that would have been sometime towards the end of 2003. There were no deaths of women with that name during the whole of 2003 or 2004. In fact, the only death record I could find for a female going by that name occurred in 1992. They lied."

Yvie was still stood by the door to the Quiet Room. She had been watching the back and forth between her team. Rank, seniority, and ego counted for nothing at times like this, each respected the abilities and opinions of the others. Every nugget of new information was weighed and measured until, by consensus, they were either discarded or placed like bricks in a wall. It should have felt like one of those moments when everything falls into place, but there was still a great big elephant in the room, or maybe even two of them, threatening to split the investigation.

"Listen, can we just take a moment?" Having noticed that Yvie appeared to be deep in thought, Joe called a halt on the chatter. "I think we need to slow down a little before we start jumping to conclusions. Let's make sure that we're all on the same page and, more importantly, that it's the right page. Boss?" Yvie went back to the table and sat down, her call to the Chief Super would have to wait.

"Thanks Joe, anyone care to summarise?" It came as no surprise to any of them that the most junior member of the team was first to respond.

"I'll give it a go Boss, if that's okay?"

"Go for it."

"Okay. Starting at the beginning, Eric Gryce swore vengeance. Is it me or does that sound a bit 'Game of Thrones' to everyone? Never mind, he swore vengeance on four people and we're fairly sure that he killed two of them with an axe. Is it likely that he's returned to kill the others after twenty years?"

"I would have thought it unlikely after that length of time," Joe said, "but Bithell was also decapitated, so we definitely can't rule it out."

"Agreed, so Eric Gryce is a suspect and has, in his opinion at least, a motive." Autumn paused for a moment while she rearranged the papers in front of her. Yvie was pleased to see the way the young DC was structuring her summary, the elephants in the room were about to take centre stage.

"Next, from what we've just heard, it's looking very much like the Bithells somehow stole the child and passed it off as their own. We still need to do some digging in order to prove it, but I think we're all in agreement. Yes?" After a quick check that there was no dissent, she continued. "It also seems very likely that Elletson recognised, or thought she recognised, her son in the photograph at Garmond's house. Given that she hadn't seen the child for around seven years, is that possible? Is it a mother thing?" All eyes turned to Yvie as the only mother in the room.

"Until we had Conor, I would have doubted it." She thought back to the happy hours she'd spent studying every last detail of her son's face, asleep and awake, marvelling at how she could already see the man that he would grow up to be. "Now though, I'm absolutely certain that it's not only possible, it's within every mother to do exactly that."

"Thanks Boss. Good job you're here or I would have had to ring my mum. So, do we think that finding out who stole your child is a motive for murder, not forgetting that there's a gap of something like fourteen years between Sophie seeing the photo and Bithell's killing?"

"Same again, I would have thought it unlikely," Joe replied, "but we can't rule it out. We have to consider her to be a potential suspect, which means we need to be looking for Sophie Elletson as a matter of urgency."

"Finally, a matter of weeks before his death, Bithell was apparently considering a second book, one that he said would be a full and frank exposure of corruption back in the day, not only in the police service but above and beyond. That has to be a possible motive and, given the time issues, it would at first appear to be the most likely. However, if his intention was to expose influential people, who may or may not have links to organised crime, surely they would have had the resources to make him disappear without drawing even more attention to themselves. I'm no expert, but hacking someone's head off with a sword is hardly normal procedure for a professional hit."

"I agree that it's not very subtle," Tom was shaking his head, recent experience had taught him that there was no end to the insult or violence that some people were prepared to inflict on others, "but remember what James said, and it certainly sends a very clear message. Perhaps that was the reason for it?"

The earlier excitement in the Clitheroe office faded somewhat with the realisation that they now had at least three potential suspects, each of whom had a possible, but completely different, motive for wanting Bithell dead. While Yvie made her belated call to the Chief Super, the team went round and round the table, putting forward ideas, building on them, and then tearing them down again. By the time she returned, Yvie got the impression that they'd managed to reach some common ground, if not full agreement, and it fell to Autumn, who was still a little heady from the cut and thrust of arguing her case while Cathy and Tom played Devil's advocate, to update her on the progress they'd made.

"They're all bollocks!" The words were out before she knew it. Another minor set-back in her ongoing struggle to put her thoughts in order before speaking out loud.

"Do you want to expand on that a little, perhaps?"

"Sorry Boss." Autumn coloured up almost instantly. "What I meant to say is that there are factors that make each scenario highly unlikely. If it was Eric Gryce, there's a gap of twenty years, I just can't see it, none of us can. If it was the child's 'real' mother," Autumn made air quotes around the word as they still had no hard evidence to confirm parentage, "there's a gap of fourteen years since she found out. If she was going to do anything, it would have been then, not now when he's a grown man. It's not like the Bithells would have been hard to track down. Finally, if he was killed to stop him from publishing a new book, then surely it would have been done less publicly and in a way that didn't attract so much attention. Also, if whoever he was threatening to dish the dirt on had been worried enough to kill him, they would have either searched his house, or burned it to the ground. They wouldn't want to take the chance of someone else finding his notes, or any other incriminating information."

"Can't argue with any of that Boss," Cathy was nodding her agreement. "Obviously we'll need to keep the different strands open, but we need to be looking for more people who had a reason to want Bithell dead."

"Yes, I tend to agree." As she'd discussed the new information with the Chief Super, Yvie had been thinking along those lines herself, but it was good to see the team reasoning it through and reaching the same conclusion. "Don't forget what we said earlier, we can't rule out an OC connection just because it was a bit showy, he could have been killed that way to send a message."

"One of those occasions when a bunch of flowers just isn't enough." Cathy joked. "We still haven't located Oliver Bithell and, up until now, we've been regarding him mostly as a missing person. I think we need to elevate him to potential suspect."

"Reason being?" Tom asked.

"I think he's either missing because he's a victim or, more likely, hiding because he's involved."

"I don't know." Tom was shaking his head, clearly not convinced. "If he found out that he'd been snatched from his real mother, would that be enough to make him kill the man responsible? Particularly when that man is the only father he's ever known."

"Another possibility could be that he knows why his father was killed, or who by," Autumn added, "and has gone into hiding because he's scared."

"Okay, either way he's elevated." Yvie agreed. "Anyone else?"

"How about the brother, Edwin Gryce?" Autumn offered. "I managed to track him down to an address in Lytham, but I haven't had a chance to speak to him yet. I've left messages on his phone but he hasn't responded. I was thinking of just turning up on his doorstep."

"Don't go to see him on your own." Tom jumped in a little too quickly, which didn't escape the notice of Yvie or Cathy. "Do we know anything about him?"

"He's been living in Spain since his brother Eric, a.k.a. the Headhunter, went missing. Which I suppose is quite understandable, the media attention at the time must have been a nightmare. According to Land Registry records, he still owns a house up at Arnside, but I don't know if it's rented out or empty."

"Joe, perhaps you and Autumn could go over to Lytham in the morning, see how he responds to the police knocking on his door."

"Will do Boss. There's a great little pork butchers just off the main street, the sausage rolls from there are amazing. If we happen to be passing, that is."

"Does Val know about your pork and pastry obsession?" Cathy laughed.

"Unfortunately, she does. And for your information Detective Sergeant, it is not an obsession, for me it's the real thing."

"Tom, I'd like you and Cathy to step up the search for Oliver Bithell." Yvie cut in, knowing that the banter could continue for some time. "Also, see if you can track down Sophie Elletson. I'm going to make a start on these box files, see if there's anything in there that might shine a light on why anyone may have wanted Bithell dead. But first, all of you, go home. Sleep on it and come back tomorrow morning full of insights and bright ideas."

Chapter Nineteen

Sophie: 2009

While she walked aimlessly through the lanes, hardly aware of her surroundings, Sophie kept reliving the moment when she'd reached out to her stolen son. As though stuck in a loop, unable to clear the sights and sounds from her mind, she sobbed uncontrollably. It was seeing the horror on Anthony's face and hearing the fear in his voice that had made her feel ashamed, more so than anything else she had ever done. The horror, the fear, and his obvious distress were caused by her actions, and hers alone. She had done that to him, her son, without a thought for the consequences. When she'd first seen him walking towards her, in those brief moments of intense joy before she'd called out the name he would never answer to, she had been so fiercely proud it had taken her breath away. He was a handsome boy, well turned out in his clean white shirt, grey shorts and school blazer. As she watched, he had mischievously loosened his neatly knotted tie and pulled it to one side, no doubt wanting to fit in with the other boys, his friends. The backpack he was carrying over one shoulder looked enormous, and he also had a separate PE bag, or it could have for swimming, she thought. He had looked happy, healthy and carefree, everything a child of his age should be. Right up until the mad woman had tried to grab him, and then started fighting with his mother as she came to his rescue.

She was snapped out of her thoughts when the driver of an old van blasted his horn at her, shouting and gesticulating as he swerved to pass by. She hadn't realised that she'd sleepwalked away from the roadside and was, if not in the middle of the road, certainly not far from it. The first thing to cross her mind was that maybe it would've been better if he'd hit her, killed her stone dead, but her next thought was of Lucy, so she banished the idea of an easy way out. Around the next bend there was a rusted iron and timber bench set back on the grass verge behind a bus stop. It was dirty and scarred with graffiti but Sophie sat, eyes on the horizon, looking out over the flat farmland but seeing nothing of it. Eventually, when she'd bottled up the sadness and the shame, locked it safely away, at least for a little while, she allowed herself to explore what, up until now, had seemed unthinkable. Anthony really had looked well cared for, and happy. He must be loved, she reasoned, Sheryl had been prepared to fight for him, putting herself in danger to protect the child that she had raised as her own. The Bithells clearly had the money to give him a better future, a better life, than she could ever offer. She asked herself a question that in her heart she already knew the answer to, what more could a mother want than the best possible start for her child? Her mind was racing, even if she could prove he was hers, could she take him away from the only home he had ever known? What would Anthony want? She had always taken it for granted that it would be his real mum but, as far as her boy was concerned, that was Sheryl Bithell. She couldn't understand how she'd been so insensitive to how he would feel if he was taken away from the only family he'd ever known. Was it a mother's love to want him back at any cost, knowing the heartache he would suffer? Avoiding the most unthinkable thought of all was becoming ever more difficult, Sophie fought against it, but it was a battle she could never win. Maybe, just maybe, she reasoned, it would be better for Anthony if she let him enjoy the life he'd been given ....and there it was! There could be no withdrawal, no second thoughts, no 'what ifs', the decision had been made simply by considering the possibility.

Sophie followed the pavement around the corner and into her street, glad that she'd be home before her daughter returned from school. Having managed to clear her head a little on the long walk home she'd decided that she would use the money she'd saved by not taking the bus to buy Lucy some sweets, a long overdue treat. It wasn't much but, along with an apology for the way she'd been distracted over the last few weeks, or maybe it had been months, it was a start. Sophie made a promise to herself that from now on, Lucy would always come first, she was a good kid and she deserved better. The two men getting out of a car parked across the street briefly caught her attention but were instantly forgotten when she noticed that her front door had been smashed off its hinges. Panic gripped her, immediately afraid for her daughter, but then relief when she realised that Lucy would still be at school. It took a moment or two for Sophie to recognise Mark Brandwood when the two men walked up behind her, it was the stench of nicotine that jogged her memory. She assumed that someone must have witnessed the break-in and phoned the police, not that there was anything worth stealing in the house. The shove in her back was completely unexpected, making her stumble, then she was pushed up against the wall and roughly handcuffed.

"Sophie Elletson, I am arresting you for the possession, with the intention to supply, of controlled drugs. You do not have to say anything, but it may harm your defence if you do not mention, when questioned, something which you later rely on in court. Do you understand?"

"My daughter, Lucy?"

"With Social Services, and a damn sight better off for it in my opinion. Leaving a kid her age alone in the house, you want locking up." Brandwood sneered as he pulled hard on her arm to spin her round. "Fucking druggies, you make me sick."

"I don't understand?" Sophie had begun to shake. "Why is Lucy with Social Services, she was supposed to be at school?"

"No shit! But I wouldn't worry about that if I was you. We found enough Class As down the back of your settee that she'll have finished school and be working for a living before you even get a parole hearing." Brandwood turned to his colleague. "Put her in the car mate, I'm going to have a ciggie before we take her in."

After being booked in at the police station, the next few hours passed in a whirl of confusion and guilty tears for Sophie. Staring at the wall of her cell, repeatedly dragging her fingers through her hair as she tried to make sense of what was going on. Struggling to understand why Brandwood had told her they'd found drugs in her house, when she knew for a fact that there weren't any. The aftermath of her disastrous attempt to reach out to Anthony had left her drained, she couldn't think straight, couldn't work out why Sophie hadn't gone to school, what had prompted Social Services to take her daughter. Apart from a few moments of joy and pride when she first caught sight of her son, the rest of the day had rapidly become a nightmare, with no prospect of waking from it. Late in the afternoon she heard the door to her cell being unlocked, she didn't look up but still recognised the man who walked in immediately he spoke.

"Aah Sophie," Bithell said softly as he closed the cell door behind him. "You really shouldn't have gone after the boy like that. You must have known that I wouldn't allow it, you left me no choice." After hearing those few words, understanding hit Sophie like a punch in the stomach. It was Bithell, the drugs, Social Services, everything. She'd overstepped the line, and now he would destroy her.

"He's my son, and you stole him."

"No, he's Oliver Bithell, and has been for the last seven years. Let's face it, who're they going to believe, eh? Ask yourself, a drug dealing ex prostitute with one child in and out of care, or a decorated police officer and his wife?"

"I'll demand that a DNA test is done, you can't fake that."

"You would be amazed at what I can do Sophie, and the people who owe me favours can do a whole lot more." Bithell softened his voice and moved closer to her. "Here's the deal, and it's non-negotiable."

"You can't do a deal for my son, he's not….."

"Call it what you want, it doesn't really matter." Bithell cut her off, he squatted down and put his face close to hers. "Fight me and, even though we both know I'll win in the end, the boy will likely end up spending time in a children's home, or farmed out to a dodgy foster carer with a thing for little boys. Neither of us want that, do we?"

"No." Sophie was again sobbing. Having already made the heart-breaking decision that perhaps Anthony would have a better life with the Bithells, she couldn't risk him being placed in care, she couldn't do that to him. "What about Lucy?"

"Plead guilty to the drugs charge, and I'll say you co-operated and push for a minimal sentence. So long as you keep your mouth shut, about everything, I'll look out for you and the girl. Do your time, and when you're out I'll see what I can do to help you get her back, again. But Oliver is ours, now and forever. Do you understand that?"

Despite confirmation of her co-operation, saving tax-payers money by pleading guilty, and even a claim by her appointed solicitor that Sophie herself was a victim of abuse whose son had been taken by the serial killer known as the Headhunter, she was nonetheless sentenced to eight years in prison, with an expectation that she could be out in four.

Shortly after lockdown on her first night in Styal women's prison, the small hatch in her cell door opened a fraction and, in a moment of déjà vu, a tiny paper wrap landed on the floor. Sophie hadn't seen whoever had posted it through, but she knew exactly what it was, and who was responsible. Andy Bithell was a belt and braces man and he clearly wasn't taking any chances on her lodging an appeal against her sentence. Less than ten minutes later Sophie was pain free and at peace with the world.

Chapter Twenty

I have great expectations of a good night's sleep tonight, after my final visit to Detective Sergeant Mark Brandwood. I've watched his house for several days, just to be sure he lives alone, I have no argument with his family or friends, if he has any. Yesterday, I was just about to go and, let's say, 'introduce myself', when I saw a car pull up outside his house. The young man who was driving it got out and, after looking up and down the street, approached the front door. He looked like a policeman, although I can't put my finger on exactly why I would think that, and I noticed that he was kept waiting for several minutes before the door was finally opened. I hardly recognised Brandwood as he stood there, he looked ill, shrunken, and close to death. I did wonder if he realised quite how close he really was? On seeing the state he was in my immediate concern was that I might not be in time, and we really can't have him popping off of his own accord. No, that would never do, he has to pay, just like the others. So, this evening I strolled around the town for a while, just to kill a little time, then waited until the flickering of a television in Brandwood's lounge was extinguished. Despite my desire to proceed I did nothing until the glow was replaced several minutes later by what I presumed to be a bedside lamp. With a growing sense of anticipation I walked up to his front door and pressed the doorbell, jamming a flat screwdriver in between the button and the casing to keep it ringing. I then turned and strode briskly down the alley that ran along the back of the terrace, a means of access that I had checked out on an earlier visit. Finding the correct house I pushed my way through a ramshackle gate and into the enclosed rear yard. While Brandwood was still making his way downstairs, and then puzzling over the screwdriver stuck in his doorbell, I placed a self-adhesive patch onto one of the small glass panels in the back door and smashed it with the butt of my axe. It still made a noise, but it was much reduced, and within a moment or two I was inside the darkened kitchen. Brandwood was still at the front door, no doubt blaming the act of vandalism on some neighbours' child he'd previously had words with and, as far as I could tell, remained completely unsuspecting. I remained still and silent in the darkness until he had slowly shuffled back up the stairs to his bedroom, only then did I follow. Tempting as it was to let the head of the axe bounce against each step as I climbed them, I decided that would be a touch overdramatic, a little too Hollywood. Quietly easing open the bedroom door, I could see him sat on the bed propped up on several pillows. His oxygen mask, which was now connected to a larger cylinder, was held close to his face while he recovered from the exertions of going up and down the stairs. It took a few seconds before he registered my presence, and longer still until I saw the realisation dawn on his face. Even when he recognised me, and I'm sure that he did, he didn't appear to be frightened. I suppose when you're as close to death as he was there aren't a lot of things to be afraid of. He reached out for a mobile phone that was sat on the bedside table nearest to me and, without thinking, I swung the axe. I hadn't intended to, it was a reflex action, but when he withdrew his hand, the severed tips of three fingers and a thumb lay on the splintered wood. Fortunately for me, he didn't have the breath for a full-throated scream of pain, but the sound he did make prompted me to finish the job without any further delay. As he tried to roll off the bed and away from me, the back of his neck was exposed, a bad mistake, you could even call it a fatal error. He didn't move after the first blow, the newly sharpened blade bit deeply, but it still took me several more swings before his head rolled clear. Afterwards, I cleaned myself up in his bathroom and used a towel to wipe down my axe. As I was making my way downstairs, it occurred to me that I hadn't been overly careful about where I may have left fingerprints, or maybe shed hair, or even droplets of perspiration – chopping off someone's head with a felling axe would make anyone sweat. Looking for inspiration, I noticed that the old gas fire in the lounge was fed by a short copper pipe connected to a brass valve with a tap on top. One gentle swing of the axe and I could immediately hear and smell the escaping gas. Leaving the lounge door open an inch, I then moved to the kitchen and switched on all four rings on the hob, fortunately it was a little more modern than the gas fire and a press of the button set the tiny blue flames dancing. I left by the same route, walking calmly and confidently, nothing to arouse interest or suspicion, my extra-long tool bag slung over one shoulder. I did indeed sleep soundly after dispatching the sickly policeman, and this morning I awoke to news of the fire which, surely, must have destroyed every trace of my ever being there. But, rather than a sense of satisfaction for a job well done, I can't escape the feeling that there are still others who deserve to die for the way they have blighted our lives. I feel that I have found a purpose, a mission, a way to make amends, and I already know who will be the next to pay.

Chapter Twenty-One

Yvie was cleaning up the fall-out from Conor's breakfast of mashed banana and pear when the opening bars of Iron Maiden's 'The Trooper' rang out from her phone. Bashing the spoon out of mummy's hand when she tried to feed him was a great new game that her son seemed to enjoy enormously, but it was worth it just to see the smile on his cheeky little face. She quickly wiped the sticky fruit from her hands, and the last few spots from the screen of her phone, before taking the call. Knowing it was Iron Annie, and with a glance at the kitchen clock telling her it wasn't yet 7am, this wasn't going to be good news.

"Morning Yvie, sorry to call so early."

"No problem Boss, what's up?" Yvie gave James a grateful smile as he took over the clean-up operation. She'd been hoping to let him have a well-deserved lie in, even if it was for only half an hour or so, but she realised he must have heard the ringtone and, knowing the implications only too well, come straight down.

"I've just been informed of an incident at Mark Brandwood's house in Longridge." Very much a 'hands-on' senior officer, there was a standing order that the Chief Super was to be informed of any significant events or suspicious deaths in the area covered by the Lancashire Constabulary. "There was a fire, and reports of several explosions, shortly before midnight. The fire crews attending the scene are still damping down and it will be at least a couple of hours before it's considered safe to enter."

"Brandwood?" Yvie asked, already knowing the answer.

"According to neighbours he hasn't left the house for months, so we have to assume he was in there. The Watch Commander apparently said that there was no possibility of anyone inside being left alive, the place was gutted."

"What are you thinking?"

"I'm trying not to until we know for sure, but it's certainly one hell of a coincidence that shortly after being interviewed by Tom his house burns down. The Fire Investigation team will hopefully be going in around eleven o'clock this morning, we can have a quick catch-up then if you'd like to meet me there? We won't be able to enter what's left of the property ourselves, but they're a decent bunch so at least we'll be able to ask questions."

"Okay, see you there Ma'am."

"Bye Yvie, love to Conor, and James of course."

After ending the call, and with Longridge only about four miles away from where she lived, Yvie decided that there was little point in driving to the Clitheroe office only to set off back again a couple of hours later. She was about to text Joe when she remembered that he and Autumn were planning to head over to Lytham first thing, so instead sent a quick message to Cathy saying that she wouldn't be in until around lunchtime. When her phone dinged a moment later she read the reply, *'No probs, can't blame you and James for wanting a bit of 'special time' while Conor has his morning nap'*. 'Cheeky cow', she laughed out loud, then thought, 'but now you mention it….'

Yvie parked her BMW behind the cordon that was preventing access to the street where Brandwood had lived. The crew of the last remaining fire appliance were packing away their equipment and a group of maybe twenty people were stood watching, presumably waiting to get back into their homes. Iron Annie was chatting to one of the Lancashire Fire and Rescue Service officers and two other people Yvie thought she recognised as working for the Coroners' Office. Showing her warrant card to the bored looking uniformed constable at the barrier immediately caused him to straighten up and try to look alert as he unclipped the tape to allow her through. As she neared the group, the Chief Super broke off from her conversation to make the introductions.

"Detective Chief Inspector Gray, Eddie here is from the Fire Investigation team, Avril and Faizan are from the Coroners' Office." She paused while the usual nods and pleasantries were conducted.

"Yvie's fine, thank you. I only get the full job title when I'm in trouble," she added with a smile. Not true, but everyone else seemed to be on first name terms.

"Eddie has just been telling us that we have a mix of good news and bad. The bad news is that the place has been completely gutted. The floors and stairs are gone, whatever is left of anything that was in either of the upstairs bedrooms, which we think is likely to include Mr. Brandwood, has mostly fallen through to the ground floor."

"It's hard to imagine any good news following that!" Yvie said. "After the fire and then the damping down I don't suppose there's much chance of us getting any meaningful forensics."

"No, it's doubtful. I'll let Eddie give you the glad tidings though."

"I was brought up in one of these terraces, just round the corner from here, actually. Some of 'em were built the best part of two hundred years ago, and they were built to last." He spoke with the softened remnants of a local accent and Yvie could sense his strong ties to the area, maybe built on memories of a happy childhood. "Like Anne said, everything inside is gone. There was a gas explosion that took out the ground floor windows and started the fire, and then three further explosions that we believe were all oxygen cylinders. However, we've had the cameras in and structurally it's as sound as a pound."

"Not sure, is that good or bad?" Avril joked.

"Oh, it's good alright," he continued. "The floor boarding has mostly gone but there's only surface damage on the heavier timber beams. A lot of the plaster has cracked and come away in the heat, but the brick and stone underneath is as good as new, none of your lightweight modern building blocks here! We evacuated several houses on either side as a precaution, there's always a danger with old terraces that the loft spaces aren't properly compartmented, but the fire hasn't broken through, which was quite surprisin'. I'll tell you what, whoever did the renovation on this place knew what they were doin', and they certainly didn't skimp on materials."

"I'm still not seeing the good news, apart from for the neighbours?" Yvie was puzzled as to where any further positives may come from.

"Well, now we know it's not going to fall down on our 'eads, once we've got the risk assessment completed we can go in and figure out what caused it." Eddie noticed her expression and shook his head. "When I say, 'we can', I mean that me and Maise can, not you guys." He pointed to where a tiny, elfin young woman wearing a bright orange tie dyed tee shirt and gym shorts had just finished removing a mound of personal protective equipment from the back of an Audi estate. Yvie thought that Maise, who was now tying back her long flaming red hair, looked no older twenty, and could easily pass for a teenager. "I know what you're thinkin', everyone does when they first meet our Maise," Eddie said with a grin, "but she's the best I've ever worked with, bar none. If there's owt to be found, we'll find it."

"Thanks Eddie," the Chief Super said, "any idea how…"

"….long it will take?" The Fire Investigator good humouredly finished off her sentence. "Same answer as every other time you've asked me that question, I'm pretty sure it will be somewhere between five minutes and five days, give or take. Now, I need to go and brief the rest of the team." With that he excused himself and began to walk towards another dark estate car that had pulled up next to where Maise was still getting kitted out. He stopped and turned. "There's no point in you two hangin' about, I know this one's important to you Anne so, as soon as I know, you'll know." He and Iron Annie exchanged nods, and he was gone.

"We're going to be here until the body, if he's actually in there, is located and can safely be removed." Avril said. "I can give you a heads-up if you want."

"Thanks love, I'd appreciate it. I'm pretty sure that he will be." The Chief Super and Yvie said their goodbyes and walked back to where their cars were parked.

"You mentioned a quick catch-up Boss?"

"Absolutely. Tell you what, why don't we do that over a cuppa back at your house?"

"Sounds good, I'll ring James and tell him to put the kettle on." Yvie knew full well that the only reason for going to hers was so that Iron Annie Atkinson could spend some quality time with Conor, her and James wouldn't get a look in. Fifteen minutes later they were sat at her dining table and, just as predicted, her boss was bouncing a giggling Conor up and down on her knee. Yvie quickly recapped where they were up to with the three potential motives, revenge for a murdered lover, a stolen child, and the threat of exposure. There was also the possibility of that number rising to four if they considered Oliver Bithell to be a suspect in his father's murder. Consensus was that the proposed exposure of some influential people having links to organised crime gangs was probably the front runner, though the way in which Bithell was murdered was uncharacteristically high-profile. While they would keep the current lines of enquiry open, the feeling was that they needed to dig deeper into Bithell's past activities and associations.

As Yvie watched her boss playing with Conor she wasn't at all sure that anything she was saying was actually going in. She finished off the briefing by explaining that they were actively seeking Oliver Bithell, who they believed to be the child stolen from the Old Vicarage, and the child's mother, Sophie Elletson. Joe and Autumn had managed to speak to Edwin Gryce, Eric's younger brother, but she didn't know the details yet. It didn't seem right to talk of death and headless corpses in front of Conor, so she left it at that.

"Are you two staying for lunch? James asked. "I've just made a panful of broccoli and stilton soup and there are some herby bread rolls waiting to go in the oven."

"Sounds great James, thank you." Iron Annie answered for them both, the first time she'd said anything other than 'How big? Soooo big!' since Yvie had begun her update. Now back in professional mode, despite Conor's attempts to grab her nose, the Chief Super demonstrated that not only had she taken in everything that had just been related to her, it was already processed and ready to be actioned. "If you need more bodies looking for Bithell and Elletson, just let me know. Also, I agree about the new book being the most likely motive, given the time lapse between events. Unlikely as it may be that an OC execution would involve beheading, we can't ignore the possibility. The problem is, we don't know who may have felt threatened, or how they found out he was planning to write a second book."

"You don't think there'd be any top brass involved do you. That's what he was implying to Garmond?"

"No, there's always going to be a couple of arseholes in any management team, but I'm confident that the senior people I work with nowadays are all above reproach. But, if anyone on the Force is involved, they wouldn't necessarily need to be senior officers to have influence, or to be influenced."

"Are you suggesting the investigation may be compromised?"

"No. I'm simply saying that it's a possibility. It's your decision, but you may want to consider relocating the team to the Great Eccleston house for the duration of the investigation. What do you think?" Yvie was silent for a long moment as she considered her reply.

"I think if Conor's first word is 'arseholes', you've got a lot to answer for!"

"Should I take him while you two have lunch?" James had been in and out of the kitchen while they were talking, taking the rolls from the oven and finishing the soup. The aroma of freshly baked bread, combined with the heady perfume of rosemary was, or at least it had been, a feast in itself, but was now failing miserably in the battle to overcome the odours emanating from Conor's nappy.

"I think that would be a very good idea James." Iron Annie carefully handed over the child. "Come on Yvie, you serve up. We haven't got all day."

Chapter Twenty-Two

Sophie: 2017

It was a typical February morning when Sophie Elletson finally stepped outside Styal Prison. The sky was grey, shower followed shower with barely a gap in between and the wind was bitingly cold. The mismatched, ill-fitting clothes she was wearing, provided by a local 'prisoner's aid' charity, were totally inadequate for the conditions, but she barely noticed. The expectation of a possible release date at the halfway point of her sentence had failed to materialise after a number of drug related altercations had led to her being branded a troublemaker. Including her time spent on remand, she had been incarcerated for almost the full eight years of her sentence, hard years, and every single day of it was reflected in her appearance. Having gone into prison as a fairly attractive young woman and, against all odds given the nature of her earlier lifestyle, a reasonably healthy one, Sophie was now gaunt, almost skeletal. With thinning lank hair, bad skin, and teeth damaged by opiate induced grinding and infection, she had the look and bearing of a sickly old woman. Her induction to prison life and the first few weeks of her sentence had passed in a blur. Each evening, the hatch on her cell door had opened just far enough for another little paper wrap to be dropped through. She'd been clean for years, ever since she'd worked so hard to get Lucy back, but the wraps were a godsend, her weakness and yet her lifeline, her escape, the only thing that was keeping the crushing, gut-wrenching sadness of her predicament at bay. Surprisingly, she had never considered for how long Bithell, she was convinced he was behind it, would continue to arrange for her to be supplied - all that mattered was the next blessed spell of peace. Her naïve acceptance lasted until the day when the hatch on the cell door failed to open, that had been a long and sleepless night. Unlike many of the other inmates, Sophie had been imprisoned with no support from family or friends on the outside, no contacts on the inside, and absolutely zero resources of her own. To obtain the drugs her body was now craving, she was reduced to doing little jobs for other inmates, providing 'favours' for anyone who was prepared to pay, giving up her meals whenever there was anything of interest in the canteen. She rapidly descended into becoming the lowest of the low, a figure of fun, one who could be cheated and abused with little fear of reprisal. Whilst the outward effects of the long days of her sentence were evident in her appearance, it was the living hell they contained that was now reflected in her eyes.

Sophie had no idea how long she'd been stood outside the prison wall, but the shivering that now racked her body and the bluish tinge to her skin, told her it was too long. They'd told her to wait; she had nowhere else to go, no one else she could call on, no other option than to do whatever 'they' said. When a small, dark blue car pulled up alongside her, she recognised the couple who had visited her in prison during the final days of her sentence, the ones who said they would help. She got into the car, glad to be out of the cold.

"Sorry we're a bit late Sophie." The woman whose name she couldn't remember was speaking to her. "Dan and I had to attend an eviction first thing. One of the residents was caught using so she had to go. Silly girl, she knew the rules, I don't know what will happen to her now. Are you okay love, glad to be out?"

"Yes, thank you." Sophie struggled to reply, conversation hadn't been a feature of her life for so long.

"We're not too far away so we'll soon get you there and settled in. We'll introduce you to Sylvia, the hostel manager, and she'll talk you through the rules and the routine. Heart of gold, but she is a bit of a stickler, isn't she Dan?"

"You can say that again! I'll tell you what Sophie, Elaine and I have both had a telling off from Sylvia, on more than one occasion." Dan laughed. "She's a bit of a dragon."

"She is not!" Elaine exclaimed, "Don't you listen to him, she just likes things done her way." Sophie had already switched off to the conversation, she was experiencing the first pangs of a need that she knew would only grow stronger.

Her room at the hostel, which was in a nice residential area on the edge of town, was actually quite pleasant. It was clean, bright and had an en-suite bathroom. There was a comfortable looking single bed and a small pile of laundered second-hand clothes had been left for her to pick through. There was even a small vase of fresh flowers and a 'Welcome' card propped up against the mirror of a small dressing table. The charity that Dan and Elaine volunteered for was clearly well funded. Sylvia hadn't seemed as demanding as Dan made out, she'd shown Sophie a chart on the wall that detailed everyone's chores for the week, nothing too arduous, and made her expectations clear with regard to acceptable behaviour. With her nerves now jangling and jumpy, Sophie almost missed the reference to the curfew. Everyone was to be back in the hostel by 7pm and to remain until 7am the following morning. Failure to observe the curfew would, in the absence of compelling circumstances, be grounds for eviction. Similarly, being under the influence of drugs or alcohol, at any time of day or night, would lead to prompt eviction. Sylvia had finished her briefing by saying that she hoped Sophie would come down to the lounge and join in with the group meetings. They were held every Tuesday, Friday and Sunday evening, a number of the volunteers would come in to chat with the residents and they would often pray together.

By 6pm on that first evening Sophie had been too strung out to eat, or even to sit still. Knowing that others would immediately recognise the signs, she had feigned a 'gyppy tummy' and excused herself from the communal meal. On returning to her room, she'd laid on the bed and tried to sleep, but that was never going to work. She'd paced around the room anxiously, looking for any distraction and knowing that worse was to come, hoping but doubting that she was strong enough to resist. Stopping by the dressing table she had picked up the card and opened it, inside was written, *'Know that you are in our thoughts and prayers. Please use this small gift to purchase any little luxuries that will help you to settle into our joyous community. Always remember, the Lord is our shepherd and will provide for his flock'.* It wasn't signed, but the twenty-pound note that fell out was better than any signature. Up until that point Sophie had considered that her only option would be to sneak out, shag the first guy who was prepared to pay, and then find a dealer. She reached for her coat.

Chapter Twenty-Three

Answering what was very clearly a 'no nonsense' knock on his front door at just after eight o'clock that morning, Edwin Gryce had been surprised to find two police officers on his doorstep. However, he'd invited them in, served them both with a cup of coffee from a freshly brewed pot, then excused himself, adding that he didn't feel it was appropriate to entertain while still wearing his dressing gown.

"This is nice." Autumn observed as they waited for the man to return. The large, detached house was set in a sizeable plot within a few minutes' walk of the seafront in one direction and Lowther Gardens in the other. The room they had been ushered towards boasted bi-fold doors with a view down the length of a lush garden, shape and foliage providing the interest rather than blooms. They were sat in matching oxblood leather chairs at either side of a small, but exquisitely inlaid, round table. The polished light and dark woods had a glow, a richness that somehow demanded to be touched, Joe smiled when he noticed the tell-tale fleur-de-lys that had been worked into the design.

"The boss would love this, it's a Stawski."

"You have a good eye Detective Inspector," Edwin Gryce replied from the doorway. "I've been collecting his work for a number of years, but the table is one of my favourite pieces." Gryce seated himself on a matching settee with his back to the garden. "Now, how may I be of assistance?"

"We're investigating the circumstances around the death of ex Detective Chief Inspector Andrew Bithell, I assume you have seen the news coverage?" Joe waited until Gryce nodded to confirm that he had. "We just have a few questions for you sir, if you wouldn't mind."

"Of course, but surely you don't think that I had anything to do with the poor man's death?" Gryce laughed. "Do I need an alibi?"

"I don't know sir, do you?"

"Of course not, I don't even know when he was killed."

"What we're really interested in sir, is when you last saw, or heard from, your brother Eric." Joe and Autumn both studied the man's face as he fashioned his reply.

"As much as I'd like to believe that my brother is still alive...." Gryce's speech tailed off, he stared at the table sat between them, his appearance was that of a man lost in his own thoughts.

"Your brother, sir." Joe prompted. "When did you last see him?" Gryce shook his head and lifted his eyes to meet and hold Joe's gaze.

"That's an easy one Detective Inspector, I can't confirm the exact date without checking, but it must be nearly forty years ago. It wasn't long after we received the Declaration of Presumed Death for my father, I'm sure you are aware of our... 'unfortunate', family circumstances."

"I am sir, and I'm sorry to bring this up after all this time, but could you tell me why there has been no further contact between you?"

"A stupid squabble that we were both too pig-headed to back down from. You know how it is between brothers, neither of us were prepared to make the first move. It is my greatest regret in life, that I let my pride come between us."

"Can you remember what the argument was about sir?"

"Is it really relevant after all this time, Detective Inspector?" For the first time, Gryce had started to look uncomfortable with the direction the questioning was taking.

"To be completely honest sir, at this moment I don't know what will, or will not, be relevant to the investigation. As you can imagine, the more background information we can collect now, the less likely it will be that we need to trouble you again." Joe and Autumn maintained their silence, waiting for Gryce to fill the vacuum, an old trick but one that usually paid off.

"Very well! It was about a house, a part of my father's estate. My father was a monster but, fortunately for my brother and myself, a very wealthy one. He left a portfolio of properties, including a house near Arnside that we used at weekends and for holidays when our mother was alive. We both had very fond memories of it and neither of us was prepared to let the other have it. Because we couldn't agree, it was sold and the proceeds added to the estate."

"Thank you for clearing that up, sir. I believe you've been living in Spain for many years?" Joe asked.

"That's correct, I found the attentions of the gutter press to be unbearable after my brother was accused of killing those three police officers. I'm only back here now because I had a difficult time with coronavirus and the lockdowns. I decided that I should return here for the good of my health."

"I understand sir, thank you." Joe closed his notebook and returned it to his jacket pocket. "I've no further questions."

"You have to understand Detective Inspector, despite the accusations made against my brother, I only ever knew him to be a kind and decent man, one who committed his life to helping others. Similarly, I found Anthony Daniels, my brother's partner, to be the gentlest, most thoughtful human being I have ever known. They were soulmates, I have never understood what happened that day, only that it was horrific, and the media portrayed Eric as a crazed killer, something I will never accept. Now, if that is everything…?"

"Could I just ask one quick question sir," Autumn asked, then immediately continued without waiting for his reply. "The property at Arnside sir, the one you and your brother fell out over, would that be the same house that you have owned for many years?" Both detectives noted the flash of irritation that passed over Gryce's face.

"It is officer, yes. It's been empty for a long time and needs significant work. I retain it simply as an investment, the value is in the land rather than the building."

"Thank you, sir. It's just that I noted from the records that when the house was last sold, it was purchased by a firm of solicitors for an unnamed buyer. Would that unnamed buyer have been you, sir?"

"Yes officer, it would. When Eric insisted that the house be sold, to my shame, I didn't want him to find out that I had purchased it from the estate, something else that I'm not very proud of."

"I can understand that sir." Autumn paused. "But if you were so keen to have it in the first place, because of your childhood memories and all, why would…?" She didn't get chance to finish as Gryce spoke over her as he stood up.

"People change officer, and it was a long time ago. Now if that really is everything, I would like to get on with my day."

The afternoon team briefing had gone on a while longer than was usual, everyone having information to contribute. Joe and Autumn had kicked off proceedings with a summary of their meeting with Edwin Gryce. The single fact they had come away with was that the man made an excellent cup of coffee, but the gut feeling of the two detectives was that he was hiding something. Not necessarily connected to the murder of Andy Bithell, but there was something about Gryce, despite his manners and apparent self-deprecating openness, they had both found distasteful. It was agreed that, for the time being at least, he should remain a person of interest. Tom reported that he had been unable to locate Sophie Elletson. There was no record of where she may have been living since she'd left the women's hostel on the day of her release from prison. She was financially inactive, any benefits she may have been entitled to had gone unclaimed, she wasn't on any social housing register or waiting list and had never attended a single meeting with her local authority supervisor. To all intents and purposes, she had ceased to exist. Cathy's report hadn't been any more positive, Oliver Bithell's friends hadn't heard from him, there were still no posts on his social media, nor had his cash and credit cards been used since the beginning of April.

"I've run out of ideas Boss," she admitted. "We've done everything bar mount a full-on stakeout at the last place he used his cards."

"Ooh, that sounds exciting," Autumn chipped in. "I won't have to wee in a milk bottle in the back of an old Transit van, will I?"

"Only if you want to dear." Cathy replied, shaking her head. "Now, if you'll all excuse me, there's an image I need to go and scrub from my brain, as a matter of urgency."

Other than informing the team of the likelihood that Brandwood had perished in the fire, Yvie had decided to wait until everyone else had finished before passing on her own information, limited as it was. She was about to begin when her phone started playing an Iron Maiden track, one which everyone in the team recognised. They watched as Yvie answered the call and, apart from a brief 'Hi', didn't speak again until the call was ended maybe thirty seconds later.

"The boss was driving, and the signal was in and out, she's going to call back." Yvie explained. "However, it seems the fire at Brandwood's was deliberate - a gas pipe had been cut in the lounge, and all four rings on the gas hob were found in the 'On' position."

"So, we've got another murder, potentially linked to Bithell and, or, the Old Vicarage case." Joe said.

"Possibly, and I have to agree that it looks that way, but they haven't found a body yet. Because so much of the heavier furniture and contents from upstairs fell through to the ground floor, it's now a painstaking process of picking through the debris one piece at a time. Certainly not a job for the fainthearted." While still on the subject of the fire, Yvie went on to discuss the routine operations in support of the investigation that were currently being undertaken by local uniformed officers. All houses in the neighbouring streets were being canvassed, particular attention being given to any fitted with doorbell cameras or cctv. Another long shot, but one that occasionally paid dividends. "Earlier, when the Chief Super and I discussed the possibility of Bithell's proposed new book being a potential motive for his murder, she suggested that we consider moving the investigation over to Great Eccleston." Yvie floated the idea. "Any thoughts?"

"It's hard to believe that there would be a leak at HQ, and we'd know if anyone had accessed our information here." Tom seemed dubious.

"Not if they managed to get into our IT systems we wouldn't," Autumn said, "or bugged the office, or used a remote camera to look through the windows and film what was on the murder wall."

"I don't know, it all seems a little far-fetched to me. We don't even know if the killings are connected, there could any number of…." Iron Maiden cut short Tom's doubts. The four of them again watching as Yvie took the call, scribbling down a few notes as she listened to the Chief Super. The one-sided conversation was ended with a brief 'Thank you, Ma'am' from a serious looking Yvie.

"They've found a badly burned body which they believe to be Mark Brandwood, but it will require a DNA test to be absolutely sure. According to the Fire Investigator, and this is an informal report provided as a favour to the Chief Super, the body was found underneath the remains of a bed which had fallen through to the ground floor. The head, however, was found in an upstairs bedroom, lodged in a corner where the flooring hadn't completely burned away."

"They think he was beheaded?" Autumn asked, then felt foolish for even asking. "Of course he was, the same as Bithell."

"I'm going over to meet the Chief Super at her house. She doesn't want any further information passing through Hutton, and relocation to Great Eccleston is no longer just a suggestion." Yvie stood and picked up her jacket and keys. "Can you start getting things together for the move, I don't want anyone staying late today, we'll finish off in the morning. Thanks."

While Cathy gathered together the case files, Autumn was busy photographing the murder wall so she'd be able to recreate it in the lounge of what they now knew to be the Chief Super's old family home. The farmhouse had been empty since her mother had passed away just over two years ago, the poultry sheds and equipment had been sold off several years earlier when her father had begun his long overdue, and all too brief, retirement. With her own retirement becoming a possibility within the next ten years or so, Iron Annie had the vague idea that she might like to move back to the house, so had chosen not to sell it. The team had used the property during a previous investigation when there were concerns of a possible leak inside Hutton HQ. Similarly, whilst the rooms they now occupied in the old Clitheroe police station were nominally theirs, other police officers still had access to the rest of the building, so security couldn't be guaranteed. However unlikely, if one of their own was passing on information the move to a private house would eliminate the possibility.

Tom and Joe were busy transferring some of the heavier equipment into the back of Joe's recently restored Land Rover.

"What do you think mate?" Tom asked.

"I think that we're going to need to tread very fucking carefully." Joe's reply made all the more chilling because apart from the occasional 'bloody' or 'bugger', Tom had never heard the big man swear before, not even on the darkest of days when they'd been fighting for their lives. "Whoever is behind this has no qualms about killing police officers. We don't know who it is, or where the threat is going to come from. Knock on the wrong door, and….," he paused, not wanting to tempt Fate by continuing. "They won't like it, but make sure none of the lasses go off to see anyone without one of us tagging along."

Chapter Twenty-Four

Lucy: 2020

The day of Lucy's graduation ceremony had dawned overcast, which matched her mood throughout the proceedings. She had been the only person in cap and gown without a face in the crowd to search for, no one there to cheer her on or to whistle when her name was called out and she stepped forward to accept her scroll. Today had been a smaller affair but had followed much the same pattern. The six-month postgraduate course had been a breeze, but there was still no one there to express their pride in her achievement or to give her a congratulatory hug on her success, not even a card. While others went off for celebratory meals with their various friends and family, Lucy made her way home alone. She hadn't had a real friend since she was ten years old, not since the day she was taken from her home by the woman from Social Services, the day her life had changed forever.

When she had been placed, temporarily they had said, in the children's home Lucy had quickly found her place in the strict hierarchy. It was brutally simple, bullied by the bigger, older children and only able to take out her frustrations on those more vulnerable than herself. The only explanation she'd been given for her predicament was that her mother was in prison, something that made no sense to the desperately unhappy ten-year-old and gave the bullies even more ammunition. When term restarted in September, she was moved up to the same secondary school as some of the other children from the home, so there was no respite. If anything, it was worse, and not helped by the fact that it took almost eight months before her first placement with a foster family. Lucy wasn't aware of the reason, no one had bothered to mention that her mother's trial had since taken place and that she'd been found guilty. The foster parents, who already had a fourteen-year-old son of their own, seemed kindly enough and did their best to make her feel welcome. She was given her own room and immediately enjoyed the solitude, the relief of not constantly having to be on her guard against attack. The boy, whose name was Ian, was civil but pretty much left her alone, preferring to spend his every spare moment playing games on his PS5 console, something which suited Lucy just fine. The new school, her third in less than a year, was better as well. A couple of girls in her year had introduced themselves and given her a quick run-down on who was nice, who was a bitch, and which boys were dicks. The three of them had laughed and agreed that, actually, all the boys were dicks. Still cautious of anyone finding out about her mum, Lucy preferred to keep herself to herself, but was nonetheless pleased to have a couple of people to chat to. She soon settled into her schoolwork and after a brief catch up period had impressed her new teachers with her grasp of a wide range of subjects. Not only that, she discovered that as well as enjoying playing football, the sport had not been an option at her old schools, she was actually quite good at it and was always picked early for the after school matches.

Sat in her sparsely furnished one-bedroomed flat, Lucy continued to replay the events of her early life that were stamped into her memory, knowing they would never, could never, be erased. The day it had all gone wrong, again, had been a Sunday. It was late afternoon and her foster parents were at a neighbour's house for drinks and a barbecue. While finishing off her geography homework project, Glaciation in the Lake District, she'd run out of printer paper. Knowing that Ian would probably have some, she had knocked on his door and called out his name. She would never have dreamed of entering his domain without permission, if he wasn't in she would just have to wait until later.

"Hang on a minute." After a short wait, the door had opened a fraction and Ian popped his head round. "I've just got out of the shower, what do you want?" She briefly thought it odd that he said he'd just got out of the shower as his hair was dry.

"I just need a few sheets of printer paper, if you've got any?"

"Okay, come in, help yourself, but no peeping." He'd laughed and the door swung open, although Ian stayed hidden behind it. Lucy crossed to the printer on his cluttered desk and took out a thin stack of paper. When she turned around, Ian was stood, stark naked, with his back to the now closed door. "You'll have to pay me for them though."

"What do you mean?" Lucy kept her eyes fixed on the floor, it wasn't the first time she'd encountered a boy who wanted her to do things for him.

"Just hold it and rub it a little bit, like this. That's all, nothing else." She raised her eyes to where his hand was moving slowly backwards and forwards.

"Please let me out."

"Not until you...." Ian had never got to finish his request. Even after all these years, and despite the consequences, whenever Lucy thought about what had happened next, it was with a rare feeling of pride in herself. One important survival lesson she had learned in the children's home was, when faced with a threat that she couldn't avoid, to embrace her temper and to go in first, fast and hard. She had taken two steps towards the boy, who was very clearly anticipating a much happier ending, before making a fist and then punching him as hard as she could, right in his unprotected, dangly ball bag. Another valuable lesson she'd learned from some of the older girls who were always keen to talk about their experiences. Ian sank to the floor and curled up, knees close to his chest, whimpering softly into the carpet. With the release of an all-consuming anger she'd never before experienced, Lucy had seized his prize possession, the PS5, wrenched the power cable out and launched the console as hard as she could towards his head. It only caught him a glancing blow before being smashed to pieces against a bedside cabinet, but the scalp wound was enough to have blood running down the side of his face. Still not satisfied, she had picked up a half empty mug off his desk and hurled it at the flatscreen TV.

"Now get out of my way, you shit." Lucy remembered her younger self spitting the words at the sobbing boy and how, despite the agony of his every movement, fear of her rage had made him shuffle clear of the door.

Her next spell in the children's home had begun the very same evening, shortly after Ian's parents had found him battered and bleeding on his bedroom floor. Whether or not they believed his version of events was irrelevant, the life Lucy had been on the brink of allowing herself to enjoy, was over.

She had been warned by her social worker that it may take a lot longer before another foster family could be found. A soon to be teenage girl, particularly one with a reputation for violence, wasn't easy to place. However, returning to the home, and to her old school, hadn't been the nightmare Lucy was expecting, largely thanks to the rumour mill. The story going around was that she'd put an eighteen-year-old would-be rapist into Intensive Care with multiple, life-threatening injuries. That bought notoriety and, more importantly, a level of respect she'd never experienced before. Lucy saw no reason to correct the much-inflated version of events, choosing instead to remain silent on the issue. When her next foster placement was eventually arranged, it was with a woman called Gill. In her early fifties, and having lost her husband the year before, Gill had been honest with her from their very first meeting. She could use the additional income but hadn't wanted the fuss of looking after a younger child. It was a set-up that worked just fine for both of them. In return for doing her share of the household chores, Lucy had her own room, regular meals, a little spending money and, best of all, the solitude she craved. After dinner, other than to top up her glass, Gill rarely moved from in front of the television. This meant that Lucy's evenings were free for her to study, she had already realised that a scholarship might be her only way of getting to university, to read, and to spend time on her new hobby – researching her mother.

Chapter Twenty-Five

"How come the post-mortem is being done in Blackpool?" Autumn asked.

"Apparently, the Home Office pathologist requested that some preparatory work was undertaken, and Blackpool was the only place with the right equipment and a consultant radiologist experienced in its use." Joe had just filtered off the M6 and onto the M55, which appeared to have sprouted a couple of new junctions since the last time he'd driven down it.

"Interesting, sounds like he'll have wanted a PMCT report."

"Go on then," he sighed, knowing he'd regret it, "tell me."

"Well, as you're asking, it stands for post-mortem computed tomography and it's used to see inside the charred remains of people who've died in fires. Particularly if it's a suspicious death."

"I knew I shouldn't have asked."

"I don't know much about it, but I think it uses cross sectional imaging techniques to help identify cause of death, as well as lots of other stuff, of course."

"Yeah, of course." Joe agreed. "And, as his head was found upstairs, and his body was downstairs, I think we can safely say it's suspicious."

"Mmm, should be a good one. Do we know who we've got?"

"No, Trina didn't say."

"I hope it's not that Ayles-Bradwell guy again," Autumn said, "he was a real arrogant prick."

"I think he might have gone off sick if he thought there was any chance of coming up against you again Constable Jackson." Joe grinned fondly as he glanced across at his young colleague. He still considered the day that she'd teed up the pompous arse, before shooting him down in flames, to be one of her finest moments. It was a good story, one that he never tired of telling, unlike other aspects of the same case that, even now, could still disturb his sleep in the early hours.

Leaving the motorway at the roundabout between B&Q and the big Tesco, Joe dropped his speed down to 30 after the lights then followed Preston New Road until the turn off for Stanley Park and the hospital. A few minutes later they were pulling into the small, private parking area that served the mortuary. Getting out of the car, they crossed to an unmarked door and both looked up and smiled into the camera as Joe pressed the intercom button. There was a short delay before the lock buzzed open and a cheery voice invited them in with a classic Lancashire greeting, 'Kettle's on, shift yer arses'. They stepped inside and waited until the door was fully closed behind them, then set off down a short passageway before stopping at the large 'No Unauthorised Persons Beyond This Point' sign.

"Hi Trina." Autumn was genuinely fascinated by the senior mortuary technician who greeted them from behind the desk. She looked old enough to remember the pyramids being built, but had the cheekiest smile and the most stunningly beautiful, fun-filled eyes she had ever see.

"Hello Autumn luv. Nice to see you again. You too Joe, have you come to sweep me off mi feet and take us away from all this then?"

"Stop!" Autumn ordered, before Joe had chance to reply. "No silly jokes and no sloppy stuff, I'm still having nightmares about last time."

"Kids today, eh Joe?" Trina smiled and shook her head. "They just don't know how to have fun."

Once they were signed in, suited, booted, masked and hair-netted Trina escorted them into the brightly lit examination room. Autumn's attention was immediately drawn to the unusual shape on the white sheeted, examination table right in front of her.

"Val and the girls all okay Joe?" Trina asked.

"Yeah, they're fine thanks. When I told her I'd be seeing you today...."

"Stop!" Autumn ordered for a second time. "If this is the 'bring home some of the special pork' joke, you did it last time."

"If you don't mind Constable, I was about to say that Val asked me bring Trina's birthday card." He reached into his jacket pocket.

"Sorry Boss, I just...." The colour rose in Autumn's cheeks, along with the feeling that she'd just made a fool of herself by jumping in too soon. Then she noticed that the hand he he'd just removed from his jacket was still empty. "It was gonna be the 'special pork' joke again, wasn't it?" She coloured up even more when the only answer was their laughter. "God, I hate old people!"

"Hello again!" The tall, masked and gowned figure said as he entered the room. "I wasn't expecting to see you here today, I thought you were based south of the Ribble?"

"Hi Stuart," Autumn answered, relieved to see her favourite pathologist rather than the pompous prick who'd attended on their last visit to Blackpool. "You know how it is, we go where the work is." Managing to hold herself back from launching straight into cadaver based questions, she began the introductions. "This is my boss, DI Joe Penswick. Joe, this is Stuart…," then realised that she didn't know his surname.

"Allenby," he finished for her. "Pleased to meet you." The two men nodded, shaking hands was pretty much out of the question for obvious reasons.

"You too, we've heard a lot about you, haven't we Detective Constable Jackson?"

"I may have mentioned your name once or twice, after the Bithell pm in Chorley." Autumn blushed guiltily under Joe's gaze.

"Ah, yes. The decapitation." He looked thoughtful for a moment. "I can only report on my findings of course, but I suspect that two such killings within a fortnight would be stretching the boundaries of coincidence?"

"Indeed, it would." Joe hadn't been expecting to get to the money question without a long preamble, it seemed that Stuart was happy to take a more relaxed approach to discussing his work than some of his colleagues. "Cause of death?"

"The actual cause, as in the Bithell case, was loss of blood pressure, anoxia and shock as a result of decapitation."

"It was the same?"

"Not exactly, no. While the cause of death was the same, the means by which it was brought about was different. With both the head and torso being so badly burned it's quite difficult to establish the exact sequence of events, hence the request for a PMCT scan."

"I was going to ask you about that, is it….?"

"Not right now Autumn." Joe instructed. "Please continue with what you were saying Stuart."

"Yes, certainly. With the aid of the scanned images, I'm fairly certain that the poor soul here was struck several times on and around the neck with a broad headed axe, something like a felling axe, but I'm no expert. Being much thicker than a sword blade it leaves very different wounds and markings on the bone. The scan picked up traces of very fine metal filings in the wounds, which would suggest that the blade of the axe had recently been sharpened."

"And he was definitely dead before the fire started?"

"Absolutely. The first cut to the back of the neck is by far the deepest and would almost certainly have been fatal. There are a further three cuts, all made at different angles, presumably to complete the decapitation."

"At least it was quick." Joe said.

"Yes, I suppose that is some small consolation. We managed to recover deep tissue DNA samples so, if the victim is indeed a recently retired police officer, you should have confirmation of identity later on today."

"Why recently retired? Autumn asked.

"The DNA records of all serving police officers are kept on the Contamination Elimination Database, and the Police Elimination Database, but they're only held for 12 months after an officer leaves the force." Joe explained. "And I'm pretty sure Tom said that Brandwood had been retired on ill health six years ago."

"In that case you'll need to examine the metal plate that I removed from our victim's left femur, quite a nasty break I imagine, and compare it with Mr. Brandwood's medical records."

"Already on it Joe," Trina confirmed, "I'll let you know."

"Would you like to view the corpse Detective Inspector? I'm afraid that due to the extent of the charring there's not a great deal to be seen, at least not with the naked eye."

"No, not necess…."

"Yes please," Autumn beamed an apology at Joe. "How else am I going to learn?"

"Brew, Joe?"

"Thanks Trina." The snatch of conversation they overheard before leaving the examination room was the start of Stuart's explanation of the pugilistic pose caused by extreme temperatures. '...muscles and tendons can shrink and stiffen in the elbows, wrists, knees, and.....' Joe let the door close behind them, knowing that he'd be hearing it all again at the next team briefing.

Joe had been mistaken; he hadn't needed to wait for the team briefing at all. From the moment they got in the car to return to their temporary base in Great Eccleston, Autumn had been buzzing with her newly acquired, and gruesomely detailed, knowledge. It was a relief to pull into the parking area at the back of the Chief Super's old house, and a profound regret that he wouldn't be enjoying roast pork with crackling for the foreseeable future.

"Chief Super's here," Autumn announced, spotting the inky blue Jaguar parked next to Yvie's BMW." Joe's phone rang as they were walking towards the back door of the farmhouse.

"You go in, I need to take this," he said after seeing the caller ID, "and get the kettle on!"

When Joe walked into the house a few minutes later, he was surprised to see the Hutton Desk Sergeant sat at the big kitchen table alongside the Chief Super and the rest of the team.

"Alright Bill," Joe nodded a greeting, "and to what do we owe the pleasure of your company?"

"I'll field that one if you don't mind," Iron Annie said before he could respond, it clearly wasn't a request. "I've just been explaining to your colleagues here that since Bithell was murdered, Bill has been travelling with me and staying over at my house. As you know, we're the only two police officers remaining who were named in Bithell's book, the other four, five if you include Julie, are no longer with us." Yvie and Cathy both noticed the hand that Iron Annie placed on Bill's arm when she mentioned his fiancé.

"But neither of you were at the Old Vicarage, were you?" Joe asked. "And at Arnside, it was Gryce who took you hostage and then dragged you into the river. Why would you be at risk, after all these years?"

"The way the press reported it at the time, and to an extent in Bithell's book, they tried to make out that we had heroically overcome the evil serial killer. Which just wasn't true. I was out of it, I would have drowned if Bill hadn't saved my life. He was the hero, but we had nothing to do with whatever happened to Gryce."

"So why....?" Joe began, then paused for a moment. "Because, if it is Gryce, back from wherever he's been hiding for the last twenty-odd years, or even some looney-tunes tribute act, they might not see it that way."

"Correct."

"With all due respect Ma'am," Tom looked uncomfortable with what he was about to say. "If you think that you need additional security, surely it should be someone a bit, well.... a bit more.... capable? No offence Bill, it's just...., you know?"

"None taken son, I know you mean well. But you're only seeing the gammy arm and the grey hair which, by the way, happened virtually overnight when Julie was killed. I'll grant you that I probably couldn't outrun you, but I'm still a registered

Taekwondo coach, mostly juniors nowadays, or if you fancy your chances on the range, I'll match any bet you care to make with a Glock 17."

"I'm sorry mate, I didn't realise." Tom looked forlorn, embarrassed at making an assumption that was so far off the mark.

"Forget it," Bill laughed, "you weren't to know."

"News just in," Joe changed the subject. "Trina rang, the plate that was removed from our fire victim's thigh matches the one referenced in Brandwood's medical records. It was definitely him."

"Cause of death?" The Chief Super asked.

"Decapitation," Joe jumped in quickly with a response, knowing that if he gave Autumn the opportunity, they'd be there all day. "The pathologist confirmed that he was dead before the fire started."

"The same as Bithell then." Yvie added.

"Not quite, this one was different in that a felling axe was used, rather than a sword." Joe went on to give a brief summary of Stuart's comments.

"It might not be the same weapon that was used on Bithell," Iron Annie exclaimed, "but it's exactly the same as the one that killed Williams and Stansfield."

Chapter Twenty-Six

The second Sunday in April was always earmarked for Val's belated birthday celebration, which some people found rather confusing as her birthday fell at the end of December. Weather permitting, it was always the first outdoor bash of the year, a tradition carried forward from when she was a child and had wanted her own special day, completely separate from the Christmas and New Year festivities. This year, because the second Sunday had been Easter Sunday, the party had been postponed for a week, which was fortunate given the events of the previous weekend. Val had decided that the 'Remaining Resolution Buster' as it had become known by friends and family, was to be an afternoon long tapas feast of epic proportions. A talented chef in her own right, with two cookbooks to her name and a growing following for her food blog, it promised to be a treat not to be missed. Late on Friday evening, with all updates discussed and recorded and a complete absence of actions requiring urgent attention, Yvie had declared that everyone was to take the weekend off. A rare occurrence during a murder case, let alone a double, but justified given the excessive hours that everyone had been working recently. Hopefully, a couple of days of down-time would help to throw off any fatigue and have the team back on Monday morning, less jaded and keen to push forward with some new ideas. Yvie was planning to take some time off herself, but that didn't prevent her photographing the updated murder wall and then printing off copies to take home, just in case she found a few spare minutes, she told herself.

Realistically, the prospect of any free time was unlikely as, for the very first time, honorary 'Uncle James' had been drafted in to help with the preparations for Val's party, a rare honour.

While James spent a pleasurable Saturday working alongside Grace and Penny, Joe and Val's young daughters, Yvie had spent the day at home with Conor, doing little other than simply enjoying being with her son. Despite it still being fairly early in the year, and in the north of England at that, the weather was dry and mild, so Yvie got Conor dressed up in his fleecy jacket and trousers before spending a good part of the morning doing odd jobs in the garden. Simply pottering around the beds and borders, checking on the seedlings in the cold-frame and doing a little preparation for the new season that was almost upon them gave her a real sense of peace, something that was definitely lacking in her day job. She laughed out loud with her son and his newfound delight at scrunching up grass and leaves in his tiny hands. Still at a stage where everything he could grasp automatically went to his mouth, she had to watch him like a hawk, it was a game he never seemed to tire of. After spending a very pleasant couple of hours, they eventually went inside for lunch and both had thick homemade soup and bread, although Yvie passed on the stewed apple and pear dessert. It wasn't until Conor went down for his afternoon nap, cheeks still rosy from his time in the garden, that Yvie allowed herself to think about the Bithell case. Not that there was a lot to think about, nothing much had changed since Brandwood's murder, no further progress in the search for Oliver Bithell or Sophie Elletson, it was beginning to feel as though the investigation had run into a brick wall. Yvie positioned the printouts she'd brought home on top of the kitchen table, then simply sat and let her eyes wander over the photos and linked notes, all the time wondering, 'What am I not seeing?' She was sensing that whatever it was, it was right there in front of her and, like so many other puzzles in life, would seem perfectly obvious afterwards. But how many more people had to die before they got to the answer? She was dragged from her thoughts by the sound of Conor waking and was amazed to find that almost two hours had passed since she'd sat down at the table. James returned home late in the afternoon, spending time working in the kitchen had the same effect on him as gardening had on Yvie, so he'd had a thoroughly enjoyable day working with Val and the girls. Conor had, as usual, been the centre of their attention until after his bath when he'd gone down to sleep in minutes. With neither of them particularly hungry, James suggested cheese on toast in front of the television. What arrived on Yvie's lap ten minutes later was two slices of sourdough bread, lightly toasted then rubbed with the cut side of a garlic clove. Thinly sliced tomato and shallot, with a sprinkling of dried 'herbes de Provence' was peaking through a browned and bubbling layer of grated gruyere. The savoury, cheesy, herby aroma was mouthwatering, as was the large glass of Argentinian Malbec that accompanied it. They ate in a companiable silence, half-watching an early evening quiz show that seemed to be based around minor celebrities showing off their lack of general knowledge. Once Yvie had cleared away and checked on Conor, she again broke the recent rule and brought them each a second glass of wine. Snuggled on the settee, in front of the final two episodes of a Scandi thriller they'd been following, Yvie reflected that it had been a good day. She made a silent promise to herself that she wouldn't think about work again until Monday.

Philip Garmond was glad of the interruption when the doorbell rang. He'd just spent his first Easter alone, something that had been much more difficult than he'd anticipated. Since the very first year that they had been married, the Easter fortnight had always been when he and his wife had taken their main holidays, like clockwork. Every year they'd gone somewhere different, even when Barbara's illness had progressed to a stage where they couldn't travel very far they'd still managed to find new places to visit. Although she'd passed away almost a full year ago, it was only during the last week that he'd decided he was going to clear her things from the drawers and wardrobes, still not a hundred percent sure that he was ready. He'd put it off on a number of occasions but knew it was time to let go of the daily reminders of a life shared; he had all the memories he needed safely stored away in his head. Looking through some old photographs he'd found in an envelope, images that he hadn't seen in years, every single one of the glossy holiday snaps brought back memories that made him smile and pushed him ever closer to putting things off for a while longer. Smiling as he made his way downstairs, still holding a photograph of the two of them taken when they'd been on a walking holiday to the Amalfi coast, he was trying to work out how many years it had been since they had completed the Sentiero Degli Dei, the Path of the Gods. On opening the door Philip was met by the sight of someone in workman's overalls, a woolly hat and a disposable mask and gloves. How the world has changed since the pandemic, he thought.

"Good morning," he began, the door now wide open. "Sorry it took me so long to answer the door. Not as quick as I…" Philip was forced backwards as the caller's arm shot out and he was punched hard in the stomach. When he managed to raise his head he was at first confused by the sight of a bloodied blade in his attacker's gloved hand, then looked down and saw the front of his pale blue polo shirt was already turning a deep crimson. Staggering backwards for a couple of steps before his knees gave way, he sat down heavily on the hall carpet, the front door was now closed he noticed, and he was no longer alone. Understanding only dawned when he saw the long-handled axe that his attacker was unhurriedly removing from an extra-large tool bag. Writing about the Old Vicarage case when he put together Bithell's book, including a detailed account of the murders of Paul Williams and Bernie Stansfield, had simply been a job, no different from any other. It had never occurred to Philip for a single moment that he might one day share their fate. Weakened by the loss of blood from his stomach wound, and for some inexplicable reason feeling desperately tired, Philp lay back on the carpet and turned his head towards the photograph that he was still holding between his fingers. In his mind, Philip reached out and took Barbara's hand in his own. He felt the softness of her skin, the two of them enjoying the caress of a cliff-top breeze as it gently tempered the warmth of the Mediterranean sun. He heard Barbara giggle as they shared a silly joke, standing together, gazing down on the azure waters far below, a perfect moment on a perfect day.

Chapter Twenty-Seven

Joe's house and garden was full to bursting with music, laughter and the comfortable, relaxed chatter of old friends and family. With the exception of a couple of Val's 'foodie pals', who they hadn't met before, Yvie and James knew just about everyone else and were greeted as though they were lifelong friends. Once again, Yvie couldn't help but compare her life now, to the one she'd left behind in London. She gave thanks for whatever it was that had made her come north on a temporary secondment, and for the people around her who had made the decision to stay an absolute 'no-brainer'. Iron Annie, just Anne outside work, and Bill had immediately commandeered Conor, and James had again been press-ganged into the kitchen to help with the serving up of tray after tray of delicious small plates. The hot fish tapas had been served first, so everyone moved indoors to sample the wonderfully soft octopus, slices of seared scallop, lightly battered goujons of haddock and garlicky king prawns, all with a selection of dressings, dipping sauces and breads. Having tried a little of everything, Yvie wandered over to where Val was taking a break and chatting to Sarah Southern and her partner James, or 'big James' as he'd been dubbed in a bid to avoid confusion, along with Cathy, Gus, Autum and Tom.

"Happy Birthday for last December Val, all the best." She hugged her friend and was surprised when Val indicated that she wanted a word in private. The two of them slipped outside, feeling the freshness of the breeze after the warmth of indoors.

"Joe's not sleeping, he won't tell me anything, but I know it's this Bithell case you're involved in. What's going on Yvie? Should I be worried?"

"I can't say there's no risk in what we do Val, because you'd know it wasn't true. But this case is no different than any other."

"No Yvie, that's not true. We got through the nightmares after what happened out at Woodplumpton," Val said, looking Yvie directly in the eye, "but this is something different, and I need to know."

"It's an old case that Anne and Bill were involved in, over twenty years ago." Yvie knew how protective Joe was with regard to his family, but she had no doubts about Val's strength and ability to deal with any given situation. The bond they had shared since standing side by side to take on the Winter Beast meant she couldn't refuse her friend. "Three police officers were killed back then. Bithell and another ex-officer have since been murdered in similar circumstances. We think the killings are linked."

"Five murders? A cop killer?"

"Not a phrase that I really want to repeat out loud, but yes, Anne is concerned that it could be. We don't fully understand the motives for the two recent murders, but we have reason to believe they may be linked."

"Thank you." Val nodded, processing what she'd just been told. "I won't ask you to look out for him but… well, you know what he's like?"

"Yes, I do, and I'll do my best." They hugged again and then went back to rejoin the party. Yvie couldn't decide on her favourite tapas, chicken and chorizo or black pudding with roasted apple, or was it the tiny spicy pork sausages, or maybe the baked goat cheese with rosemary and honey. So many dishes and so little time, there was still an array of salads and a huge serving dish of patatas bravas that she hadn't sampled, but was valiantly working her way towards. By the time the desserts came out everyone was already stuffed to the gills, the Resolution Buster had once again lived up to its name. Nevertheless, Yvie still took her place in the queue to sample Val's take on cannoli, one of her all-time favourite pastries. Smaller than the traditional Sicilian version, Val flavoured the sweetened ricotta filling with either pistachio or rhubarb and ginger, they were absolutely irresistible. Juggling two of the delicious pastry tubes on a side plate, and with a coffee in her other hand, Yvie was momentarily at a loss when her mobile rang. It wasn't one of the ringtones she reserved for family or friends, so she knew it was unlikely to be good news. After quickly offloading her coffee to James, she reached into her pocket for her phone and noticed that John from FIT was doing exactly the same thing. A moment later, a grim looking Iron Annie was crossing the room towards her. While Bill handed Conor back to James, her boss mouthed a single word, 'Garmond'. It was time to leave. Yvie ignored Joe's protests and insisted that he stayed with his family, similarly she dismissed Cathy and Autumn's offers to assist, saying that with her, Tom, the Chief Super and Bill, they would already be getting in each other's way. Quick kisses for

James and Conor, a hurried goodbye wave to Val, and they left, a mini-convoy en route to yet another crime scene.

Tom drove quickly, but not excessively so, and on their arrival at Garmond's house in Penwortham they saw that both the Ambulance Service and John's FIT colleagues had beaten them to it. Parking directly behind Tom and Yvie, John went straight over to the van to be briefed and to begin donning his PPE. There were two uniformed officers guarding the front of the house but, after showing their ID and being signed in at the tape barrier, the Chief Super and Yvie were allowed to approach just far enough to see through the partially open front door. One glance at the carnage in the hallway had been enough to confirm their worst fears. Exchanging a solemn, knowing look they retraced their steps to join Tom and Bill with the two uniformed officers who had been first to arrive at the property. The young male constable looked decidedly unwell, as if he might keel over at any second. His female companion appeared to be nervous, but was managing to hold it together, at least for the time being.

"PC Blackledge and PC Carter, Ma'am. We we're first on the scene and I told Daz, PC Carter Ma'am, to…" the young police officer stopped immediately when Iron Annie raised a hand, the gesture unmistakeable.

"What's your name, love?"

"PC Blackledge, er Karen, Ma'am."

"Okay Karen, take a breath. You've both had a nasty shock and, no matter what anyone says back in the locker room, this part of the job doesn't come easily to any of us. I'd be worried about you if it did. Now, don't rush, use your notes, just take us through it from the top. Okay?"

"Yes Ma'am, thank you." Karen removed the notebook from her pocket and took a moment to familiarise herself. "PC Carter and I received a call from Control at 15:50 asking us to proceed to this address once we'd finished dealing with a minor altercation at the golf club."

"What was it you were you on with?" Yvie and Tom both knew that the Chief Super wasn't really interested in the answer, she just wanted to give the young PC a chance to settle down a little.

"It was just two old guys, had a drop too much to drink and started playing silly buggers Ma'am. Nothing really, it took us a few minutes to settle them down and then we were on our way here. There were no real details available, we were just informed that concerns had been raised by a neighbour, at number 42. Apparently, the occupier," Karen again checked her notes, "a Mr. Philip Garmond, hadn't turned up for their usual Sunday afternoon card game, and had also failed to answer either his mobile phone or his doorbell. The neighbour was concerned because when she rang the doorbell and he didn't answer, she tried his mobile again and could hear it ringing inside the house. She thought maybe he'd had a fall or something."

"Okay, you're doing fine Karen."

"We arrived here at 16:02 and, after ringing the bell and knocking on the door didn't get a response, I told PC Carter to wait at the front while I checked the rear of the house. I managed to climb over the side gate and when I got round the back I noticed that there was a strong smell of gas in the garden. I could see that one of the kitchen windows was open and when I checked the back door it was unlocked. The smell of gas was much worse when I opened the back door, I know I shouldn't have gone in Ma'am, but I thought that maybe the owner had been overcome by a gas leak or something."

"I'd have done the same Karen, you did the right thing."

"Thank you, Ma'am. As soon as I opened the door I could see that the cooker had been pulled away from the wall and that the connector hose had been cut. I could hear the gas escaping, so I unplugged the bayonet fitting."

"How did you know what to do?" the Chief Super asked.

"Me and my partner are doing up our own place Ma'am and, well, you just learn about stuff like that don't you?"

"You do, but it was quick thinking, well done!" With the young PC now much more at ease, the Chief Super finally got round to asking about the true purpose of their visit. "So, who actually found the deceased?"

"I suppose it was PC Carter, Ma'am. While he was waiting for me, he got down on his hands and knees to try and look through the letterbox, it's one of those really low ones. When I came back he was throwing up over by the bushes, he was white as a sheet and couldn't really get his words out. He held my arm and tried to stop me looking, but I needed to know." The young officer paused and her voice began to break, just a little. "It's the first time either of us have seen anything, you know.... like that."

"We've all been there Karen, and we all find our own way of coping," Yvie and Tom both found themselves nodding in agreement, "just don't bottle it up, and don't try and do it all on your own. If ever you need someone to talk to, feel free to call me, any time." Yvie watched as the Chief Super smiled and handed the constable her card, another example of why Iron Annie Atkinson had become a legend within the ranks of the Lancashire Constabulary. "Now, see to your partner, give your reports, then the pair of you clock off and get yourselves home, on my orders." While Karen gratefully departed to go and check on her colleague, the Chief Super made a mental note to make sure someone was keeping any eye on the pair of them for the next few days.

"Big soft bugger!" Bill said after leaning in close to her ear, then nodded towards the lounge window. Moving a little closer, and shielding the sun from her eyes to see into the lounge, she could make out a gas fire burning merrily away. "Damn near the same set up as at Brandwood's, only this time it didn't work."

"No, not for want of trying though, was it?"

Chapter Twenty-Eight

Lucy: 2022

Over the eighteen months that had passed since her graduation and, as she acquired the skills and resources that would enable her to push on even further, what had begun as an interest, a teenage hobby, had developed into nothing short of obsession. Ironically, Lucy even recognised the same trait from those last few weeks and months before her mother had been imprisoned. Whatever the reason, she was powerless to overcome the need to find her, to see her again, to hear answers to the questions that burned in her mind. Unable to analyse or even identify her true motivation, was it the unconditional love of a child for her mother, or the white-hot anger she felt when she thought of her own lost childhood? She decided that it didn't matter, confident that everything would be okay when they eventually came face to face once again. And so, several evenings every week, all her rest days, the weeks when her work colleagues thought she was away on holiday, were spent in the pursuit of what had become her single goal in life. Her approach was simple and methodical, travelling from area to area, searching in ever increasing circles emanating from Leyland, the last home they had shared. Walking the streets, seeking out the homeless, the disadvantaged, the vulnerable, the very people that everyone else avoided. The best photograph she owned of her mother was ten years out of date, before prison had taken its toll. It had come from the meagre box of personal possessions presented to her when their house had been cleared by the housing association. Regardless, she still handed out copies and the promise of a reward, there was little else she could do.

After all the study, research and endless hours of legwork, her first real nugget of information came about by sheer chance. Lucy had spent a fruitless weekend working some of the estates to the north-east of Preston. Walking back to where she had parked her car, it was safer on the main road, she became aware of an elderly woman sat on a bench by a bus stop. As she drew nearer she noticed the empty cans of super strength lager scattered at the woman's feet. Closer still she picked up the sour smell of body odour and, after moving ever so slightly upwind of the woman who she now realised might not have been much older than herself, she held out the photograph.

"I've seen someone who looks a bit like her, but a lot older. Sal, or Sophe, or something like that, she calls herself. What's it worth?" The woman's bleary eyes were drawn to the £10 note that had suddenly appeared in Lucy's hand.

"When did you last see her?" The possible mention of her mother's name was making it difficult, but Lucy was trying to keep the urgency out of her voice, knowing that if she seemed too anxious the price demanded for information would skyrocket.

"Could have been last week, yeah, it was last week." Dirty fingers reached out for the note, but Lucy held it out of her reach.

"Where?"

"There's a food truck, you know, burgers and stuff. If the dark-haired woman is on her own when they close up in the afternoon, she lets us have anything that's gone out of date. That's where I've seen her, a few times lately, but I ain't saying any more 'til I've been paid." She held out her hand for the note and this time Lucy handed it over. Then took another from her pocket.

"So where does this food truck park?"

"Thing is, it's gonna cost you a lot more than that sweetheart." The words had barely left her cracked lips when she was slammed into the back of the bench. Within a second, a forearm was pressed hard across her throat and her left wrist was being forced backwards against the joint. After pausing long enough to be sure there would be no underestimation of her ability to cause a whole new level of pain and suffering, Lucy released a fraction of the pressure on the woman's scrawny throat, just sufficient to allow her to speak.

"Okay, okay, please!"

"Where can I find it?" Lucy snarled into the panic-stricken face an inch from her own. "Don't be in any doubt, if you lie to me I will find you and I will fuck you over."

"It parks in the layby outside the industrial estate," she waved her free hand vaguely in the direction of a small business park over the road, "the one with the big carpet place."

In the last week of October, on only the fourth occasion she'd sat in her car watching people approach the burger van, Lucy finally located her mother. Her first glimpse was through the windscreen, and she wasn't sure, not one hundred percent. She got out and walked towards the gathering group of vagrants, all patiently waiting for a share of the out-of-date pies and sandwiches, still not sure. It was only when she forced herself to ignore the premature aging, the greasy hair and the bad posture, and finally got a good look at the woman in profile, then she was taken back to being a little girl. Before she knew what was happening tears were streaming down her cheeks, her pulse was racing and her voice cracking with emotion as she took the last few steps towards her mother.

"Mum," she said softly, reaching out her arms, nervous and unable to hold in the intense wave of joy that threatened to take away her ability to move or speak.

"Fuck off and wait your turn," the woman staggered slightly as she turned, unsteady but ready to fight.

"Mum, it's me, Lucy. I've been looking for you, for so long."

"Well whoever you are, now you've found me, you can just fuck right off and leave me alone again." Lucy could see that her mother was struggling to focus on her, then she realised that she was drunk, she could smell the cheap booze on her breath. This wasn't the joyous reunion she'd been imagining at all, she decided to try something else.

"Mum, I've got money for you. If you come with me in the car we can stop at the off-licence and then maybe get some fish and chips on the way home. I've got enough money for whatever you want." Lucy watched the puzzlement play out on her mother's lined and grubby face as she struggled to comprehend what she'd just been told.

"You really got money for me?"

"Yes." Lucy held up the notes from her pocket.

"Okay," her mother took a wobbly step towards her, "but stop calling me Mum. My child was fuckin' stolen from me."

The following weeks weren't the fairy tale that Lucy had been hoping for. The small relief that her mother was now using alcohol rather than heroin didn't last beyond the first night. After downing a full bottle of vodka and most of a bottle of white wine, her mother was not only drunk and passed out of the settee, she'd managed to drink herself into a state of uncaring incontinence. Over the following days, Lucy resorted to watering down the cheap supermarket vodka that she purchased almost daily, not wanting to have more than one bottle in the house at any time. She also supplemented her mother's prodigious intake with lower strength lagers, reasoning that there had to be a limit to how much the woman could drink. Surprisingly, the phased reduction in her alcohol intake, no doubt along with the provision of regular meals and a comfortable bed, seemed to be making a difference. Sophie had recognised and accepted Lucy as her daughter within the first seventy-two hours but wasn't yet ready for any meaningful conversation. When the alcohol began to take hold of her in the evenings was the only time she ever expressed any emotion, and that was always tears for her stolen son, never for her dutiful daughter. By the middle of December and with Sophie now largely coherent, if not fully sober, for longer spells, Lucy finally felt they were approaching the point when she would be able to ask the questions that had troubled her for as long as she could remember.

With her annual leave entitlement used up, and afraid to take any additional sick leave, Lucy had returned to work for the first time since she had found her mother. All the way home that evening she'd been dreading what she might find waiting for her when she stepped into the flat. She realised she was holding her breath as she opened the front door, and then immediately burst into tears. The place was spotless, not a thing out of place, the carpets had been vacuumed and she could even smell shepherd's pie, fresh from the oven, always her favourite as a child. Sophie met her in the lounge, shaky but sober, and they hugged, both now in tears.

"How did you manage all this?" Lucy was close to being overwhelmed.

"I decided that I wanted to do something for my daughter, more than I wanted to start drinking. So, I cleaned up a little and then had a walk to the shops. I hope you still like shepherd's pie." Lucy was too overcome with happy tears to answer right away but they talked late into the night and, gradually over the following days, all of Lucy's questions were answered.

"When I read Bithell's book, he made out that Gryce and Daniels were like some evil baby traffickers."

"No, they were the kindest, nicest men I've ever met. Anthony in particular was an absolute saint, that's why I named your brother after him."

"And are you sure that it was Bithell who took him, it's not what the newspapers said at the time, or what's in the book."

"It was him, he admitted it when I tried to see Anthony, before…. you know? He'd already warned me to keep my mouth shut as a condition of helping me to get you back."

"Me, you chose me? I always thought…."

"It wasn't like that, not a straight choice. But yes. I agreed to keep quiet, and he helped me to get you out of care."

"We can talk to Anthony, we can tell him…."

"No love, not now. It was too late even back then; I just didn't realise in time. I'm so sorry."

Lucy had known for several weeks that she was rostered to work some of the most unpopular shifts over the holiday period, the unspoken rule was that those with children would get first pick of any time off. But it didn't dampen her mood in the slightest, for the first time since she was ten years old she was looking forward to Christmas, determined to make it one to remember. Late on Christmas Eve she returned home from the afternoon shift, tired but happy. Swapping with a colleague who wanted New Year's Eve off meant that she would have all of Christmas Day at home with her mum. Lucy just hoped she liked the present that she had agonised over for weeks. It had meant bending the truth a little, more than a little if she was completely honest, but she'd managed to get hold of all of Anthony's, or Oliver's, senior school photographs and a copy of his university ID photo. Really pleased with herself, she'd made a collage of his younger photos with his current one in the centre. The whole thing was set in a heavy glass frame, wrapped and ready in her tote bag.

Immediately she unlocked the door to her apartment Lucy could sense that something was wrong, very wrong. The place was untidy, a mess, she could smell the sharp tang of vomit and noticed that the old-fashioned piggy bank she kept pound coins in had been taken from its shelf in the kitchen and lay in pieces on the floor. The empty vodka bottle on the settee provided all the explanation she needed. As she approached the bedroom, the one she'd gladly given up for her mother, she could hear the drunken sobbing.

"Anthony, I'm sorry son, I'm so sorry. I should have fought for you, I should have chosen you." As much as it stung to hear her say such words, Lucy put it down to the effects of drink. She knew her mother loved her and appreciated everything she was doing for her.

"Ahh Mum! You were doing so well." Lucy put her bag down on the floor and placed a hand on her mother's shoulder. "Come on, let's get you cleaned up and I'll change the...." Lucy recoiled in surprise when her mother leapt up from the bed, her lips were drawn back, a look of abject hatred making her face almost unrecognisable.

"It's your fault, if it hadn't been for you I could have got him back. I hate you! It should have been you who was taken, not my Anthony." As Lucy backed out of the bedroom Sophie rushed at her in a blind, drunken fury, hooked fingers clawing for her daughter's face. Stepping to one side, Lucy could only watch with horrified disbelief as her mother tripped on the bag containing her Christmas present, then propel herself forwards for two or three giant stumbled steps, before finally losing her balance and launching herself headlong into the lounge wall. Her arms and legs continued to jerk spasmodically for several seconds, then she lay unmoving, her neck at an impossible angle.

Chapter Twenty-Nine

31st March 2023 - Oliver

Never a dancer, at least not until getting on the wrong side of half a dozen pints, Oliver had volunteered to look after the drinks and bags. The friends he'd come out with, four girls and one other guy who were also home early for the Easter break, had melted into the Friday night throng fifteen minutes earlier. He was already starting to wonder if he dared leave the table unattended for a few minutes while he got himself another drink. Moments later, his beer related problem was miraculously solved by the pint glass of Wainwright's Gold that was plonked on the table in front of him. Unfortunately, the tall, dark, young woman who delivered it then took one of the girls' seats and smiled at him, which left him in something of a quandary.

"That's really nice of you, but these seats are taken. Look, can I pay you for the drink, would that be…?" When he looked at her properly his good intentions began to wane. Probably a couple of years older than him, he reckoned, but she was hot and, better than that, she was still smiling at him.

"No need, I only wanted to get your attention. I asked the guy behind the bar what was a popular beer, hope it's okay. She held out a hand for him to shake. "I'm Lucy."

"Erm...yes, thank you." He took her hand gave it a very brief, embarrassed squeeze. "I'm Oliver." He felt his cheeks flush under her gaze. He'd always been a little bit shy around girls but, even so, had still enjoyed a few boozy brief encounters, and one or two relationships that had lasted a little longer, but he'd never met anyone quite so direct.

"Do you have any plans for this evening Oliver?"

"No, we're just, you know, home from uni, out for a drink and…" he was waffling and knew it. Pull yourself together man, he thought to himself, don't cock it up.

"Would you like to come home with me?"

"Yes, please." Oliver's mouth was suddenly dry, he couldn't believe his luck. That this really fit looking woman was coming on to him, and coming on strong, was way beyond his limited experience. On the verge of living his every teenage dream, and more than a few since he'd turned twenty, he got up without a second thought. After a quick, unsuccessful look around for his friends he followed her out of the busy city centre pub, drinks and bags forgotten as he watched the way her short skirt clung like a second skin as she walked ahead of him.

After the short drive back to her flat, during which she'd good naturedly slapped the back of his hand when it had strayed onto her thigh, Lucy unlocked her front door, keyed in the code for the alarm, and pointed him towards the settee.

"Would you like a glass of wine? Red, white, any preference?"

"Er… yes, no, whatever you've got is fine." When she returned a few moments later, armed with a bottle of pinot gris and two glasses, rather than sitting beside him she sat on an armchair with the coffee table between them.

"There's something important that you need to know about me Oliver."

"Oh shit! You're not a guy, are you?" The words were out before he could stop himself. "Sorry. I mean, not that there's anything wrong with that, if you are like, but, I'm not, you know, into.... guys. Sorry."

"No, I'm definitely a woman," she smiled at his confusion, the look on his face was priceless. "In fact, I'm your big sister."

"What? I haven't... I'm an only child, I don't understand?" He paused, then grasped for the most obvious answer. "You mean like, you're my dad's daughter with another woman?"

"No, we have different fathers, but the same mother. I think it's time you knew the truth, about both of us." Several times over the next couple of hours Lucy thought her half-brother was about to get up and leave. To be told that the woman whose cancer diagnosis had devastated him, whose funeral he had shed tears at, the only mother he had ever known and loved, had stolen him from another, was beyond comprehension. The only thing that prevented Oliver from dismissing her as a fantasist, the thing that had rocked him back on his heels, was when she'd told him that his real mother had named him Anthony.

"Does the name mean something to you?" Lucy asked when she saw his shocked reaction.

"There was this mad woman, when I was on my way to school, years ago. She called me Anthony, and then she tried to grab me, but Mum stopped her. They both fell on the pavement, I was so scared, I thought she was going to hurt Mum, but she got up and ran away crying. Was that... her?"

"Yes, and because she tried to reach out to you that day our mother was sent to prison. I never saw her again."

"People don't get locked up for something like that, no one was hurt, it wasn't a crime. It sounds more like she needed help."

"Oh yes, she needed help alright. But instead, she crossed Andy Bithell, the man posing as your father, once too often."

"What's that supposed to mean?"

"Speak to him Anthony, Oliver. I don't know what to call you." She shrugged and stood up. "Don't take my word for any of what I've just told you, ask him, ask Bithell. But look into his eyes when you do, and don't be fobbed off with any of his lies." Even though she could see look of the hurt and confusion on his face, Lucy still wasn't sure if he would ever share the anger, the hatred, that she felt towards the man who had used and then destroyed their mother. "After that, if you want to know any more, come and see me again." Lucy took the empty bottle and glasses into the kitchen, when she came back out he hadn't moved from the settee.

"You can sleep on there if you want, I'll give you a lift home on my way to work in the morning." She brought him a pillow and the spare blanket that she'd used herself while their mother was occupying the only bedroom, until Christmas Eve. "If you can't sleep, you can read the lies they told about our family, and the men Mum named you after, in here." She handed him her copy of Andy Bithell's book. "Goodnight Anthony."

When Lucy was awakened by her alarm the next morning, she wasn't at all surprised to find that her half-brother had already left, probably with little or no sleep, she thought. How odd to think of him like that, her brother, after all the years she'd spent wanting him dead, hating his very existence. How certain she'd been that without him the happy, carefree life she had briefly enjoyed would have continued unchanged. Her mother wouldn't have been sent to prison, she wouldn't have been taken into care, her mother would still be alive. Lucy slowed her breathing, as she had learned to do whenever the feelings threatened to overwhelm her. It wasn't his fault, she told herself repeatedly, he was a victim of Bithell as well, stolen from a family that would have loved him. It was Bithell and, if Anthony truly was her brother, together they would make him pay for what he'd done.

Oliver had never challenged his father before, it would have been unthinkable. From being a young boy, he'd always known that while a cheeky smile was enough to get round his mum, his father wouldn't tolerate any backchat or bad behaviour. As he'd grown older, he'd realised that his father prided himself on being a 'man's man', he would always be, or perhaps needed to be, in charge, the alpha male in any group. Having walked the streets since the early hours of the morning, desperately wanting to dismiss everything he'd been told the evening before, Oliver was tearing himself apart. He kept going back to the morning when the mad woman, that's what they'd called her, had reached out for him. He had wracked his memory for hours, before eventually remembering the few words she'd spoken that day, *'Anthony, Anthony, it's me. I'm your mum.'* In the end, it was as simple as that, hard to believe, harder still to accept, but he knew it was true. When he walked into the house that morning his father was having breakfast at the kitchen table.

"Hello, dirty stop-out! Look at the state of you?" Andy Bithell looked up from his plate and pointed with his knife. "You should have let me know you wouldn't be home."

"You didn't need to worry. I stayed with my sister, Lucy. She sends her regards." He watched as the man he'd always thought to be his father stiffened momentarily, then it was gone.

"What the fuck are you talking about boy?"

"Surely you remember Dad?" Oliver kept his voice level. "Sophie, my real mother, and my big sister, Lucy?"

"Don't talk fucking daft, have you been on drugs or something?"

"I wish I had, I really do, Dad. Tell me the truth, I want to know. Who am I Dad? Who the fuck am I?"

"Stop this nonsense now, you don't know what you're talking about."

"No? I know about the Old Vicarage, I've even seen the book you wrote about it. What I didn't know was that I was the kid you fucking stole. How could you do that?"

"You want the truth?" Andy got up from the table, pushed back his chair and was shouting, angry. "You think you're fucking ready for it? Okay! Your birth mother was an addict and a whore, she'd got one kid in care and you would have gone the same way as soon as she got money for her next fix. Me and your Mum took a chance and saved you, we raised you and gave you a life, a good life at that. How do you like the truth now, big lad?" Andy took a step forwards; regret was an emotion he rarely experienced but in that moment, seeing the expression on Oliver's face, he would have given everything he owned to take back his words. "Son, you don't understand."

"Don't ever call me that again. I'm not your son, I never was." Oliver turned and walked out of the kitchen, a few seconds later Andy heard the front door slam.

Chapter Thirty

1st April 2023 - Oliver

Later that morning, after storming out of the house that had been his home for as long as he could remember, Oliver, or should he now be thinking of himself as Anthony he wondered, finally began to calm down and think more clearly. He'd been putting one angry foot in front of the other without a thought for where he was going or what he was going to do, and now found himself almost in Walmer Bridge. He had no recollection at all of how he'd got there, it was a complete blank, something he found to be greatly unsettling. Taking several deep breaths he decided to carry on walking, this time with a little more purpose, and try to unravel his tangled, turbulent thoughts. Continuing on Gill Lane he followed the roads he and his friends used to take when cycling to Midge Hall, or onwards as far as Worden Park, completely unaware that he was following the same route his mother had taken the day she'd found him. Rage had prevented him from listening to anything that his father, 'No', he corrected himself, anything that Andy Bithell, had tried to say, deaf to even the prospect of an explanation. With a cooler head, he acknowledged that his feelings for the woman who had brought him up weren't affected by her part in his abduction, she had been the only mother he had ever known, and he had loved her unconditionally. After what Lucy had told him, the way his birth mother had been so cruelly mistreated, he couldn't bring himself to extend the same understanding towards the man he had believed to be his father. Even so, he was forced to admit that Andy Bithell had provided for him his entire life, he had wanted for nothing. In fact, he realised, he was still being supported while at university, something that he could no longer allow to continue. He was due back in Cardiff in a couple of weeks' time and decided he would have to make other arrangements for the coming term. But could he bring himself to hate the man who had helped to raise him, supported him, really? He wanted to, but knew he couldn't, it just wasn't there. What he needed was someone to talk the whole sorry mess through with, someone who might understand, but all he had here were drinking buddies, good for a few laughs on a night out, but nothing like this. Lucy had told him she was working this morning so there was no point in going back to her place just yet, maybe later. When his stomach began to rumble he checked his phone and was amazed to find that it was already approaching mid-day and that he must have been walking for several hours. Oliver or Anthony, he pondered as he continued along the road? Anthony didn't feel right, which he supposed was only to be expected, but did he owe it to his birth mother to use the name she had chosen for him? It was the simple realisation that he was beginning to think more constructively about what amounted to the trivia of the situation, the minor fall-out from the bombshell that had been dropped on him, that provided the first faint glimmer of confidence he would find a way through all this. Boosted by the knowledge that he could, and would, work this out, he decided on a simple course of action, find somewhere to eat, then go and have an honest conversation with his half-sister. Once he'd explained that the Bithells weren't bad people, that they'd given him a good and loving home, done what they had with the best of intentions, he was sure Lucy would understand.

Having walked the quiet lanes since leaving Longton, first towards Midge Hall, then south through Moss Side and the long trek down towards Ulness Walton, with Garth and Wymott prisons off to his right, the noise of heavy traffic on the A581 came as an unwelcome interruption to his thoughts. The pub he'd last visited with his parents, he'd never be able to think of them as Sheryl and Andy, for a final Sunday lunch before he went off to university, wasn't far down the road. He was also pretty sure he could get a bus up to Preston from nearby so, with his immediate needs catered for, all he had to do now was work out what he was going to say to Lucy.

By four o'clock Oliver, he'd made the decision that he was sticking with the name during the bus-ride back up to Preston, had parked himself on a bench outside the newish development of one and two bedroomed apartments where Lucy lived. It seemed like quite a nice area, on the edge of town and still a little bit countrified, but not too far out. With a decent lunch and a couple of pints inside him, he was feeling a lot more mellow than when he'd left her flat early that morning. It wasn't long before the combination of lack of sleep, food and alcohol, and a little spring sunshine, had him dozing on the bench.

"Jack! Jack! Come out! Jack" The repeated shouting from only a few yards away roused Oliver from his slumbers. Stretching and turning his neck to ease the stiffness, then rubbing his eyes, he tried to make sense of the scene in front of him. It was a little old lady doing the shouting, she was poking about in the overgrown shrubbery that filled the triangle between Lucy's block and the one next to it, but he couldn't fathom out who Jack was or what he'd done.

"Can I help?" Oliver's offer was met with such a look of mistrust, almost fearful, that he immediately felt guilty. Asleep on the bench, wearing jeans and a hoody under his army surplus jacket he must have looked like a tramp. "I'm sorry if I startled you. I just thought that maybe I could help. I'm Oliver, I'm just waiting for a friend to come home from work, Lucy," he pointed a finger in the general direction of her flat, "she shouldn't be long." The old lady relaxed immediately, her frown changing to a smile.

"Such a nice girl, I didn't know she had a boyfriend."

"No, were not…"

"It's my Jack," she said, cutting off his reply, "I let him off his lead for a little run and he's got his coat caught up on something in there." She pointed with her walking stick into the tangle of shrubs. When he leaned in, Oliver could see an increasingly angry little terrier type of dog in an eye wateringly bright tartan jacket. "I can't get in there to help him, not since my operation. Do you think…?"

"Sure. Could I borrow your stick for a moment?" Oliver was happy to help, but didn't fancy getting within range of the snappy little bugger's teeth. He pushed his way into the bushes and then used the stick to lift the edge of the dog's coat free of the cut branch it had become snagged on. He had a nervous moment when the terrier shot between his legs on its way out of the bushes and was relieved to see it safely clipped back on the lead before he handed back the walking stick.

"Oh! Thank you. He's such a comfort to me now that I'm on my own, I don't know what I'd do without him."

"Glad to help, honestly." Oliver gave her his best smile and made his way back to the bench.

"You shouldn't have too long to wait. Lucy is usually home by five o'clock when she goes to work on a Saturday." Oliver got the impression that the old girl could have related from memory the comings and goings of everyone on the small estate. "I'll stay and keep you company for five minutes, but I'll need to be home for the start of 'The Chase'. I remember when Bradley was in Coronation Street, did you ever…." Aggie proved to be capable of keeping a conversation going singlehandedly for a whole lot longer than the promised five minutes.

When Lucy drove up to the small block of resident's garages at a couple of minutes after five, she was thrilled and relieved to see Oliver sat on the bench waiting for her. He must have spoken to Bithell, she thought, must have realised that the man who'd snatched him and destroyed their mother was nothing short of a monster. They'd gone up to her flat where, after a brief exchange of pleasantries, the conversation hadn't gone at all the way Oliver had been hoping. Since the moment Lucy had placed two cups of instant coffee on the table, he'd not been given the opportunity to put forward any of his own thoughts, or explain his acceptance of the Bithells as essentially well-meaning, if misguided, people. Instead, Lucy had insisted on telling him their mother's life story, becoming increasingly animated as the injustices stacked up. The loss of their grandmother, how she'd been pushed out of the family nest by an evil stepmother, the drift into drugs and prostitution, used and abused by a succession of men.

"How do you know all this, if you haven't seen her since you were ten?" Oliver asked.

"What I meant was that I never saw her again while I was a child," she covered her lie from the previous evening. "We spent some time together, real mother and daughter quality time, when she was released from prison. That was when she told me everything."

"Okay, I just thought you said…." he paused when his mobile rang, taking it from his pocket he angled the screen away, not wanting her to see that it was 'Dad' calling. He cancelled the call then made a show of switching off the phone and placing it on the table. "Sorry."

"It doesn't matter what you thought," she snapped irritably, ignoring the apology, "just listen, then you'll understand what she had to go through, what he did to her." Lucy launched into a description of how their mother had very nearly been killed by a 'client', and how she'd found out, while she was in hospital, that she was pregnant.

"She got herself clean, free of drugs, for me." Lucy's manic smile was beginning to make Oliver feel a little uneasy. "Can you imagine how hard that was for her, and she did it just for me? Then some evil fucking scumbag got her hooked again, to stop her giving evidence against him. Because of that, I was taken into care." Her worrying smile disappeared, replaced by a look of animal ferocity. "When I find out who was behind it, and I will, I will tear their fucking hearts out." After a long pause, one that Oliver was frightened to interrupt, Lucy's breathing calmed as she moved the story on to the time when Sophie had been taken in by Eric Gryce and Anthony Daniels after finding she was pregnant again.

"Mum said they took such good care of her, that they were the nicest, kindest men she had ever met. That's why she named you Anthony. She joked with me that, as much as she loved them both, having Eric as a first name was just too much to lumber a little boy with. Fancy that Anthony, you could have been called Eric." Lucy laughed and the shrill sound chilled him. In the book she'd given him the previous evening, Oliver had read that Gryce had been struck off as a doctor, had severe mental health issues, and that both he and Daniels were suspected of trafficking in babies. He wasn't going to contradict her, he'd already realised that he was way out of his depth here and just wanted an opportunity to leave.

"Mum said they even talked about helping her get me back, so we could all be a family, together." When Lucy stopped speaking, wrapped up in the dream she'd held for years. Oliver was tempted to make a dash for the door but, even as he watched, her features again contorted into a mask of pure malevolence. "But then, when Bithell snatched you and Anthony Daniels was killed, decapitated in the fall that Mum always protested wasn't an accident, everything changed. How could I ever compete with a stolen child?"

"I'm so sorry, that must have been a terrible time for...." Oliver shut up when Lucy carried on as though she hadn't heard him.

"He made her keep quiet, Bithell, told her he'd help her to get me back if she didn't make a fuss. So she didn't, not a word. She let you go Anthony, she chose me, she stayed off drugs again, for me." The manic smile had returned, Lucy's eyes were wide open but whatever she was seeing was for her eyes only. "We were happy, just the two of us... we were so happy," tears were now flowing down Lucy's cheeks, "until one day I came home from school and she was too busy to even speak to me, she just told me to leave her alone, and the next day, and the next, it got worse and worse." Lucy turned and, for the first time since she'd begun speaking, looked deep into his eyes. "She was looking for you. It was like I was no longer there, I'd ceased to exist since the moment she saw a photograph of you."

"Lucy, I really am sorry, I had no idea."

"You're not to blame Anthony, it wasn't your fault." The mounting anger in her voice told a different story and she began to rock slowly backwards and forwards. "You didn't know what Bithell had done." Lucy was gradually raising her voice, she was still holding his gaze and he didn't dare look away, terrified at what she may do. "It wasn't your fault that the same day Mum came to find you, Bithell's crony planted the drugs that would get her sent to prison, I'll never forget the stench of cigarettes on his clothes. It wasn't your fault that I was back in care that very same day. It wasn't your fault that they wouldn't let me visit her, not once. It wasn't your fault that she came out of prison with a worse drug habit than ever before, or that it took me years to finally track her down." She was shouting, almost screaming, spittle flying from her mouth with every word. "It's not your fault she died!" Oliver was ready to take his chances and make a run for it, but her next words, delivered in a cold, level voice, pinned him to his seat.

"It was Andy Bithell's fault, all of it, everything. He destroyed her, he didn't care what happened to me, it's his fault our mother is dead. But he's going to pay for what he did, we're going to make him pay, the same way they killed the man she named you after."

Chapter Thirty-One

2nd April 2023 - Oliver

"Lucy, I… You can't mean that, it's…." despite being momentarily stunned by the threat, Oliver was still able to stop himself from completing the intended sentence, realising that 'madness' may not have been the best choice of words at that particular moment. He glanced over to where Lucy was gently rocking in her seat, trancelike, with her eyes wide open but unseeing, lost in her own personal world of anger and hatred. Wary of taking his eyes off her for even the briefest moment, Oliver took a deep breath to steady himself before rising on shaky legs, grabbing his jacket and making a dash for the door. His hands were shaking even more than his legs as he fumbled with the lock but, after the longest couple of seconds he'd ever experienced, he was outside her flat and running down the stairs. A couple more seconds and he was out on the street, still accelerating. Five minutes later, and with no sign of pursuit, Oliver stopped to get his breath back and, more importantly, to try and work out what to do next. In comparison to Lucy's chilling meltdown, not to mention the threat to kill his father, the revelation that his real mother was dead left him unmoved. Sad as it may be, he'd no memory of her, she was a complete stranger to him. Realising that he was now involved in something far beyond anything his limited life experience had prepared him for there was only one option, he had to warn his Dad, he'd know what to do, he always did. He reached into a pocket for his phone, then swore when he remembered placing it on the coffee table. Well, one thing was for sure, he thought, he certainly wasn't going back for it, now or ever. In fact, as far as he was concerned, he never wanted to set eyes on his bat-shit crazy half-sister, ever again. He thought briefly about trying to thumb a lift, but there was hardly any traffic this far out and nobody in their right mind was likely to offer a lift after midnight. Besides, he'd seen too many movies where the serial killer was driving the only car that stopped on the dark and lonely road, and that never ended well. Instead, he decided his best option was to simply keep walking until he could get a cab into town, he'd borrow a phone and ring his dad then. With the temperature falling, the cool night air already tingling his ears, Oliver pulled his hood up and set off purposefully down the road.

The sound was considerably louder than Lucy had been expecting. The initial impact against Anthony's legs and lower back was drowned out by the thud of his upper body bouncing off the car bonnet before he was tossed high into the air. She'd been careful not to drive too fast, or to rev the engine too much, she didn't want to alert him, or draw attention to herself. Knowing the route he would almost certainly have taken, she'd held back until he'd had enough time to make it as far as a long, empty stretch of road without any footpaths or houses. Lucy had run through the checklist in her head, seatbelt, a final check in the mirror, a last-second flick of the steering wheel, avoid the temptation to touch the brakes, and it would be over in an instant. She'd caught him neatly, slightly left of centre of the bonnet, exactly as planned. Another check in the mirror, just to be sure it was safe to reverse back towards the crumpled body of her half-brother, and she was nearly done. A few minutes work and it would simply be another closed box in her mind, another one to be sealed and stacked up, along with all of the others. It was something she'd learned to do years earlier in the children's home, whenever something bad happens, just put the feelings in a little box and close the lid tightly, then they can't hurt you. Lucy was relieved to find that Anthony, or should she now call him by the name he was christened, she wondered, was already dead. One of the few thoughts she'd allowed herself was the hope that it would be quick and as painless as possible for him, he was still her little brother. Despite her relief, she soon discovered that getting a corpse into the boot of her car may not be quite as straightforward as she'd anticipated, and then there was the.... mess, something else she hadn't really considered. Working quickly, she raided the stash of supermarket shopping bags in the driver's door pocket of her car before crouching down beside his lifeless body. Carefully placing a bag over his now misshapen head, in an attempt to contain the blood and brain matter leaking from a horrible looking wound, she used another to seal it off by tying it tight around his neck. Once that was done, and she'd hoisted his upper body over the boot sill, she managed the rest of him without too much trouble. A quick walk around the car revealed less damage than she'd been expecting to find, given how noisy the collision had been. The bonnet had bowed slightly under the impact and there was what looked a crease in the metal towards the front edge, apart from that there were only scuff marks. The lights and indicators were untouched, which was good news, the last thing she needed now was to be pulled over by a traffic car, although she could probably show her warrant card and talk her way out of it. Less than fifteen minutes later, Lucy was closing the door of her garage, job done. Once back in her apartment, and having quickly tidied round, not forgetting to remove the battery and sim card from Oliver's mobile, Lucy quickly showered then went to her bedroom. She was shaking slightly as she got her clothes ready for the morning, the usual white blouse and black trousers. The tears broke through before she'd set her alarm, her legs now shaking so badly she was forced to sit on the bed. Reaching for a pillow, she pressed it hard against her face with both hands, then silently screamed at the wall, over and over until she was utterly drained. Too weak to hold herself upright she toppled sideways onto the bed, exhausted, but knowing that sleep would not come. Sometimes, the little boxes just wouldn't stay closed.

Chapter Thirty-Two

Arnside 2002

Whether it was the cold of the water lapping around his thighs, or maybe it was the aftermath of the huge wave of adrenaline that had driven him to the edge of madness, something gave Eric Gryce his first real moment of clarity since the two policewomen had reached out for him on Morecambe promenade. Was it really only that morning, he wondered? He couldn't be sure, without medication the red mist of his temper blotted out all rational thought and made true recollection nigh on impossible. He understood his condition all too well, unlike Edwin who had always been in denial, and for many years had been able to maintain a level of control that allowed him to function highly in his chosen profession. However, without access to the drugs he needed he was prone to unpredictable flare-ups, often at the slightest provocation. Events of the last few weeks, by far the worst times in a life that had already seen a surfeit of grief, had tested him to the limit, and then beyond. Shaking his head, almost in disbelief at his current circumstances, a single glance at the near shore told him all he needed to know. The lights and the growing crowd, some of whom were also beginning to venture out into the water, meant no return. He was now fully committed to the panicked impulse that had made him take the woman hostage and then attempt to cross the river. He remembered how, as children, they had spent long and happy summer days in the house a little further down the estuary. Edwin hadn't liked the water and always stayed back from the shoreline, but Amy, fearless Amy, the most adventurous of the three, had loved to wade and swim across to the far shore with him. That had all ended when their mother had disappeared, left them for another man their father had said, 'didn't love you enough to stay', he'd said. That was also the time when his father had begun coming to Eric's bedroom at night, hurting him, making him do things he didn't want to. He remembered the words his father always used afterwards, '…if you tell anyone, I'll go to prison and you'll all be sent to an orphanage. If you do this, I'll leave the others alone, they'll be safe, I promise…' Lies, all lies.

Eric looked across the darkening waters of the estuary, searching for the man he'd just fired the pistol at, hoping, praying, that his shots had gone wide of the target. When he saw the man was injured and struggling to stay upright in the rising tide, knowing that in his panic and his rage he had intentionally harmed an innocent human being, it was almost too much to bear. The policewoman he had dragged into the river was failing fast, shock and blood loss taking their toll. Eric flipped her over onto her back, she would have a better chance of survival that way, if she could remain afloat. He did his best to edge her towards the wounded man, then said a silent, heartfelt prayer for the two of them. Since fleeing from the home he and Anthony had shared, his actions had been unforgiveable, disastrous in the extreme. With the single goal of putting an end to the insanity, Eric had never intended anyone else to be harmed, it went against everything he had ever believed in, had ever worked for. Not that good intentions counted for anything when, in a supremely ironic act of treachery, his brain could be flooded by an overdose of the very chemicals that were meant to protect, not to enrage. The unbidden flash of a memory, the young policewoman crashing through the windscreen of the car, came without warning. The harsh and violent images of her broken body, scenes he was powerless to prevent playing out again and again before his eyes, doubled him over and he cried out in anguish. He'd caused untold pain and suffering, damaged too many lives, it was more than he could take, much more. Turning to face the incoming tide he leaned back in the water and said a prayer for his dead sister, apologising once again for not being there when she'd needed him most. As the swell lifted him off his feet he finally allowed his thoughts to turn to Anthony, the love of his life, and smiled as he let the river take him.

Chapter Thirty-Three

Yvie and the team had spent a frustrating Monday morning reviewing progress, or at least that had been the intention, as it turned out there was precious little to get excited about. Three dead bodies, Andy Bithell, Mark Brandwood and now Philip Garmond, and they weren't a single step closer to finding out who was responsible. So many people had been in and out of the marquee where Bithell was found that any trace evidence was meaningless. There was plenty in his background to suggest possible motives, but all agreed that they were unlikely at best. No forensics from Brandwood's house, the fire had taken care of that. Was the man's past association with Bithell sufficient to warrant his murder several years after an ill-health retirement, they didn't know. Any hope of a breakthrough arising from the crime scene at Garmond's house had soon been dashed by John's unofficial heads-up that the killer had been gloved and careful. FIT had worked through Sunday afternoon and well into the evening to analyse clothing fibres that had been collected, analysed, and then found to be from a common brand of workwear that sold by the tens of thousands. News that tiny particles of dried blood had been found in the wounds inflicted on Garmond's neck had very briefly seemed as though it may be of importance. However, even though DNA results weren't back yet, and there wasn't sufficient for typing, given the similarities in the method of decapitation it was strongly suspected that the same weapon had been used, which gave them precisely nothing that they hadn't already thought likely. Not a single step forward in the search for Oliver

Bithell or Sophie Elletson, in itself a cause for growing concern over their safety. Their final person of interest was Edwin Gryce and, other than Joe and Autumn finding the man to be somewhat unpleasant, or 'downright fucking creepy' as Autumn had confided to Cathy, they had nothing else. Unlikely as the various scenarios had at first seemed, concerns over the content of any proposed new book had to be regarded as a front-runner in at least two of the murders. The death of Philip Garmond, the ghostwriter behind Bithell's first book and approached about the second, was a connection that couldn't be ignored. Killing Brandwood didn't entirely fit the theory, but could possibly be seen as general housekeeping, the tidying up of any loose ends. The Chief Super and Bill had sat in on the session, looking long and hard at the notes and photographs Autumn had positioned on the murder wall, but neither had been able to add anything of value. Yvie had just called for a comfort break and Cathy was on her way to the farmhouse kitchen to put the kettle on when her mobile rang. They all heard her whoop followed by a shout of 'Yes!'

"Boss, we've got the person using Bithell's cash card." A broadly smiling Cathy came through from the kitchen. "Uniform just picked him up, they're taking him over to Ribbleton as we speak."

"Brilliant, tell them we'll be there as soon as poss."

"Was it the surveillance cameras?" Autumn asked.

"No, and it was nowhere near town centre either, sounds like it was a complete fluke. The kid was hanging about near an ATM outside the shops at Longsands. When a couple of local bobbies stopped off to pick up the sandwich order he fled, they followed, the rest is, as they say, history."

"A kid?"

"Yeah, fourteen. He broke down as soon as they picked him up, gave them Oliver Bithell's cash card and the £20 he'd just withdrawn, said he's got the wallet hidden in his bedroom. They're stopping off at his home to collect it."

"Shouldn't he have been at school?"

"Inset day, teacher training or something like that."

"Okay. I'm not really seeing where this is going to lead us, but right now I'll take any lead we can get."

Yvie's first thought on arrival at the old estate office, it certainly didn't warrant the title of 'police station', was that she'd somehow slipped back in time by about fifty years. The interview room they'd been allocated was not a pleasant place, and that was being kind. The scarred floor tiles, peeling paintwork and mould in every corner of the ceiling was an embarrassment, a strong smell of drains didn't help either. It would have depressed a hardened criminal, let alone a distraught fourteen-year-old boy sat with his mother's arms wrapped protectively around him. Yvie took one look and shook her head.

"Do you think you could find us a different room, perhaps something a little less gulag like? Do you have a canteen maybe?"

"You asked for an interview room, you've got an interview room, Detective Chief Inspector." The middle-aged sergeant lingered over her title and looked a little too pleased with himself for her liking.

"And the canteen?" Yvie asked again. She'd met one or two of his type before, misogynistic jobsworths who'd do whatever they could to show off in front of their mates and score their petty little victories. She gave a barely perceptible nod to Cathy who had guessed what was most likely coming next and had her mobile phone out and ready.

"This is a working nick and my lads are entitled to a break. We've caught the little scrote for you, what else…" He stopped and took a step back when Cathy thrust out her phone, directly in front of his florid face, leaving him no choice other than to take it from her.

"Chief Superintendent Atkinson would like a quick word with you, sergeant." They watched with interest as, without even having had the opportunity to speak, the colour began to drain from the man's face. Within a matter of seconds he was mumbling his apologies and bobbing his head in agreement. Cathy was pretty sure the apologising continued well after the Chief Super had ended the call, now that was bloody impressive, she thought. He handed back her mobile before turning to one of the uniforms stood behind him.

"Constable, get everyone out of the canteen, now. I want it clean and tidy and get some tea on, and some cans of pop and something to eat for our young guest. Don't just stand there doing nothing man, get a move on!" He risked another look at the two detectives. "Sorry about any misunderstanding Ma'am, Ma'ams," then turned and marched away, reminding them both of a little clockwork soldier.

"Is it wrong that I enjoyed that quite as much as I did?" Cathy whispered to her boss.

"Only if you enjoyed it more than me, which I doubt."

Within five minutes they had been ushered upstairs to a brighter, less unpleasant room. There was a lingering smell of hot vinegar in the air, but it would suffice. A young constable placed four mugs of tea on the table, along with a half full bottle of milk and a crusty sugar bowl, he even checked if there was anything else they may need before closing the door behind him. The boy seemed to have recovered somewhat and was already getting stuck into a can of cola and a packet of ginger biscuits. Yvie introduced herself and Cathy, and was about to begin the interview when the boy's mother couldn't contain herself any longer.

"Will he have to go to a…, you know, a young offender's place?" The words came out in a rush as she grasped her son's hand. "They said downstairs, the one in charge, he said that he could get five years for this. He's always been a good lad, never been in trouble, his dad hasn't been around for years, and there's just the two of us, and I have to work, and…"

"Mrs. Wilcox, please. We just want to ask Karl a few questions, that's all." Her first look at the boy had been enough for Yvie to tell that, whatever childish mischief he may get up to, there was no way he had any involvement in the Bithell case. "Afterwards, we'll run you both home, and you have my word that Karl will not be going anywhere. Except maybe to his room." The woman's shoulders dropped as the knife blade of worry deeply embedded between them melted away.

"Are you sure? He did take some money out the man's account?"

"Mum, I told you, I just wanted to see if I could do it. I was going to put it in his wallet with the rest. I haven't spent any of the money in there." While Karl was speaking, Cathy leafed through the contents of the wallet, there was ninety pounds in notes along with a credit card and driving licence.

"How did you get the right pin number Karl?" Yvie asked.

"Got it first time, it was easy," he smiled and looked pleased with himself, until he received a nudge from his mother. "His driving licence was in there and it's got his date of birth on, so I tried the first four digits, date and month. I was going to try the credit card next, but I wouldn't have kept anything, I thought that I might get a reward for finding it."

"He's always been into mobile phones and tablets and things, anything electronic, you know what they're like."

"Okay," Yvie nodded, "we believe you, and you're not in any trouble. I promise. Now, can you remember when and where you found it?"

"Yeah, it was just lying there on Longsands Lane. I was going to Tariq's house, he's my mate, on my bike and I just saw the sun shining on something in the grass by the side of the road. I couldn't believe it when I saw what it was."

"Why didn't you tell me?"

"You'd have made me hand it in right away. I thought I might get a reward if I took it back to the owner myself."

"So why didn't you take it back?"

"The address is in Longton and I'm not allowed to go that far. Tariq's older brother has a car and he was going to take us last weekend, but he had to work and he said the earliest he can do it is next weekend." The admission earned an angry look from his mother. Yvie had no doubt that Tariq's parents would be hearing from her.

"And when was this, exactly?"

"It was early on Sunday morning, not last Sunday, it was the week before."

"Are you sure Karl? This is important." She and Cathy shared a glance. If something had happened to Oliver Bithell, as now seemed very likely, it had occurred before his father's murder.

"Defo!" Karl replied. "You can ask Tariq, I showed him the wallet."

"Do you think you'd be able to show us exactly where you found it?"

"Sure. I know exactly where it was, there's a gap in the hedge where you can…" he stopped mid-sentence and glanced guiltily at his mother, the boy was learning fast.

"Okay, I just need to have a quick word downstairs, I'll let them know that you're being released without charge." She didn't add that whoever had threatened a vulnerable child with five years in a young offender's institute would be facing an interview of their own, at HQ and in the very near future.

"Cool!"

"No, it's most certainly not cool, Karl," his mother disagreed, "and I haven't finished with you yet."

Chapter Thirty-Four

The FIT van stopped a good fifty yards short of the spot Karl had identified half an hour earlier. Yvie had walked up and down the road alongside the hastily barriered off stretch of grass and hedgerow while she'd been waiting for Cathy to return from dropping off the boy and his mother. John joined her briefly while three of his technicians were getting suited and booted in preparation for a fingertip search of the area. After the usual exchange of pleasantries, she gave him a brief update on the wallet that had been found, and where, it was the 'when' that presented a problem.

"Got to be honest, Yvie. After the rain we've had this week, it's not looking good for any fluids or trace evidence, we'll need to be lucky."

"Right now, it's all I've got John, so let's keep everything crossed!" She looked over to where Joe and Autumn had just parked behind the FIT vehicle and were deep in conversation with Cathy. "Looks like the cavalry has arrived, I'll get out of your way." Strolling back to her team she noticed the unmistakeable smell of coffee drifting her way, she realised it was late afternoon and she hadn't had anything to eat or drink since an early breakfast.

"Hi Boss, thought you and Cathy may be in need." Joe handed her a takeaway coffee and pointed to a selection of supermarket sandwiches on the back seat of the car.

"Thank you Joe, you're a lifesaver," Yvie took a sip and savoured the rich, almost smoky, aroma, "that is so good."

"We were having a chat on the way over, and Detective Constable Jackson here would like to put forward a suggestion as to what we do next."

"Okay, it's not like we're overrun with ideas. Go for it."

"Erm, there's an awful lot of assumptions Boss," the young detective began, "but, I think we should start canvassing the area."

"That's pretty much standard procedure Autumn," Yvie was surprised at the obvious proposal.

"I know that, but I mean something much more specific. It's unlikely that Bithell's wallet was thrown from a vehicle, at least not with cash, cards and ID still in it, so assumption number one is that he was on foot when it was lost."

"No, assumption number one is that something happened to Oliver Bithell that caused him to lose his wallet." Yvie corrected her. "We still don't know for sure that it did."

"Okay, so assumption number two is that he was on foot."

"Or on a bicycle?" Cathy offered, causing her colleague to think about the possibility for a second before continuing.

"Yeah, that would still work. Assumption three is that the wallet was most likely lost during the hours of darkness. It was out in the open so, if it had been lost during the day, it would probably have been found straight away."

"Okay, so far so good. But why was he walking, or cycling, down here at night?"

"That's the thing Boss, it was Saturday night and he's young, free and single. There's no pubs, clubs or anything round here, so assumption number four is that he was probably going to or from someone's house."

"That may be a bit of a stretch, but carry on."

"I checked with Traffic, and they reckon there's still a good number of cars using this road as a shortcut to the new Tesco up until around half past ten, then it tails off quite a bit. Assumption number five is that whatever took place, it happened after eleven o'clock. If he was seeing someone, that's late to be arriving, so I think he had to be leaving, walking back towards town, maybe they had a row or something."

"Are we counting those as mini assumptions or are we sticking at five?" Cathy asked.

"I get what you're saying Autumn, but all that suggests is that he was walking in the direction of town late at night when he lost his wallet." Yvie tried to be as supportive as possible, Autumn's sometimes quirky take on events had paid off in the past, but she just wasn't seeing where this was going.

"But that's just it, Boss. Apart from the road up to the superstore there's nothing in that direction apart from building sites and one small estate of flats and starter homes. That's where we start knocking on doors, not the odd isolated places up and down the road here."

"Joe, Cathy, any thoughts?" Yvie asked. There were a lot of potential points of failure in the theory but, then again she thought, weren't there always?

"I think we should give it a go." Joe said.

"Me too," Cathy agreed, "but we could do with some photographs of Oliver Bithell for the door to door."

"I er, took the liberty of ringing Tom," Autumn began awkwardly, "and asked him to print off some enlargements of Bithell's student ID photo. Just in case you agreed with my theory, Boss. He should be here any minute."

"Just remember Jackson," Cathy was grinning at her friend, "nobody likes a smart-arse!"

They were still laughing when one of the FIT technicians shouted over to them. She led them over to where John was lying full length, flat on his back and halfway under the overgrown hawthorn hedge. They noticed that a further section of roadway had also been taped off.

"Must be your lucky day after all Yvie. Excuse me if I don't get up." He was pointing with something that looked like an overgrown Q-Tip towards the underside of a tangle of gnarled branches. "Blood. We found the faintest traces on the roadway over there, detectable but useless for analysis. However, under here we have definite blood spatter."

"What are you thinking John?"

"Best guess, and that's all it is at the moment, is that the victim's head impacted with significant force on the tarmac over here," he pointed to the newly fenced area a couple of feet from where he was lying, "and the resultant spatter, or splashes, were generated at the time of impact. The spatter we managed to find was all emitted at a relatively shallow angle, there would have been considerably more, but the rain has washed away any that was exposed. We'll take some soil samples to confirm."

"Could it have been a simple fall?" Yvie asked.

"Unlikely." John was shaking his head. "The force required to cause a severe head wound, one capable of spreading splashes of blood over several feet, as part of a single impact, I very much doubt it. And, before you ask, I don't know if the victim could have survived. But I'd be very much surprised if they did."

Yvie excused herself, and walked back to the car, she wanted a couple of minutes to get her thoughts in order before updating the Chief Super. It was still possible that no one had died here, it could conceivably have been an accident, maybe a driver who was over the limit had panicked and hidden the body, it wouldn't have been the first time. Realistically though, if this was indeed where Oliver Bithell had died, it was much more likely that this was the fourth murder over the course of not much more than a few weeks. Was it significant that Oliver had died a week before his father, had his father even known, she wondered. More to the point, unless it was the coincidence to end all coincidences, why would a student home for the holidays have been targeted? Seeing Tom arrive, she decided to wait a little longer before ringing her boss, it was getting quite late in the afternoon and they needed to organise the canvassing of the area Autumn had suggested. She wasn't familiar with the locality and unsure what was meant by a 'small estate', the only way to be sure was to go and have a look. Leaving John and his team to continue their work under the hedgerow, they drove the half-mile up to the small development. After a quick look around they agreed that it appeared to be easily manageable without pulling in any additional resources. Yvie estimated that there were maybe ten low-rise blocks, each made up of six apartments and around twenty pairs of semi-detached houses. Assuming they were all occupied, that left them with approximately a hundred separate addresses to be visited.

"Twenty each Boss?" Tom asked hopefully, fully aware of Yvie's standing order that no one was to carry out lone visits.

"Nice try Tom, but I think you'll find that's fifty for you and Autumn, and the same for Joe and Cathy. Just do what you can," she replied. "As I'm the odd one out I'm going back to the office for an hour or two. Give me a call if anything comes up," she paused briefly, "or not, either way, let me know." She got back into her car and gave them a wave before following the road back to where John and the team were packing away their equipment and used protective clothing. She stopped briefly to again thank them for the prompt response, and then set off back in the direction of the A6. Twenty-five minutes later she was pulling into the parking area behind the house, unsurprised to see the Chief Super's Jaguar hadn't moved. They were still sat at the kitchen table an hour and a half later when Joe rang.

"Hiya Boss, we've knocked on every door but only about one in four or five has been occupied, and so far no one's recognised the photo of Oliver Bithell. We need to come back either later this evening or, preferably, first thing in the morning. I'm thinking that we might have more success if we're here nice and early, before people leave for work or the school run."

"Makes sense. Are you all okay with an early start?"

"Yeah sure. I'll pick Cathy up on my way through and Tom said that him and Autumn will be travelling in together. He did look a little sheepish when Cathy asked him if that included travelling all the way downstairs from the bedroom." Joe laughed. "Subtle as a kick up the arse, that one!"

"Hey, good luck to them both, I don't know what he'd have done without her."

"Yeah, you're right. Anyway, I'll give you a call in the morning."

"Thanks Joe." Yvie ended the call.

"Nothing yet, Ma'am." Yvie shook her head, "they're going back first thing in the morning, trying to catch people before they start their day."

"Do you think Autumn's right, there were a lot of ifs and maybes in her theory?"

"I certainly hope so. As Joe would put it, we've got bugger all else to go on."

"Indeed. It's time you got yourself off home as well. The little fellow will be wanting some attention."

"James is…."

"I was talking about James. Now away with you."

"I think I will," Yvie said with a tired smile. "We'll see what tomorrow brings."

"Well I hope your day turns out better than mine is likely to be! Our esteemed Assistant Chief Constable is concerned about the rising body count and wants a full report. He wanted you in on it, but I told him you were close to making an arrest and couldn't be dragged away."

"Thank you, Boss. Much appreciated." ACC Gregory Chaperon had never been one to whom the phrase 'forgive and forget' could be applied. He remembered every perceived slight or challenge to his authority, every supposed misdemeanour, and in Yvie's case, that was already proving to be quite a long list. He was, most people suspected, a man who would carry a grudge to the grave, and then beyond. "What if we don't make an arrest?"

"Don't worry, I'll distract him with something shiny, it usually works," she laughed. "Now go home."

Chapter Thirty-Five

With hindsight, it wasn't really surprising that not everyone was at their best at seven-thirty on a weekday morning, particularly in the type of estate where almost everyone had children and both parents were working full-time. Getting unwilling kids out of bed and ready for school, forcing food down unappreciative throats, checking that homework had been completed and they were properly washed and dressed, all came before even thinking about getting themselves ready for a job they didn't really want to go to but had no choice. On the plus side, almost every door they knocked on was answered, usually by a harassed looking parent who was already running late. By the twentieth door, Autumn's initial, cheery introduction of, *'Good morning Madam. I'm Detective Constable Jackson and this is my colleague Detective Inspector Barron. We're seeking assistance with an enquiry into a potentially serious offence and would like to ask if you, or any member of your family, has seen this person in the area.'* Had now been reduced to a more streamlined, time efficient offering.

"Morning, Police. Have you seen this man?" With her ID in one hand and the photo of Oliver Bithell in the other, Autumn waited while the young mum who answered the door took a little longer than the current average of three seconds before deciding that she'd never seen him. It was the same answer at every home they'd tried, the only difference being how the response was delivered. The majority of people had been civil, some looked suspicious, a few looked guilty, but no one recognised the face in the photo. By eight o'clock, the daily exodus was in full swing and the number of doors that remained unanswered was increasing exponentially, at eight-thirty Joe called a temporary halt.

"I think we've pretty much exhausted the pre-work and school crowd. If you two want to get the paperwork up to date, me and Cathy will go and pick up some coffees from the supermarket café."

"Sounds like a plan," Tom agreed. He and Autumn had been up later than planned and had dashed out without any breakfast.

Twenty minutes later, the four detectives were sat in Joe's car finishing off the sausage and bacon rolls that he insisted were mandatory on any workday commencing before seven o'clock in the morning.

"What do you think, should we have a last round-up and then maybe come back tonight, or tomorrow morning to finish off?" Cathy asked, licking the last trace of brown sauce from her fingers.

"Yeah, not much more we can do really." As Joe spoke, the four of them were idly watching an elderly lady with a scruffy little dog that was pulling hard its lead, it was the bright and bold tartan of the dog's coat that caught the eye. "Tonight may be better, I didn't feel particularly welcome this morning." The dog appeared to want to dive into every shrubbery, no doubt looking for rats and rabbits to chase, while its owner seemed equally determined that it didn't get the chance. She settled on a wooden bench, presumably for a break from the dogs constant pulling, situated about twenty yards from where they were parked.

"I'll go," Cathy offered, "I need to walk off that sandwich." She brushed the crumbs from her jacket as she got out of the car and approached the bench, ID and photo at the ready. What she hadn't been prepared for was the barrage of information that she was immediately subjected to. The lady, who said her name was Agatha, 'but everyone calls me Aggie', was keen to show off her prodigious local knowledge.

"Oh yes, that's Oliver, such nice young man, he helped me get Jack out of the bushes, when he got his coat stuck on a branch. He was waiting for Lucy, he said she wasn't his girlfriend, but between you and me I think he's sweet on her. Good luck to them I say, it's not like it was in our day, is it dear?" The full impact of fifty years instant aging hit Cathy right between the eyes. She quietly signalled for one of the others to join her, not wanting to slow the torrent of information but wary of anything important being lost in the flood. "Lucy keeps herself to herself, but I suppose you have to in your job dear, it must be difficult. Her mother was a funny woman, she only stayed a couple of months, I think she used to drink," Aggie had lowered her voice and leaned in a little as though this was a confidence not to be broken, "but she doesn't live with her now, it must have been a temporary arrangement."

"What do you mean, 'in my job'?" Cathy jumped in fast when there was the briefest of pauses, convinced it was the first time Aggie had drawn breath since she'd sat down.

"She's a policewoman dear, just like you. Although she wears a uniform, looks very smart in it too."

"You don't happen to know Lucy's surname by any chance, do you? That would be really helpful."

"Of course I do dear," she half turned and pointed to the small block of apartments directly behind them, "it's Elletson, it's printed beneath her doorbell, just over there."

"Wow, that's great, thank you Aggie, you've been a real help. Can you remember when you last saw Oliver?"

"Oh yes, it was April Fool's Day. I remember saying to him that children today don't celebrate it like we used to, none of the japes and jokes." Autumn, who had not long since joined Cathy at the bench, jogged back to the car where she spoke quickly to Joe.

"Oliver had been to see Lucy Elletson, a police officer, on the evening of the first of April. It all fits."

"Do you remember the spaghetti tree, dear? That was one of my favourites, lovely Cliff Mitchelmore, I think it was." Cathy spent another five minutes being chatted at before being able to make a note of Aggie's address, telephone number and, to her surprise, an e-mail address.

"Thank you Aggie, you've been really helpful. We may need to contact you again, just to ask a few more questions, if that's okay with you?"

"I shall look forward to it dear. And thank you too, I've had such a lovely chat, people don't seem to have the time nowadays do they?"

"Lucy Elletson, why didn't we clock the name?" Yvie said, it felt as though they'd missed something obvious.

"No reason why we should have done Yvie." The Chief Super and Bill had already been at the Great Eccleston house when Yvie arrived shortly before eight that morning. Bill had put mugs of tea on the kitchen table for them both and then gone off to busy himself somewhere else in the house "It's not an uncommon name, there are two other Elletsons on the force besides her. The Next of Kin information in her personnel file refers to a Gill Masterson, the woman fostered her for several years, in fact she continued to support her right up until Lucy went to university. There's no mention of Sophie Elletson, or any link to the Bithell family."

"And she's at work right now?"

"Yes, I've spoken to her Chief Inspector, I've known Dave for years, and he's going to keep an eye on her. He says she's a good officer, a bit quiet and doesn't mix particularly well. Not one for the occasional Friday night piss-up - his words, not mine."

"We still don't know for sure that she's involved, it could be coincidence."

"You don't believe that any more than I do. I've asked Dave to take a stroll through the car park and have a crafty peek at her car. You never know your luck."

"Yeah, maybe she thinks she's above suspicion." Yvie agreed, then changed the subject. "How come you and Bill were here so early?"

"We decided to stay over last night, it just seemed easier." Iron Annie raised her eyes to meet Yvie's, challenging her not to push her enquiry further. Her poker face was on the verge of being defeated by Yvie's knowing grin, when she was saved by her mobile. She snatched it up and looked away.

"Hi Dave." She listened for a short while, lips pursed and her head nodding gently. "Okay, don't do anything just yet, maybe give her a job that will keep her in the office for an hour or two. I'll let you know immediately we find anything. Thanks Dave, I owe you one." Yvie watched as her boss placed her mobile on the kitchen table.

"The bonnet of her Hyundai i30 is slightly bowed in, and there's a dent in the metal that looks like impact damage, close to the leading edge." She paused and once again met Yvie's gaze. "I think we may have just found our murder weapon, or at least one of them."

"Okay, I've got the team on standby, just out of sight of her apartment. I'm going to get over there myself. Joe's already been on to the developer and, provided she hasn't changed the locks since she moved in, they can get someone to him with a master key in twenty minutes or so."

"Good, that's better than breaking down the door and drawing a lot of attention, it would probably take just as long to get a door entry team out to them. Dave's going to keep her in the office for now so there's no immediate hurry."

"How long do you think it will take to get a warrant?"

"Do we agree that it's possible a severely injured Oliver Bithell may be in the apartment?"

"I think it's highly unlikely, but yes, I agree that it's possible." Yvie already knew what her boss was suggesting and reached for her own mobile.

"In that case I'm authorising a Section 17 entry, 'to protect life and limb'. Tell Joe they can go in as soon as the key turns up."

"If we wait for the key, wouldn't a half decent barrister be able to undermine the whole 'threat to life' aspect of the entry, which would make any findings inadmissible in court?"

"True." Iron Annie thought for a moment then beamed a smile at her colleague. "I'm going to seek the advice of our esteemed ACC. By the time he's got his head out from up his arse, and then sought half a dozen separate legal opinions before dodging the question and telling me that I should use my own judgement, the man with the key should have arrived. Just make sure Joe understands that the time they receive my authorisation to proceed, which I'm very confident he will have written down in his notebook, will be shortly after the arrival of the key."

"Got it, Boss."

It was unusual for Lucy to receive texts or e-mails at work, or at any other time, so she slipped her phone from her pocket and glanced at the screen. The cheap and cheerful burglar alarm system installed by the developer didn't have video, or even the capability to send a still photograph to her phone, but it did let her know that her alarm had been accessed, and a new override code added to her settings. She pushed her chair away from the desk where she'd been given three large filing boxes to sort through, apparently a witness statement had been mislaid and an important case hinged on it. Her sergeant was on a call so, after catching her attention, she laid a hand above her stomach and pulled a face, then headed off in the direction of the toilets. She ran down two flights of stairs and then out of the rear door, directly into the car park. Within moments she was behind the wheel of her car and accelerating towards home.

"We'll take it from here, thanks." The developer's Security Supervisor, who'd only been in the job for a few weeks, appeared disappointed that he wouldn't be contributing further to the investigation, particularly after doing such a good job on the alarm. Joe had quietly placed himself between the man and the rest of the apartment while the system was deactivated, and then ushered him out to the landing where the others were waiting. "If you can stay nearby though, we might need you to lock up again." As agreed with Yvie, and in accordance with the 'protection of life and limb' justification for entry, only Joe was going to enter the apartment. He quickly looked in each room to ensure that there was no sign of Oliver Bithell, not that anyone was really expecting him to be there, and then took the opportunity to have a good nosey round, pausing longer in the bedroom to take several photographs of the newspaper clippings, printouts, photographs and a plethora of neatly handwritten notes that covered the whole of one wall. He'd seen enough. Leaving the apartment, he instructed the still inquisitive security man to lock up but to stay around, and they all made their way back down the stairs and out onto the street.

"Do you want to check the garage while I'm here with the keys?"

"I need to make a call," Joe replied, turning to Tom and Autumn. "Do you want to go and take a quick look?" Tom nodded and the two of them followed the security man as he set off towards the garage block.

"You're on speaker Joe, the Chief Super is with me. Anything?"

"No sign of Bithell, but I'd say Elletson is definitely our prime suspect. I'll send you the photos in a minute, but her bedroom wall is covered in clippings and references to both Bithells, her mother, and the Old Vicarage case that you mentioned Ma'am. We need a warrant, and she needs picking up."

"Thanks Joe, I'll let you know as soon as we've got it, and her." Yvie ended the call and saw that her boss was already on with things.

"Hi Dave, we think it's her. Can you do the honours and put her in a holding cell, make sure she's watched," she was silent a moment, listening. "Anything, failing to report an accident will do for starters. Got to go, and thanks again." They both took a couple of moments to look at the photos Joe had sent through to Yvie's phone. It wasn't conclusive, there were no threats or ravings, but what was there clearly pointed in the direction of obsession, towards someone deeply, and very possibly dangerously, troubled.

"Dave's going to put her in holding, awaiting charge. I'll get on with the warrant, do you want to get off to the house?" After a quick trip to the bathroom, Yvie was getting her things together and was about to leave when the Chief Super's phone rang.

"What do you mean, gone?" she turned to face Yvie, shaking her head in disbelief. "Half an hour! For fuck's sake man, I thought you were keeping an eye on her." Iron Annie was silent for several moments, Yvie presumed that Dave was either explaining or apologising, or if he'd any sense, both. "Okay, I understand, get an alert out, we'll speak later."

Yvie ran to her car, knowing it would take her at least twenty minutes to get to Elletson's apartment. The Chief Super would already be ringing Joe but, if Lucy had gone straight back home she could be almost there by now, and God only knew what she might do.

Chapter Thirty-Six

Lucy had watched from her car as two men and a young woman split off from the group and walked in the direction of the garages. That had been at least ten minutes ago and they hadn't yet reappeared, but she knew they would, sooner or later. The big guy who'd been on his mobile phone most of the time was still standing on the pavement outside her block, in between calls he was chatting to a slim, younger woman with shoulder length dark hair. She recognised these two immediately, the same as every other member of the Lancashire force would have done. Detective Inspector Joe Penswick and Detective Sergeant Cathy Bell worked for Iron Annie Atkinson, and if they had already linked her to either of the Bithells, it meant that her time was very nearly up.

Looking back over recent years, Lucy realised that she'd never given any real thought to life beyond the day when she would find her mother, never considered what might actually happen afterwards. She had simply expected to be happy, to be part of a family again, to love and to be loved. It had never occurred to her, not for one second, that the outcome may be anything other than that, it couldn't be surely, but it had. The emptiness, the despair she experienced following her mother's death on Christmas Eve had never really lessened. She had only a vague, hazy memory of how she had taken the still warm body and crammed it into one of the big, wheeled suitcases that had been purchased for her move to university. Similarly, she had little recollection of dragging the heavy case down the stairs and along the footpath to the small block of garages; hardly big enough to park a car in they were almost all used as storage space or utility rooms. Her most vivid memory of that night was when she'd closed the lid on the big chest freezer. Gill had bought it for her as a flat-warming present and, up until that night, it hadn't held more than fish fingers and a few packs of frozen peas - not any more! It hadn't been until that moment, the thud of the lid as it closed, that she'd realised her own hopes and dreams of being part of a family again, of having a mother who loved her, were lost forever. Throughout January and February she had been operating on autopilot, work, eat, shower, sleep, repeat. Before she slept, and as soon as she awoke, she was mocked by the photographs of Andy Bithell taped to her bedroom wall, but she would never, could never, remove them. A part of her needed to see the face of the man responsible for the suffering that had been heaped upon her mother, the man whose evil had blighted her own life. As her sense of loss transformed into anger, her hatred of the man festered to become an all-consuming, intense loathing. It became a struggle to present a false front during the hours she was at work, away from the station she could think of little other than the justice she was desperate to receive.

Quite by chance, Lucy came across the heavy glass frame intended to have been her mother's Christmas present. As she studied the photographs of the smiling young man, looking for any sign of a family resemblance, it had occurred to her that maybe she wasn't entirely alone after all. She had a half-brother, perhaps there was still a chance to be a family. Knowing his 'real' name, and that he was a student at Cardiff University, meant that within an hour Lucy was using his social media postings to plan for their first meeting. She'd been surprisingly nervous the evening she had lured him back to her home, albeit under false pretences, and given him the bare bones of their family history. In fact, that first night she hadn't been at all sure of him and thought she may have made a mistake. However, when he returned to her the second day, she was jubilant, convinced that the stolen child would now share her hatred of the monster pretending to be his father. With the benefit of hindsight, she now realised that she'd confided in him way too soon, he hadn't been strong enough to accept the deception of his past, or to share her vision of their future. He had run from her, she couldn't risk him warning Bithell of her intentions so had no choice other than to stop him, to kill her half-brother, her last remaining hope. Every night since his death, every time she closed her eyes, she saw the shy smile on his face when she'd first introduced herself, and then the image would morph into his battered corpse as she pulled a Tesco bag over his ruined head. Even Bithell's death, just one week later, had done nothing to ease her sense of desolation, of complete and utter loss. The newspapers and television presenters had made him out to be a harmless old man, playing war games in his retirement, rather than the vile, shameless beast who had brought nothing but misery and death to her family. If Iron Annie's team thought they could bring her to justice, portray her as the wrongdoer and him as a victim, they were mistaken, she would not let that happen.

After racing across town, Yvie felt the tension leave her when she saw Joe and Cathy stood outside one of the neat apartment blocks. Having been forced to park fifty or sixty yards away, she even gave them a little wave as she got out of her car, about to set off to join them. From where she was stood, Yvie could see further round the bend in the road than either of her colleagues, their view being obscured by a huge tree. The sound of an engine being revved hard caused her to look up, just as a green Hyundai sped towards where Joe and Cathy were stood chatting, oblivious to the danger rushing towards them.

Lucy ran through the same checklist for a second time, get the speed right, seatbelt, a final check in the mirror, a last-second flick of the steering wheel, avoid the temptation to touch the brakes, and it would be over in an instant. Finally hearing the approaching vehicle, Joe and Cathy both turned just as Lucy pulled hard on the steering wheel and the car became momentarily airborne as it mounted the pavement at speed, her target directly ahead of her. Lucy closed her eyes, and for the briefest moment was transported back to her happy place, her eighth birthday, when her and Mum had their own little party, a cake with candles to be blown out and a wish to be made.

The majestic oak tree, after which the entire housing development had been named, stopped the vehicle's forward motion dead in its tracks. The forces generated at the moment of impact pivoted the car upwards, causing the roof to be crushed flat against the massive trunk and lower boughs, before falling back onto all four wheels. As Joe and Cathy ran across from the opposite side of the road, stunned by what had just taken place within a few yards of where they were stood, they could see Lucy's broken body lying half in and half out of the car. Having unfastened her seatbelt, the first action to follow her final, fateful decision, the driver's airbag had impeded her journey through the windscreen, but not fully prevented it. Without restraint, the momentum of her own body had pushed Lucy forwards, snapping her neck like a twig, a merciful instant before her head and shoulders were crushed as the roof of the vehicle was flattened against the ancient tree. Yvie arrived a few seconds later, breathless, partly from her dash down the road, and partly from the adrenaline surge she'd experienced when she'd thought Joe and Cathy were about to be mown down by the speeding car.

"Are you both okay? I thought…"

"Yeah, is it Elletson?" Cathy asked, as they both watched while Joe approached the wreckage and very cautiously checked for signs of life, even though all three of them could tell there was absolutely no chance of her surviving the impact. Yvie finished speaking to the emergency services operator before answering.

"It's her car, and the Chief Super sent me her most recent ID photo," she held up her phone so that Cathy could see the image, "I'd say there's not much doubt. Joe?" Yvie noticed that he'd removed his ancient Barbour jacket and draped it over the dead girl's head and upper body. It was the wrong thing to do, but no one would deny her the dignity offered by his act of kindness.

"It's her, I'm sure of it. What a waste, she was a bonny girl, could have had a good career ahead of her. You've got to wonder what sort of demons she had inside her head."

Alerted by the noise of the crash, Tom and Autumn had sprinted back from the garage block.

"There's more... freezer… in the garage," Tom managed between breaths. "Two bodies, I think the one on top is Oliver Bithell. I don't know about the other." All four looked over towards the garage block where they could see the security man was now sat on the grass outside the garage, his back against the wall. Even from a distance he looked ashen, shaken.

"Oh shit! He must have gone in for a look when we heard the crash and came running over here." Autumn turned away from the sorry looking spectacle. "Sorry Boss, I never gave him a thought. He lent us some tools to get a big padlock off the freezer and I told him to stay in his car. I'll go and make sure he's alright."

"No matter, it's probably better that he was over there, rather than over here. Lock up the garage and hold on to the keys, we're going to need them."

"Okay, will do."

"Oh, and ask to see his phone, we don't want any photos appearing on social media." The first of the approaching sirens could be heard in the distance, Yvie couldn't help thinking that they were too late to help Lucy Elletson, maybe years too late.

Chapter Thirty-Seven

It was early evening by the time the Forensic Investigation Team completed their work in Lucy's apartment and garage. The bodies had been removed from the old chest freezer and taken to the mortuary where they would be allowed to thaw before the post-mortem examinations could take place. Yvie was fairly certain Tom was correct in identifying one of the frozen corpses as Oliver Bithell, but the older female found lying beneath him was, as yet, not in an identifiable condition. From Cathy's report of her conversation with Aggie, Yvie remembered that the elderly lady had said, '*her mother was a funny woman, she only stayed a couple of months*', so the smart money was on it being Sophie Elletson. Within minutes of the FIT examination commencing, one of the technicians had opened the wardrobe door and immediately seen the handle of what turned out to be a long bladed sword. It was still carrying traces of dried blood and hadn't even been hidden away, just left in the only cupboard large enough to hold it. Similarly, Oliver Bithell's phone, battery and SIM were found in a kitchen drawer - whatever else Lucy may, or may not, have done, she'd made little effort to hide the evidence of her crimes. It was almost as if after each murder, if in fact that was what they all were, Lucy had simply ceased to think about it, and moved on to her next objective. The psychologists would no doubt have their own opinions, but it was unlikely they would ever know for sure. After painstakingly photographing every image, note and newspaper clipping attached to the bedroom wall, individually and as a whole, they had been removed, leaving the walls bare. Lucy's lap-top and mobile phone had been taken away for examination, along with some clothes, shoes, the sword and Oliver's mobile phone. The only remaining item of interest was still being checked over by one of John's technicians. The cardboard box, found in one of the drawers under the bed, was half full of thick A4 writing pads. Different colours and styles, every single one contained page after page of neatly handwritten notes, some items took only a line or two, others ran on for several pages, but all were dated. Yvie realised that these were Lucy's diaries, a detailed account of the events that had transformed a happy eight-year-old girl into a deeply troubled killer, and eventually led to her death by suicide. Reluctantly overriding the urge to immediately delve into the notebooks, Yvie called a halt. It had already been a long and difficult day, despite her team's insistence that they were fine to continue, everyone needed to switch off for a while. The books were sealed into tamper evident bags and taken out to the FIT van, tomorrow would come around soon enough.

Having spoken to James earlier to warn him she'd be late, and knowing Conor would already be fast asleep in bed, when Yvie parked up outside her house she took a couple of minutes to call the Chief Super about arrangements for the following day. Knowing her boss would be every bit as keen as she was to understand the motivations behind Lucy's behaviour, and any possible links to Bithell and the Old Vicarage case, Yvie told her she'd arranged to have the notebooks delivered to the Great Eccleston house where they could go through them together.

"No problem. Bill and I decided to stay over again." There was a short pause. "It saves on the mileage."

"Is that the best excuse you can come up with, lady?" Yvie laughed out loud. "It saves on the mileage."

"I don't know what you're talking about. We..."

"Yeah, you do. Just make sure he takes precautions, Ma'am!" Yvie was still chuckling to herself a few minutes later when she quietly closed the front door behind her, not wanting to disturb their son. After a quick apology and a peck on the cheek for James, she went upstairs to Conor's bedroom and stood, simply watching him sleep. Home, husband, son, followed by a quick shower and a change into an old rugby shirt and jogging bottoms, now she was ready to put the day behind her.

"Table or knee?" James asked when she walked into the kitchen.

"Well, I was thinking of having something to eat first, but..."

"Ha ha, very funny! You know exactly what I meant."

"Knee then, thank you. Shall I get the glasses out?"

"Already done, pour one for me too. The food will take about another ten minutes, I just need to get the temperature up a little and I'll be with you." Yvie settled on the settee then poured them both a large glass of Malbec.

"So how was your day?" James asked

"Not very nice. The woman we believe is responsible for the killings committed suicide by driving her car into a tree. I thought for a minute she was going to run down Joe and Cathy."

"My God, that's awful. Was it definitely her, the one who killed herself?"

"Yeah, she'd not tried to hide anything, we found one of the murder weapons in her flat." Yvie decided that there had been enough misery for one day and decided to change the subject. "And, you're not going to believe this, but I'm pretty sure Anne and Bill are getting it on."

"Whoa! That's even more disturbing than your serial killer!" The two of them were still laughing when the kitchen timer went off and James got up from the settee. "Won't be long."

"Good, I'm starved." As she sat back against the cushions, thoughts began to pop unbidden into her mind, 'Why only one murder weapon?', was quickly followed by, 'Where's the axe?', when James returned with the food she was already reaching her phone.

"Whatever you're about to do, stop," he said firmly, "eat first, we'll discuss anything you want afterwards. There's nothing you can do tonight that's going to make a difference." He handed Yvie a tray on which there was a large bowl of vegetable chilli and brown rice, and a smaller shallow bowl containing homemade salsa and guacamole.

"You're right. It's just…"

"Eat first, then talk."

A little later, after they had eaten and James had loaded up the dishwasher while Yvie tidied round, they both settled back on the settee. Over the remains of the bottle, yet another rule broken,

Yvie had voiced her concerns that Lucy may not be responsible for all the killings. Once again, in line with what had become their accepted roles, she used James as a sounding board to test her ideas and bounce her thoughts off, relying on his instinctive ability to know when to support and when to play Devil's Advocate.

"Yvie, If we set aside the stuff from twenty years ago and just think about the recent murders, what are the odds of two serial killers, operating entirely independently, targeting people who are so closely linked, and both choosing to decapitate their victims?"

"Realistically, next to no chance. But why haven't we found the axe that was used to kill Brandwood and Garmond? In fact, why bother with an axe at all when you've still got the sword that you killed Andy Bithell with?"

"There could be a million and one reasons why the axe hasn't been found, and maybe it was easier to get close to Bithell with a sword. You did say that everyone and his dog were carrying them where he was killed."

"I can't explain why, but it just doesn't feel right. As far as we can tell, Elletson didn't make any real attempt to hide anything, but whoever killed Brandwood and Garmond tried to destroy the evidence."

"Okay, I agree that's something that doesn't quite fit." James glanced at his watch. "Listen, it's getting late, can we leave it at that for tonight? You might find all the answers you need in her diaries tomorrow. And, if you don't, we'll pick up where we left off. Just promise me one thing."

"What's that?"

"Please, whatever else you do, don't put any more images of Anne and Bill into my head, especially at this time of night. I don't think I'm going to be able to sleep for hours."

Chapter Thirty-Eight

By seven-thirty the following morning, Yvie was already on her way to Great Eccleston. She'd risen early so that she could spend a little more time with Conor, careful not to dress in her work clothes until he'd finished decorating the immediate surroundings with his breakfast. James had appreciated the extra half hour in bed, something that nowadays amounted to a 'lie in', so she felt slightly less guilty about leaving them both. The Chief Super's Jaguar was, as expected, still parked at the rear of the house and she had only just closed her own car door when Joe pulled up alongside, having picked up Cathy on the way.

"Morning Boss. We've been talking about the case on the way here and…" Cathy began.

"…and it doesn't feel quite right?" Yvie hazarded a guess.

"Great minds, eh!"

"Yeah, I was thinking exactly the same thing myself. Trouble is, as James pointed out late last night, what are the chances of having two separate killers, choosing victims so closely linked, and cutting their heads off?"

"Yeah, way beyond coincidence and just this side of impossible." Cathy nodded. "But it could happen. We didn't come up with an answer for the linked victims but, what if the same MO was used simply to make it look like it was the same killer?"

"Or," Joe added, "two killers working together." A bright red Mazda turned into the parking area and lined up alongside Joe's Land Rover.

"Eh up! Love's young dream have arrived." Cathy announced as Tom and Autumn got out of his car. Before the greeting could be returned, the back door of the farmhouse opened and the Chief Super waved them in with a shout.

"Tea's up people, get a move on, we haven't got all day!"

"Hello, sounds like the Boss has had her Weetabix this morning." Cathy joked.

"No, I think it was more likely her oats!" Yvie enjoyed the look of shock on her friend's face, then set off at a brisk walk towards the door, leaving no opportunity for the inevitable interrogation. Once inside the kitchen, she was surprised to see all nine of the A4 notebooks from Lucy's house had already been delivered and were sat on the big oak table. Each one was still sealed inside an individual tamper evident bag bearing a completed exhibit label.

"Morning Ma'am, I wasn't expecting to see these just yet."

"I had them couriered over last night after having a word with John, and speaking to Angela from CPS, of course." Iron Annie explained. "There's no requirement for further forensic examination, and the evidentiary status of the diaries will be minimal unless we come across a detailed, signed and dated confession inside one of them. Apart from that, without adequate corroboration, anything that's in there is likely to be regarded as little more than hearsay. We'll maintain the chain of evidence as a matter of course, but it's probably unnecessary."

"Okay," Yvie had been thinking much the same, but was still intrigued to find out what Lucy had written over the years. "I imagine the police psychologists will be keen to get their hands on the diaries of a serial killer."

"No doubt they will, but they'll have to wait their turn. Anyway, tea is in the lounge, along with enough biscuits to keep even Joe happy, so I suggest we settle down in there and have a read."

"No Bill this morning Ma'am?"

"Yes, he's upstairs. I'm thinking of having some work done on the house, fitted wardrobes, and maybe knocking through to make an en-suite. Bill's measuring up."

"Glad to hear it Ma'am, although that may be a little bit too much information!" Yvie gave her a cheeky wink then picked up the bagged diaries and followed the others through into the lounge where Autumn was already at work updating the huge murder wall. "I suggest we take one each, do an initial read through and stick a post-it on pages containing anything of interest, and then circulate them."

Cathy took the first bag, signed the exhibit label and asked Joe to countersign it, before settling into an armchair with a mug of tea on a small table at her side. By chance, she had picked up the first of the diaries, all that was written on the front cover was 'PRIVATE'. There was no date by the first entry, which was decorated with colourful little drawings of cakes, candles and balloons. The already neat writing described how Lucy had enjoyed her eighth birthday party, her first one at home with her Mum. Page after page was covered in drawings and memories of happy times, here and there were a more lines of handwriting, usually describing something good or funny that had happened at school or with her friends, but nothing to give even the slightest indication of the dark times that were to come. Cathy was about to select another from the pile when Joe stood up and quickly left the room, diary still in his hand. Having grown to love the big man like an older brother, Cathy immediately knew when something was wrong. She waited a couple of minutes, understanding he'd need a little time to settle himself, then went to look for him outside. He was stood, as she knew he would be, staring out over the flat Fylde plain towards the western edge of the Bowland fells, the cone of Parlick and the grassy hump of Fair Snape clear on the horizon. She stood patiently by his side, waiting until he was ready to speak.

"Sorry lass, it just took me by surprise a little bit."

"No apology needed here Joe. Was it anything in particular?" Despite his size, his strength, his farming background, and even the job they did, Cathy had always thought Joe was the most sensitive, compassionate man she'd ever met.

"In the diary, she talks about everything changing after her mother had seen a photograph of Anthony. She'd always heard his name, been aware that there had been another child, but it hadn't seemed real to her until one day she came home from school and had to fend for herself. In that moment her whole life changed, no meals, no food in the house, no clean clothes, no input at all, nothing. The joy she'd experienced at being reunited with her mother was suddenly snatched away from her Cathy. She actually wrote this," he opened the diary and began to read out loud. "*Since Mum saw the picture of Anthony it's like I'm not here, she can't see me or hear me. I wish she'd never seen that picture, she wouldn't care if I was dead, all she cares about is him'*. That was dated 2009, so she would have been ten or eleven, the same age as our Penny is now." They stood for a while, neither of them really seeing the hills in the distance. "I'm all right now lass, thank you. Come on, let's go back inside."

No one questioned the temporary absence when they returned to the lounge. As police officers they'd all experienced things that had, on occasion, made them feel the need to *'take a moment'*, it was a part of the job. Settling down to read again, it was only a couple of minutes before Joe broke the silence.

"Lucy refers to the policemen who came to search the house on the day she was taken into care. There are no names, but it says here, *'the one who wasn't in uniform stank of tobacco smoke. The smell made me feel sick when he was asking questions about Mum. He was horrid, he laughed when he said Mum was going to prison and I would be better off without her. I wanted to cry but I didn't want him to see my tears. He was like the devil, and I hate him for what he said about Mum being a druggie and a bad person.'* I'm guessing that's Brandwood she was referring to."

"He's named in Bithell's book as being at the Old Vicarage," Tom agreed, "and even though it was years ago it would have been fairly easy for her to find out who was in charge of the raid on their home."

"Ten years old, poor little bugger never stood a chance!"

Little over an hour later, by which time they had each read several of the diaries, the Chief Super received a summons to attend a meeting at Hutton HQ.

"Surprise, surprise!" she said after reading the e-mail. "Despite my asking them to wait until tomorrow, they've arranged the press conference for this afternoon, in time for coverage on the tea-time news. I've been instructed to drop everything, go immediately to Hutton, and make myself available to brief the ACC. Well, if the useless bugger can't be bothered to speak to me in person, he can bloody wait. Anyone fancy another cup of tea?"

"Don't antagonise him Ma'am, you know he'll only take it out on someone else." Yvie smiled as she got up from her chair. "I'll make some tea, then I think we need to pool our thoughts before you leave. We've all read enough to be sure we haven't missed anything of significance."

As interesting as many of the entries were, particularly the blame Lucy attached to the photograph of Anthony, and her declared hatred for Brandwood, the consensus was that there were three specific sets of references that stood out above the others, the ones that resulted in death.

The first, was the years long search for her mother, which accounted for many pages across several of the diaries. Detailed descriptions of how, after eventually finding and attempting to wean her off alcohol, they had talked, often late into the night. It ended with a surprisingly short description of how Sophie had died, a fall after she had been drinking, on Christmas Eve.

The second set of references, confined to the last few months, was about her half-brother and included her hopes that she and Oliver, although sometimes she called him Anthony, would become 'a close and loving family'. The same phrase cropped up time and again throughout the diaries, so it clearly had special significance to her. In one entry she wrote about how she had passed on their mother's kind words about Gryce and Daniels to him, and the accusations about his false father's raid on the Old Vicarage. The very next day, she wrote of her realisation that she had confided in him too soon. This section culminated in another very brief, frank account of how she had no choice other than to kill her half-brother. How she had run him down with her car, simply to stop him from warning Andy Bithell.

The lengthiest, and by far the most damning, account had a single theme and had been added to on an almost daily basis. Since her mother's death, she had documented her every agonised memory of Sophie's repetitive, and often rambling, claims – stories that must have been seared into Lucy's brain. How she had lost her mother, then been forced out by her stepmother, only to be used and abused, her daughter taken from her, her baby son stolen, falsely accused and imprisoned, losing her daughter for a second time, a guardian angel murdered. The references to herself, the daughter in and out of care, had been underlined, a glimmer of recognition that she hadn't been forgotten.

Between the recollections of her mother there were occasional glimpses of her own feelings, sadness at first, then a growing determination that Bithell must be made to pay for what he had done, for the lives he had blighted, the misery he'd caused. For destroying her mother, for snatching Anthony from his true family, for stealing her childhood – HE MUST PAY.

In another entry she wrote how her mother had never believed that Anthony Daniels had jumped to his death, she knew in her heart that the kind, funny, angelic man had been murdered. How in Bithell's book of lies it stated that Daniels had been decapitated in a freak accident and, in subsequent revenge attacks only a few days later, two policemen had been beheaded by his grieving partner. Eric Gryce, her mother's other guardian angel, had been accused of the murders and hounded to his death. In a final stripping away of his dignity they had labelled him the Headhunter. Lucy had written that for there to be justice, there must be fitting retribution, it wasn't until a later entry that she detailed her preparation to deliver it.

Having researched Bithell thoroughly, and knowing he would not be an easy target, Lucy had devised a way to get close to him, one where she could, if necessary, carry a weapon in plain sight. Obtaining the sword and an appropriate uniform had been expensive, but nonetheless a simple matter of two on-line purchases made with a one-time only email address, cash on collection. Practice with the weapon had been a little more difficult given the lack of space in her apartment, but she had persevered, stabbing and hacking her way through cardboard boxes stuffed with old cushions. Finally, from the Facebook page of the Civil

War society Bithell was a member of, she learned that they would be staging the Battle of Naseby on Easter Saturday, she decided that would be the day.

Reading her matter-of-fact commitment to kill a man in cold blood, whatever his perceived sins, wasn't easy. The fact that it was written in the same neat hand that had made up poems and declared undying love for Joe McElderry after seeing him on The X Factor, made it almost unbelievable.

The final entry in the diary was Lucy's account of simply watching and waiting for her opportunity, and that had come about much more easily than she had been expecting. Seeing Bithell turn away from the mock battlefield, she had correctly guessed that he would go back to the marquee. Making sure to get there first, she was pleased to see that there was no one else inside when she arrived, not that it would have stopped her if there had been a dozen people in there. She described walking towards him when he entered the tent and raising her blade at the last moment, just as she'd practiced in the apartment. How, with a single thrust she had plunged it into his stomach, throwing all her weight behind it, and her surprise at just how deeply it penetrated, much further than her usual box of cushions. As he fell to his knees, there had been a moment of concern that she might not be able to pull the blade out again, and had to resort to putting one booted foot against his chest and then jiggling the sword until it came free. Lucy had concluded her account with another simple, factual description of how she'd hacked off Bithell's head, finding it more difficult than she'd anticipated, and then just walked away.

The cold and clinical wording of her account at odds with the ferocity of the act.

Yvie had been holding the notebook containing the final entry when they began brainstorming the key points and had quoted from it several times during the discussion. She opened it again.

"Her final words, written that same evening, were, '*It is done, the monster is dead, but I fear I have taken his place*'.

"Bloody hell!" Joe exclaimed. "That doesn't sound like hearsay to me."

"Me neither," Cathy added. "It doesn't even sound like she got any sense of relief or justice from it either. It's just.... cold, empty."

"I don't know about you lot, but her reference to 'jiggling the sword' certainly made me feel a bit queasy." Autumn shuddered. "Stuart was right about the bruise on his chest though."

"I wonder why there were no more entries, nothing about Brandwood and Garmond?" Tom queried. "You'd think that after everything else she's written, well, it's not like she's shy or anything, is it?"

"Maybe they just weren't important enough to her." Autumn replied. "Andy Bithell was the main man, and Sophie and Anthony, or Oliver, were family."

"Or maybe, it wasn't her. A few of you were saying it just didn't feel right." Tom added.

"Okay, I suppose I'd better go." Iron Annie cut through the speculation. "I'm still struggling for a clear motive, something that links the victims. Any thoughts?" It was left to Yvie to provide a response.

"Jealousy, hatred, rage, revenge, could be any of them, or all of them. But I'd also put total, abject, desolation and plain bloody misery up there."

Chapter Thirty-Nine

Iron Annie had completed her briefing with the Assistant Chief Constable and was back in Great Eccleston before any of the team had gone home for the evening. When ACC Chaperon had appeared in his best dress uniform it had been pretty clear who would be leading the televised press conference, which was absolutely fine by her. What wasn't fine was the news that she had to break to the team, something she preferred to do in person rather than by phone.

"Quite simply, they want the investigation closed down, as of right now," she held up a hand as if to ward off any anticipated protestations. "As far as they're concerned, we have our serial killer. This isn't just coming from Greg, I could have bullied him out of it," no one in the room doubted for a second that Greg Chaperon, the illustrious ACC, would have shrivelled under the angry gaze of Iron Annie Atkinson. "The Chief Constable himself is insisting that we have sufficient, irrefutable evidence that she was responsible for the deaths of her mother, and both Bithells. Additionally, from the briefing I gave on the diaries, they have also concluded that Lucy Elletson had, in her own troubled mind, a clear motive for the murders of Brandwood and Garmond. The method, decapitation, was the same as Bithell senior, and even reflected the killings of Williams and Stansfield, as per the copy of Bithell's book found in her apartment. She also had adequate opportunity." The Chief Super paused for a moment to let the unwelcome news sink in. "When you put it all together, and with no other suspects, it's quite difficult to argue with."

"Is it a political decision, do you think?" Yvie asked,

"I don't think so, not this time. There's always pressure, the Force gets a hammering from the media, particularly when they can run with a serial killer story. But with no one else in the frame, not a shred of evidence that doesn't fit, and all we've got is a missing axe and a 'feeling'… I can understand why they think it's time to take a bow and accept the applause for a job well done."

"Motive, method and opportunity, the classic combo." Joe closed the notebook he'd been using and laid it on the table in front of him. "Listening to it put like that Ma'am, I'm starting to wonder if maybe we are guilty of overthinking it."

"Yeah," Cathy agreed. "We started off by hunting the cold, calculating killer who decapitated Andy Bithell, and yet, after all she undoubtedly did, I can't help thinking of Lucy as more victim than murderer. Possibly that could have skewed my judgement a little, I don't know."

"If any of you feel strongly enough about it, tell me now and I'll go back and push harder. I can't promise it will change anything, but I'll certainly make them sit up and listen." The Chief Super noted the slight shaking of heads as she made eye contact, one at a time, with everyone around the table. "Yvie?"

"The missing axe troubles me, it really does, and the inconsistency. However, apart from that, I can't come up with anything else that would cast doubt on Lucy being responsible for

Brandwood and Garmond...." she paused and shook her head. "Maybe they're right, perhaps it is time to close it down."

Since returning to work, it had become a rare occasion for Yvie to have the pleasure of giving Conor his breakfast in the morning, and also being home in time for his bath in the evening. While James was in the kitchen getting dinner ready, she was blowing soapy bubbles for their son to pop, relishing his laughter but also increasingly aware that these days wouldn't last forever. Her son was growing, changing, almost by the day it sometimes seemed. As she watched him play, and not for the first time, she wondered how many milestones and simple pleasures she would miss out on, and for what?

"What should I do Conor?" A question that she'd never voiced before, not even with James in the early days of her pregnancy. Following completion of his book and film deal, they were financially sound, mortgage free, and she had no real need to work for a living. Although he'd never done more than hint at it, she knew James would prefer her not to work at all, and would like them to spend more time at his house in Ireland. "So, you tell me young man, why am I going to work every day and missing out on you growing up?" His happy, smiling, gurgling response as he splashed water, just because he could, didn't provide any of the answers she was looking for.

"Dinner will be ready in about thirty minutes." The shout from the bottom of the stairs was enough to break her out from the not entirely unexpected, but still quite unsettling, chain of thought.

"Okay, I'll get his Lordship dried and settled."

Twenty-five minutes later, Yvie came downstairs and went through to the kitchen where James was laying two places at the big farmhouse table. After checking Conor's gentle breathing on the baby monitor, she poured them both a glass of wine.

"Do you miss Ballycotton, James?"

"Yes, I do, but we get over there fairly regularly, it's not like it's the other side of the world. Why do you ask?"

"I didn't just mean the house; I meant the life you had there before we met. Being able to write whenever you wanted, walking the cliffs above the bay or taking a stroll along the beach, meeting a few friends in the pub, all of it really?"

"Now you've got me worried!" He turned off the heat under the large saucepan he'd been stirring and replaced the lid before turning to her. "Yes, I enjoyed doing all those things, even more so when we were able do them together. Apart from the writing, I suppose it's a bit like being on holiday when we spend time there, it's nice for a while, but it's not real life. What's the matter, tell me?"

"Nothing, honestly. I was just thinking that you gave up everything to be here, and I've never really asked you about it before, not properly. You've not been able to write since we had Conor and that was your career, something you loved."

"I don't see it like that, I really don't, and I'd do it again in a heartbeat. I met the woman I love, and now we have a beautiful child." He reached out and put his arms around her. "There is nothing else I want in the world Yvie, nothing. You and Conor are the centre of my very being, I want to spend the rest of my life with you and to watch our amazing son grow up and have his own family. I want to be wherever you are, and that will never change."

"Thank you," she looked deep into his eyes. "That was a bit of a flowery speech though. Especially the 'very centre of my being,' part, that was just plain cheesy."

"Sorry," he laughed. "I was working on the script reviews while Conor had his nap. It takes me a while to get the added drama out of my system."

"No problem, I forgive you." Yvie laughed with him, it seemed that neither of the men in her life was going to be much help with her dilemma. "Now, more importantly, what are we eating and when is it ready?"

Chapter Forty

Arnside 2002

At first, I could only hear the sirens, a short while later there were lights in the sky above the village. I watched as a police helicopter slowly made its way down the river, towards where I was sitting on the raised decking at the rear of the house. The intense shimmering brightness of its powerful searchlight, split and reflected by the waters of the rising tide, imprinted patterns behind my eyes. The noise from the aircraft's engines as it tracked slowly back and forth above the estuary was so great that I could feel the vibration running up through the timber decking and the legs of my chair. Two small inflatable boats had also joined the search, adding to the display of flashing lights and disrupting what had been, up until all the fuss started, a peaceful evening. No doubt some holidaymaker had gone missing or got themselves into difficulties chasing after a wayward dog, or failed to heed the ample warnings that are provided. I struggle to understand why people feel the need to venture into the water at all, and why they expect others to come to their rescue when they get into trouble. Well, they would be disappointed this time, because the search teams were looking in the wrong place. I had been using my binoculars to observe the birds rising as the incoming tide forced them from their feeding grounds and had watched as the man, I'm fairly certain it was a man, dragged himself from the water and then slithered and crawled his way across the mud and sand. He was making slow but steady progress until I lost sight of him when he slid into a deep channel on the near bank. I've checked occasionally, but seen no further sign of him, I assume he's drowned. I take no joy in his demise, but nor do I feel any sense of sadness, it means nothing to me. I have lived a life without the need for others, removing the opportunity for deceit and disappointment, for hurt and ingratitude, makes everything so much simpler.

Father hadn't got very many things right, in a life seemingly devoted to making others subservient to his will, but I had to give him grudging credit for this one special place. The house wasn't particularly grand or large, but it sat on a four-acre plot that sloped all the way down to the banks of the river. The decking ran almost the full width of the house and looked out over a broad, lawned expanse, with just a single flowerbed in the exact centre. But it was when you raised your eyes above the garden and looked higher, that the exceptional beauty of the setting really came to life. The estuary, which sometimes seemed to hold little more than a vast expanse of undulating sandbanks and at other times was filled by the waters rushing in from Morecambe Bay, was crowned by the majestic Cumbrian fells rising not far beyond. At night, when the skies were clear, billions of stars and distant nebulae were there to be observed, or simply marvelled at. Eric had never shared my passion for the house, I think for him it would always be the place where my father's unwanted attentions first began. He was twelve years old. We only ever discussed it once, that was when he came home from medical school after Amy had taken her own life. He was so angry, unlike I'd ever seen him before. He told me that our father had always proclaimed that if he did as he was ordered, Amy and I would be spared the same fate, the same pain and humiliation. I had always been a little in awe of my older brother, but I loved him more than life itself for that, for trying to save us in the only way he could, no matter the cost to himself. Eric thought he was protecting us but, first I, and then Amy, were fed the same lies. We all suffered in silence, and we all thought we were protecting each other. For all of his anger, I couldn't tell him that father hadn't really run away when Amy died, not then. It was seven years later when I tried to explain to him why we couldn't sell this house, when I told him that I had killed our father immediately after finding Amy's body and reading her tragically brief note. How, I had struck him over the head with a single blow from my cricket bat, and then taped a plastic bag over his head while he was unconscious, how I had watched him die. I had secretly hoped Eric would be proud of me, would understand how I had been strong beyond my years, how I had acted for the three of us. Though I was too young to legally drive a car, I had already learned how on the muddy tracks of a friend's farm, so I had taken father's keys and brought his body up here to our holiday home. I explained how I had buried him under the roses in the centre of the lawn, the same ones I am looking down on now, and had then driven back towards home in the early hours of the morning. How I had left father's car, with the keys still in the ignition, in a rough part of town and walked home. Then waited for several hours, until it was time for Amy and I to be getting ready for school, before raising the alarm. I can still recall the 999 call I made to the emergency services operator, and my tears as I said that my sister was dead, and my father was missing.

The day I eventually told Eric the truth, seven years after I had taken revenge for the three of us, was when he told me I had to leave the home I had shared with him and Anthony. I had lived there ever since Amy's funeral and I loved them both, they were my only family, the only people in the world who ever mattered to me. I had killed our father for what he'd done to us, all of us, but Edwin couldn't, or wouldn't, bring himself to understand. In some ways my brother was weak, I saw it then and knew I had to be the strong one, but he would always be my hero. I didn't argue, I simply packed my things and left the house. Anthony was in tears, but Eric was adamant, in his eyes I had crossed a line, one that there was no way back from. I never returned to his house, or to medical school where I had followed Eric's example. We didn't speak again, but my love for them both has never diminished.

When I looked back towards the channel, I could see fresh tracks rising up the bank, less than a hundred yards from where I was sitting. The helicopter and the small boats were further down river now, thinking they were searching for a corpse carried by the tide. The light was failing but there was still sufficient for me to pick him out with my binoculars, slipping and sliding on the muddy bank. As I watched, he made it as far as the firmer ground and then looked directly towards where I was sitting. My chest tightened and my breath wouldn't come, I thought my heart had stopped, it was Eric. In that moment, I knew without any doubt whatsoever why my brother was here. My brother, who had never harmed a soul in his life, a life dedicated to healing and helping others, intended to break all his vows and override his good intentions. He was here to kill me, and I knew why. For all his rage when lovely, sweet

Anthony was killed in such a horrendous manner, for all his letters to the press and his accusations, and even his empty threats, Eric would have done nothing. He would have mourned the loss of his soulmate and eventually accepted whatever whitewash Bithell and his team came up with. His weakness would allow Anthony's murderers to go unpunished, I would not. I had not. The two policemen, Williams and Stansfield, were the first ones I was able to follow from outside the police station in Blackpool. Once I knew where they lived it really was a simple matter to pick a time and place for them to die. I had decided, after dispatching the first two with such ease, that Brandwood was to be next, I wanted Bithell to fear for his life a while longer. Unfortunately, I hadn't anticipated the media frenzy that followed their deaths, or that I may be questioned by the police and stalked by tabloid reporters whose sole intention was getting their angle on the 'Headhunter' story into print. So, I had retreated back here to the house while I bided my time, doing little more than watching the river, observing the birds and the heavens.

I was transfixed as Eric straddled the low wire fence, a token barrier only, before walking up the lawn towards me. I wanted to speak, to explain why the terrible revenge I had taken on the policemen was for Anthony, and for his loss, but I couldn't form the words. I wanted him to tell me that he understood, but he remained silent. When he was no more than a few feet away from me I could see the tears streaming down his face, washing the mud from his cheeks. His whole body was trembling as he raised father's old pistol and pointed it at my heart. I couldn't move, my brother was about to kill me, and I couldn't move a muscle.

I watched his finger whiten as it tightened on the trigger and waited for the bullet to slam into my chest, but nothing happened. Eric looked down at the gun and again tried to pull the trigger, but it was merely a dead weight in his hand. The silt and sand of the estuary had found its way into the tiniest of openings, jamming the mechanism and rendering the weapon useless. In his frustration Eric drew back his arm as though to strike me, the look of intense sadness upon his face will stay with me forever. Instinctively, I swung the heavy binoculars, more in self-defence than to cause harm, but they struck him hard on the left temple. As Eric fell, I experienced a jolt of indescribable fury as my body responded to the chemicals released in my brain. I raised the binoculars and brought them down on my beloved brother's head again and again until the rage subsided. Eric's body convulsed for several moments on the timber decking, and then lay still, my big brother was dead. The brother who had suffered at my father's hand in the belief he was protecting me, the brother who had given me a home for many years. The brother who was so utterly appalled by my actions that he had taken it upon himself to stop me, was dead by my hand.

In the days that followed I made the decision to close up the house, I could no longer live here, not after what had occurred, what I had done. I arranged for a local contractor to keep the grounds tidy, the newly turned soil of the rose garden in particular, even though I doubted I would ever return.

Chapter Forty-One

"I can't believe we're going out for the evening," James said, "just like proper grown-ups!"

"I know, it feels strange doesn't it? What time is the table booked for?"

"Half past seven, but we'll need to leave soon if we're picking Joe and Val up on the way. What time are the babysitters coming?"

"Anne said they'd be here by six-thirty, so they must be running a little late."

"Are you sure they'll be okay? I mean, if we were talking armed robbers and murderers, I'm confident they'd manage just fine, but neither of them has much experience with kids do they?"

"Trust me, Anne and Bill will be absolutely fine, you've seen how they dote on him. If they're not here in the next ten minutes, I'll give her a call." Thirty minutes later and, despite repeated attempts, still not having been able to contact Anne or Bill, Yvie's mobile rang. However, instead of a delayed and apologetic Chief Super, it was Joe, wondering where they'd got to.

"Stomach's rumbling lass, you can't promise a man food and then let him down."

"Sorry Joe, Anne and Bill haven't turned up yet. I've been trying both of their phones, but they just keep on ringing until voicemail kicks in."

"Both of them, that's a bit odd. Were they still over in Great Eccleston?"

"No, she definitely said they'd been staying at her place in Catterall for the last couple of days, she's been thinking about selling up there since they started building all the new houses. They'll just be stuck in traffic somewhere, probably be here in a minute."

"....and not answering their phones, how likely is it that they both forgot them? No, this is the Chief Super we're talking about; if they were delayed by an accident or something she'd have found a way to get in touch, even if meant commandeering the police helicopter." Despite the lightness of his words, Yvie could sense the concern in Joe's voice, it was a feeling she was beginning to share. "Cathy and Gus are with our two, they're staying over tonight so it's already pyjama party time in here. Why don't me and Val nip over to Catterall, just to make sure everything is okay?"

"Tell you what, we'll do the same and meet you at her house. We'll take the Beacon Fell road, then we'll have covered both routes between here and there, just in case they've broken down somewhere or gone off the road."

"Okay lass, we'll see you there in about half an hour. I'm sure they'll be fine."

"I hope so Joe, I really do." Yvie ended the call, took off her jewellery, then changed out of what Joe would have called her 'posh frock' and back into jeans and a sweatshirt. Dressing up had been fun, for as long as it had lasted, but she had the feeling it was no longer going to be that type of evening. "James, are you okay to cancel the restaurant and look after Conor? I think something may have happened to Anne and Bill, so I'm meeting Joe at her house in Catterall."

"I'll come with you; just give me a minute and I'll ask Jenn if she'll sit in for an hour or two."

"There's no need really, I'll be fine."

"There's every need, this isn't work, this is your friend, our friend. I'm coming." It was a fraction over half an hour later when James pulled up behind Joe's Land Rover, outside the neat, detached bungalow in Catterall. Joe and Val were stood in the driveway, in front of the Chief Super's Jaguar. When she saw Joe put his phone away after making a call, Yvie feared the worst.

"Both doors were unlocked when we got here, both mobile phones were on the kitchen worktop, and there are signs of a struggle in the hallway." There was no trace of humour in the big man's voice now, this was a time when nothing less than deadly serious would do. "There are droplets of blood on the timber floor and a larger patch has been smeared on the wall around waist height." He paused for a moment, his expression grim. "I think they've been taken." Neither wanted to say the words, but both knew the only current case the Chief Super and Bill each had a direct connection with was the Bithell, Brandwood and Garmond murders. The implications were too awful to consider. "I've put a call in to FIT, John's on his way now, the rest of the team will follow asap. Uniform will be here shortly, so will Tom and Autumn." Joe completed his report and turned to where his wife was waiting with James. "I was planning to start going door to door, see if anyone saw anything, or maybe we can get a lead on a vehicle. I just need to speak to Val first." Yvie nodded her understanding, her mind racing, there was no time for a single error of judgement, they may already be too late.

"I'll take Val home while you two go and find them." James said, crossing to where Yvie was standing next to the inky blue Jaguar before giving her a hug. She could feel his hands shake ever so slightly as he leaned in and whispered into her ear. "They'll be okay. I know you've got to do this, but please, please, be careful. I love you." He kissed her on the lips, gave her shoulders a final gentle squeeze then walked over to the car and waited until Val and Joe had gone through an almost identical goodbye. As James pulled away from the kerb, the empty space was taken moments later by a dark green Mini Cooper. John jumped out of the driver's seat and walked briskly towards them, already pulling a full set of protective clothing from the grab bag in his hand. While Joe briefed the Head of FIT on what he'd seen inside the house, Yvie made her way to the kerb to meet the six uniformed police officers who had just arrived in a trio of liveried patrol vehicles. It was time to be professional and practical, the emotion would just have to wait. Fortunately, the sergeant who arrived in the lead vehicle was an experienced old hand. Once Yvie had brought him up to speed, he quickly dispatched two constables to the rear of the property, had two of the patrol cars moved to provide a fifty-yard vehicle exclusion zone to either side of the house, and then had his remaining officer begin setting up a tape perimeter. All of the officers attending knew Bill and, even if they hadn't actually met her themselves, all were aware of the legendary Iron Annie Atkinson. There was a quietly efficient urgency to their actions, this wasn't a time for the graveyard humour that was often a first line of protection for emergency services personnel. Yvie had only just rejoined Joe when a fully suited, booted and hooded John reappeared at the front door. He handed Joe a sealed evidence bag containing what looked to Yvie like a long, narrow plastic strap.

"I found that in the hallway and I've sent a picture of the blood smear to both of you." While they fished for their phones, he went back into the house.

"Cable tie or zip tie," Joe held the bag up for Yvie to see. "We use them for all sorts of jobs around the farm, ones that size are also used as disposable handcuffs."

"Yes," Yvie nodded, "on the plus side, that means whoever took them wants them alive, at least for now. What do you make of the blood smear photo?"

"I don't know, it looks like a circle, maybe?" Joe passed his mobile to Tom and Autumn who'd just reported back after canvassing the nearby houses. One lady thought she might have seen a dark blue van parked in the street when she nipped out to the shops sometime mid-afternoon, but she wasn't sure of the exact time or which house it had been outside. Apart from that, no one had seen anything, nor did they have door-cams or cctv that took in the roadway or overlooked the Chief Super's house.

"Possibly, but does it mean anything, or is it just a smear?" Tom handed the phone to Autumn.

"It's a funny shape, it doesn't look like someone has accidentally brushed against it. If you forward it to me, I've got a laptop in the car and it might show up better on a bigger screen." Handing the mobile back to Joe, she jogged back up the street to where Tom had parked his Mazda. Five minutes later, laptop in hand and wearing a thoughtful expression, she rejoined the group.

"If you were handcuffing two people with ties like that one, how would you do it, Tom?"

"I would probably get one of them to secure the other's hands behind their back, and then tell the first one to cuff themselves using one tie around each wrist and interlinking them. That would have to be hands in front though." When Yvie and Joe both nodded their agreement Autumn placed her hands behind her back, as though cuffed.

"Waist height, yes?" She didn't wait for a response. "If you had blood on your hands and backed into the wall it would just leave a single mark, but this has been dragged nearly into a circle," with her hands still behind her back she mimicked how much movement that would take. "It has to be deliberate; I don't know what it means, but one of them tried to tell us something." She opened the laptop and placed it on the bonnet of the Chief Super's car so that they could all see photograph.

"Is it a letter 'O' do you think?" Tom studied the picture. "Maybe it was going to be OC, Bithell told Garmond that he was going to expose some influential people with links to organised crime."

"The circle isn't fully closed, it looks more like a 'C' to me." Joe thought for a moment, "Chaperon, surely not the ACC?"

"No," Yvie said, "Anne was adamant that whatever else he might be, he isn't bent." They all watched as Autumn enlarged the image as far as she could without losing clarity, and then viewed it section by section. "Stop! There."

"What is it? Joe asked, "I'm not seeing it."

"Everywhere else the blood has been dragged round in a curve, but just there, is what looks like a tiny downstroke."

"Yeah," Autumn increased the magnification a fraction and a narrow line could be seen, as though someone had dragged a fingernail through wet paint. "It's not a 'C', it's a 'G', definitely."

"Gryce, it has to be," Yvie was excited, relieved they finally had something to go on and desperate to get on with the chase. "But which one, could they both be alive?"

"We only know where one of them is, so that's where we need to start." Joe was already moving towards the Land Rover.

"Wait Joe," Yvie shouted to her colleague. "Tom, I want you and Autumn to go to his house in Lytham. Get a local unit to meet you there and break the fucking door down if you have to." Yvie paused for a second. "And Tom, I want you both in vests and I want you carrying your firearm."

"Got it Boss." Tom and Autumn acknowledged the instruction, and the implications behind it, then sprinted for his car

"So what are we going to do?" Joe asked, perplexed.

"Gryce still owns a property at Arnside. Whichever brother it is, if this personal, that's where it links to Anne and Bill. How long to get there?"

"In the Land Rover, forty minutes, maybe forty-five."

"Sergeant, any of your team qualified in that?" Yvie shouted, indicating the liveried Audi A6 Avant pursuit vehicle parked by the kerb.

"Yes Ma'am, I am."

"Excellent! Fancy a trip to the seaside?" As soon as they were strapped in the back of the big car, both started making calls. Yvie's first call was to the Chief Constable, partly to update him on the situation but mostly to ask him to sort out any issues that may arise over jurisdiction. They would be right on the border between Lancashire and Cumbria, or maybe it was Westmoreland, she wasn't sure. Either way she didn't want any delays or confusion over who was in charge on the ground. Joe rang Lancaster Police Station to ask for an unmarked support unit to drive by the house on Sandside Road and report back on any sign of activity. He then put a call in to HQ for an Armed Response Vehicle to be dispatched to a position at the top of Sandside Road. Although, judging by the speed they were already travelling at, he reckoned they would probably be there long before the support unit or the cavalry arrived. After joining the motorway at Lancaster, and a brief spell heading north at 120mph, they rejoined the A6 as far as Milnthorpe.

"Bit quicker than your old Landy, mate." The sergeant, who'd said his name was Gary, grinned as they were leaving the motorway.

"Yeah," Joe grudgingly agreed, "but how many sheep can you get in it?"

The final leg of their journey, now travelling within the speed limit and without the blue lights, took them briefly west and then south along Park Road, the River Kent estuary on their right-hand side. As they drew level with Storth, Joe asked Gary to pull over just after final the turn-off towards the village.

"I'm going to take a stroll past the house, see if anything's happening."

"Not on your own you're not, and you'll stand out like a sore thumb dressed like that. Take your suit jacket off and roll up your sleeves." Yvie was already getting out of the car.

"I've got PAVA spray and an extending baton in the glove box, if it's any use to you." Gary offered.

"Cheers mate, I'll take whatever you've got." Joe pushed the baton into his trouser pocket and passed the canister of PAVA to Yvie. "When the ARV and the support unit arrive, I want you to tell them to hold position here until further contact."

"Will do. Bill's a tough old bugger and, from what I've heard, so is Iron Annie. Whoever's got them is the one with the problem." Joe knew the man was trying to be positive, for them, and appreciated the gesture. More than anything else, he hoped it was true.

"You can say that again!" Joe and Yvie stepped away from the car and walked slowly down Sandside Road, giving their eyes time to adjust to the failing light. It wasn't yet fully dark, and there was only patchy cloud, but neither wanted to miss the tiniest detail as they approached the house. There were only a few properties on the estuary side of the road, and they were well spaced out. After walking for around quarter of a mile, they saw the house number they'd been looking for fixed to a brick pillar gatepost.

"This is the one," Yvie said, "no lights on that I can see."

"If it's been empty for a long time, the services might have been isolated. He told us that he only kept it for the land, as an investment." Joe suddenly slowed down and lowered his voice as they got near to the long driveway. "Look! Tyre tracks, and they've been made today. Anything older would have been washed out by last night's rain, these are sharp, clearly defined."

"Okay, keep walking, engage me in conversation in case anyone's watching." They walked a full hundred yards past the house, talking absolute rubbish to each other, until Joe spotted a gap in the tall hedge and what appeared to be a dog walkers track leading through the trees and towards the sandy scrub that topped the banking.

"If we go through here, we can cut back along the bank and check the rear of the property." They picked their way carefully through the thin line of conifers, then turned sharp right, hoping to stay hidden against the trees as they again approached the house. The low, barbed wire fence that marked out the boundary was their first indication that they had arrived. Dropping down low before moving forward another five yards, Joe was able to scan the rear windows and the broad stretch of timber decking, looking for any sign of light or life, but finding neither. He was about to return when he caught the faintest glimmer of reflected light off to his left, away from the house. After moving a little closer still, he could just make out the shape of a vehicle, almost invisible against the wall of conifers on the far side of the garden, a shaft of moonlight caught on the windscreen had given it away. He made his way silently back to where Yvie was stood.

"There's a van parked up against the hedge across the other side," he waved in the general direction. "They're here."

"I just hope we're in time Joe."

"If I stay here and keep an eye on the van, can you make your way back up to where Gary is parked. You'll need to brief the firearms team when they arrive?"

"Okay, but no heroes!. Promise me, you won't do anything....."

"Rash, reckless, downright bloody stupid?"

"I was going to say something a little more tactful, but that about covers it, yes." There was genuine warmth in their smiles. Their relationship went way beyond friendship, it had been forged at moments like this, and worse. They were comrades in arms, a bond that could only be earned, and never broken. As Yvie turned to leave, they both heard a male voice, somewhere behind them. It was coming from lower down the bank and maybe fifty or sixty yards beyond the house. They crept slowly forwards towards the point where the coarse grass that topped the rocky bank petered out and the vast expanse of sand began, then stopped dead as they tried to take in the scene playing out before them. Joe reached for his phone.

"Gary, I want the Armed Response Unit, an ambulance and anyone else nearby, to the near bank behind the Sandside Road address. Speed not stealth!"

Chapter Forty-Two

"Can you get that Bill," Anne shouted from the kitchen. "I'm ironing."

"No problem," he called back as he left the lounge and entered the short hallway leading to the front door. "Are you expecting anything?" Swinging the door open he was faced with the barrel of a handgun pointed directly at his chest.

"Not that I know of, it's probably just…." The rest of her sentence was cut off by the slam of the front door and a voice she didn't recognise.

"Get in here now or he dies. Three… two…" Immediately in full-on professional mode, the Chief Super took a deep breath and carefully put the iron back on its stand, after briefly considering it as a weapon, before doing as she was told. Right now she needed information, who, why, and what the intruder's intentions involved. Opening the door into the hall she could see he wasn't wearing a mask, which meant he had no fear of identification, bad news.

"You," he gestured towards Bill with the gun, "face the wall and put your hands behind your back."

"Do it Bill." Anne ordered. This situation could rapidly turn from bad to worse, the least provocation the better. The intruder threw some long cable ties onto the floor behind Bill.

"Secure his hands, any tricks and he dies." Thinking rapidly as she picked up two of the plastic ties, she quickly fastened one around his left wrist and then used another around his right, threading it through the first one before pulling them both tight. The double tie would give him slightly more flexibility than a single used across both wrists, but not much.

"Now do your own, any tricks and he dies."

"It will have to be in front." She picked up two more ties then raised her hands, drawing his eyes upwards. "I can't reach behind my back." As she spoke, she slid the remaining tie up against the skirting board with the side of her foot.

"Do you know who I am?" The intruder asked.

"Should I?" Bill used the question as an opportunity to turn and face the man.

"I know who you are." Anne said coldly, looking him in the eyes, wanting to judge his reaction to her words. "You're Edwin Gryce, your brother Eric was the Headhunter. He killed three police officers."

"Oh dear! You had no idea then and you have even less idea now." What she hadn't been expecting was for him to laugh, although there was little humour in it. "Eric never harmed a soul in his life."

"Apart from killing my fiancé, putting two bullets in me, and very nearly drowning my friend here." Bill spat the words at him. "Your brother was an evil bastard; I hope he's rotting in hell." Gryce's face changed in an instant, he stepped forward and smashed the long barrel of the pistol across Bill's mouth. Blood immediately ran from his split lips and stained the floor. Another objective achieved Iron Annie noted, leave readily available evidence of violence.

"My brother was a good man who would never, could never, intentionally hurt another human being. The events at Arnside were the panicked actions of a frightened man, chased down, driven to the edge, by the two of you. The female officer was an accident, one in which he could have been killed himself. If you had left him alone none of it would ever have happened, you are the ones responsible for her death, not him."

"Dress it up however you like, your brother was a murderer." The blood was still dripping from Bill's chin as he spoke.

"No, you hounded him down and then drove an innocent man to his death, just the same as Bithell did to Anthony when he pushed him out of the window. You are all going to pay for what you did to them."

"Are you saying that it was you who killed Andy Bithell?" The Chief Super knew she was taking a risk but needed to stop Bill from saying anything else. Gryce's voice was rising and falling, one minute he was highly agitated the next moment he was icy calm, one wrong word could easily tip him over the edge.

"No, and that is my one regret. I left the country shortly after my brother's tragic death. I had no wish to hear more of the lies and accusations levelled against him by Bithell and his motley crew, or what was left of them. It was only when I read about his death that I allowed the memories to return. That was when I decided that my duty towards my brother, was… unfinished."

"Your duty? Unfinished? So it was you who killed Williams and Stansfield, not your brother?"

"Finally, you begin to understand what had to be done, why there was no other choice if Anthony was to have justice." Anne was watching Gryce closely. Although he was speaking to her and Bill, his focus wasn't fully in the here and now, his thoughts, his mind, was somewhere else. It was as if he felt compelled to explain, hoping for forgiveness, but from whom, she wondered, his dead brother? "When they killed Anthony I saw my chance of redemption. I knew there was finally something I could do for my brother, to make amends."

"What was that, Edwin? What did you need to make amends for?" Anne spoke softly, not wanting to interrupt but anxious to understand what had gone on.

"Because father is buried in the garden, that's why we couldn't sell the house." There was a long pause, Edwin was swaying, ever so slightly backwards and forwards. "Eric thought he was protecting us, that was how good a man my brother was. But father used and abused all his children, there were no favourites for him, he was a monster. I waited seven years to tell Eric what I had done, hoping he would be ready to understand. But even after everything father had done, the pain he caused, raping and impregnating our sister who then took her own life, Eric said that I was wrong. He said I had to leave, that I could no longer be a part of his life or he of mine. There was a longer pause, Anne could see the wetness of tears on his cheeks.

"So you killed Williams and Stansfield, for him. To gain justice for Anthony and make amends for killing your father?" Anne noticed that Bill was pressing himself back against the wall, rubbing his hands against the painted plaster. What neither she nor Gryce could see was that he'd been using his thumbnail to rip at a fingernail on his right hand until he could feel the blood run, now he had something to write with.

"Eric never harmed a soul, he always walked away, would never face confrontation. I needed to be strong for him, for all of us."

"I understand. You punished them because Eric wasn't able to do it for himself." Anne wasn't sure where to take this next, or how it would help them overpower him, but in this state the man was vulnerable. When he nodded, she decided to push a little more. "What about Brandwood and the journalist, Garmond? Did you punish them for Eric as well?"

"Of course, I had no choice. I knew he wouldn't forgive me, not until they had paid, I owe it to him to make them all pay." Anne didn't miss the implications of his final words, unfortunately Bill chose that moment to speak up.

"What I don't understand, is that if your brother was such a great guy, why did you let him take the blame for the first two murders? Remember them? When you hacked two coppers heads off with an axe. Or are you just as spineless as he was?"

The change in Gryce's expression and posture was instant, the faraway look gone as he snapped back into the moment. Whoever or whatever had been in his head was no longer the focus of his attention.

"Well, we'll find out soon enough, won't we." His smile was chilling. "It's time we left, I'd hate for us to miss the tide, that would never do."

"What's that supposed to mean? Bill asked.

"We are going outside and you will climb into the back of the van and lie flat on the floor. If either of you makes any attempt to escape, or attract attention, I will immediately shoot the other one." He gestured with the pistol. "This belonged to our father, it's the same one my brother armed himself with all those years ago, and I can assure you that this time it will work just fine."

The light was beginning to fade when they heard Edwin's footsteps returning. After driving for what they estimated to be around an hour, he had turned off the road and onto a short track before parking. When they were able to sit upright, a struggle as he'd cable-tied their legs once they were in the back of the van, they could just make out a tall hedge to their right, but nothing else. Before he'd left them, which was several hours earlier, Edwin had warned that if there was any noise, or any attempt to attract attention, he would silence one of them with the same axe he'd used on the others. When the rear doors of the van opened, Edwin was stood well back to avoid any potential attack. It was unnecessary as, even after he'd removed the plastic ties from their legs, both were too cramped to move quickly. His nose wrinkling at the smell of their urine soaked clothing, he gestured impatiently for them to clamber out. Looking towards the

Cumbrian fells on the far bank, Bill immediately recognised where they were, only about quarter of a mile further down the river than their last encounter with one of the Gryce brothers. The sirens they had heard some time earlier now made sense; the warnings were sounded to announce the imminent tidal bore.

"I think it's only fitting that we return to the river, where they hounded you, where they caused your death."

"We didn't…" Bill began but was quickly shushed by Anne who had again caught the faraway look on Gryce's face. He was here, but not entirely, she was pretty certain that he was talking to his dead brother. With her hands tied in front of her she was hoping for an opportunity to grab for the gun, and a distracted Gryce was preferable to an angry alert one. In the long hours in the back of the van they had agreed, first chance they got, Bill would try and barge into him and knock him off his feet, and Anne would go for the gun.

"This is the final thing I can do Eric, then they will all have paid, for you and for Anthony." Gryce stood for a moment then shook his head, as if to clear his mind. The expression on his face changed, and they could see he was back, and alert. He smiled, then pointed with the gun and, carefully keeping his distance, walked them down the stretch of lawn, over the wire fence onto the rocky bank, then down onto the sand. The tide was still out as he urged them further into the estuary, gesturing with the pistol until they were both knee deep in the water.

"That will do. I checked the times carefully; we shouldn't have long to wait." Gryce had stopped at the water's edge, maybe twenty yards away, the muddy sand sucking at his rubber boots.

"Keep moving your feet, Anne." Bill said quietly as soon as he was sure Gryce wouldn't be able to hear him. "Whatever you do, don't stay in the same place. Try to stand sideways on and brace yourself when the tide hits us, if you're lifted off your feet, float on your back and let it take you. Okay?"

"Okay," Anne replied, her thoughts going back to the last time the two of them had been in the river together. "Bill, after this…"

"Thought you'd never ask." He grinned back at her, pointing at an angle towards to the near bank. "Make your way slowly in that general direction, the estuary widens out quite a bit so the bore drops off fairly quickly."

"What are you going to do?"

"I'm going to make sure Gryce doesn't go anywhere. Try and put some distance between us, and don't forget to keep moving your feet." As Anne cautiously made her way across the uneven sand, the flow of seawater now noticeably quicker, Bill turned to face Gryce. Even in the failing light he could see the white crest of the mini tidal wave in the distance as the bore swept down the estuary towards them, already closing on the railway bridge, churning and filling the channels as the water flowed in from the bay. From where Gryce was stood, still as a statue and now ankle deep in water himself, Bill thought there was a good chance he wasn't yet aware of how soon the bore would reach them. All he could do now was hope the man, who was seemingly lost in his thoughts once more, didn't suddenly wake up to his surroundings. He'd no sooner thought it than Gryce's head snapped up, and with it the gun. He looked first at Bill then over to the Chief Super who was now a good thirty yards away, but still in range.

"You said, 'this time the gun will work', so tell me, when did it not work?" Bill shouted above the hiss of the incoming wave, desperate to draw Gryce's attention away from Anne and away from the bore. "Let me guess, Eric was really coming for you wasn't he, he was coming to stop you." From the way Gryce stiffened, Bill knew he'd just scored a direct hit.

"No," Gryce turned his head towards Bill and raised the pistol, then faltered as if suddenly realising where he was. "He just didn't understand why I…"

"Oh, I think he understood only too well." Bill jeered, a last attempt to keep Gryce's attention on him and away from the low wall of water that was nearly upon them. "You killed him, didn't you? He must have got out of the river and come after you, there's no other way you could have got hold of the pistol. You killed your own brother." He was still shouting at Gryce, provoking him, when he saw Joe and Yvie appear on the bank behind him.

"I… no… I didn't mean to, the pistol was full of sand and when I…"

"I'll bet he's buried up there somewhere. I'll dig up every inch of it if I need to, but I'll find his rotting corpse if it's the last thing I ever do." Sensing that Anne was in danger of being bowled over by the relentless pressure of the rising waters he began to wave frantically at Joe, hoping he'd understand. Needling Gryce had worked, the man's attention had remained solely on him, but his expression was now murderous. Bill saw the pistol raised and pointed directly at him, but with his hands tied behind his back he was powerless to move, it was taking his every effort just to stay on his feet. Still shouting at the top of his voice, Bill braced himself, ready for either a bullet or the full force of the tidal bore, not sure which would come first. The water was still only waist deep but, just like a mini tsunami, it kept coming, unrelenting, pushing forwards. Gryce fired two shots, both of which went wide, before seeming to realise that even though he was much nearer the bank he was also in danger from the rising tide. He tried to take a step but couldn't move his feet, the mud and sand had a hold on his boots that he was unable to break no matter how much he tried to twist and turn. Standing still had allowed his boots to sink, almost imperceptibly, ankle deep into the grabbing wet sand. Something that would often result in nothing more harmful than the embarrassing loss of a boot or shoe, took on an entirely different nature in the rapidly rising waters of the tidal bore. Edwin struggled to pull his feet from his trapped boots but only succeeded in losing his balance. Defenceless against the push of the tide he fell over backwards, bending at the knees, unable to free his feet from the vice-like grip of the sand. Arms flailing, he tried to keep his head above the rising water, but the constant pressure of the tide repeatedly forced his upper body below the surface. Each time he managed to snatch a partial breath he was immediately pushed back down as the tide flowed over him, again and again, filling his mouth and lungs with sand-heavy saltwater.

Having seen Joe go sprinting down the bank, Yvie kicked off her shoes and waded out to where Bill was somehow still managing to stay upright. The full force of the tidal bore had passed them by and, although the water was still growing deeper, it was much calmer. The tiny penknife that she kept on her keyring made short work of the cable ties on Bill's wrists and they began to make their way back to the safety of the bank.

"Did you see Anne?" Bill asked fearfully. "Was she still on her feet?"

"I think she was floating on her back, but Joe's gone after her."

"He'll never find her in this. Her hands were tied, and it must be half a mile wide with the tide full in."

"Trust me Bill, Joe will find her." Yvie prayed to a God she didn't believe in that she was right.

At that moment, Iron Annie Atkinson was rolling helplessly in the estuary and fighting a losing battle to expel what felt like gallons of seawater. She had briefly regained her footing on a sandbank before once again losing her balance and being turned over in the main flow of the river. With her arms pinioned in front of her, she was finding it almost impossible to regain a stable position floating on her back. Coughing and retching, becoming progressively weaker and taking in more water than air, she was still hopeful that Bill may have survived, even if she didn't. The choking sting of salt and sand in her nose and throat was becoming unbearable as she again rolled and slipped beneath the surface. Unable to right herself, or to hold the meagre breath she'd managed, she was slammed hard against a tree trunk. Even as the last of the air was forced from her body by the collision, a part of her brain was wondering what a tree was doing in the middle of the estuary, until the tree raised two powerful arms and hoisted her clear of the water.

"I've got you, lass. You're safe now." Joe stood like a colossus rising from the deep, the waters churning around his waist no more than a minor inconvenience. He gently placed his friend over one broad shoulder to help drain the water from her lungs, before striding out for the shore.

Chapter Forty-Three

In the few minutes it took for the firearms team to arrive at Gryce's house, and then make their way over the long lawn, Yvie and Bill had waded to the bank. Holding up her badge and explaining the situation to the team leader, two of the officers had immediately handed their weapons to a colleague and then set off at a run, in the same direction as Joe had not long before. One of their own was at risk, maybe two of their own. Bill recovered quickly from his spell in the river and was insisting that he should go and join the search for the Chief Super and Joe. He'd barely gone a dozen steps when, with the last of the sun's rays reflecting off the newly replenished estuary behind them, the unmistakeable figure of the big detective inspector appeared, flanked by the two firearms officers. Yvie saw the tears of relief on Bill's cheeks, and shed a few of her own when the hoarse, but nonetheless unmistakeable, voice of Iron Annie Atkinson cut through the magic of the moment.

"I'm telling you Joe Penswick, if you don't put me down right this minute, there'll be trouble!"

"Yes Ma'am."

"Never mind, 'Yes Ma'am', just do as you're bloody-well told and put me down!"

"Give the man a chance, love." Bill steadied her as Joe carefully lowered her from his shoulder. Putting an arm around her, he suddenly found he had no more words, his throat was tight and, for once, he couldn't speak. Instead, he grasped Joe's forearm with his left hand, the nod of gratitude, the smile through the tears, said it all.

With the sound of multiple sirens gradually increasing in volume, it was unlikely to be long before officers from the Cumbria Constabulary arrived to take control of the scene. In the meantime, two of the firearms team remained posted on the rocky bank, at a point in line with where it was expected Edwin Gryce would reappear, once the tide had receded sufficiently. As everyone made their way back onto the lawn at the rear of the house, they were met by two Community First Responders who had arrived shortly after the Armed Response Unit but had been held back pending confirmation that it was safe for them to proceed. Whilst CFR volunteers often played a vital role in emergency situations, on this particular occasion, with one casualty currently underwater and the other, as Joe put it, 'not ailing, but as mad as a bag of wasps', there was little for them to do.

Having given brief statements to the newly arrived officers, Yvie and Joe were provided with some towels and dry clothes before being taken home by Gary, at a far more sedate pace than their journey north. Bill had chosen to accompany the Chief Super to hospital where, much against her wishes, she was to be kept in overnight as a precaution after ingesting so much sand and seawater.

Eventually arriving home, Yvie had kept James up until late into the night, knowing that she needed his help to process what had happened before there would be any chance of sleep. Apart from anything else, it was becoming difficult to keep up with who had done what, and to whom. The following morning, she had spent an extra couple of hours with Conor and James which, as nice as it had been, had done little to help with her, 'Do I stay, or do I go?' decision, something that was troubling her more than she'd realised while focussed on the investigation. After breakfast, she received a call from the Senior Investigating Officer now assigned to the case. It was a courtesy call to confirm that the cadaver dogs had been in at first light and three bodies had been found buried under the rose bed at Gryce's house. At this stage they were presumed to be Eric Gryce, his father Victor Gryce and a female presumed to be Annabelle Gryce, his mother.

Her next call, one that she'd been expecting, had been from ACC Gregory Chaperon. Despite daily progress updates from the Chief Super, and no doubt having had access to all of the accounts and statements from the previous evening, it was a 'request' to brief the Chief Constable on the events at Arnside, and the associated Gryce family murders. Although it was still early days, and many details had yet to be confirmed, the two cases combined appeared to reach a scarcely believable body count. While there may never be sufficient evidence to be absolutely certain, Yvie was fairly sure they were looking at somewhere between eight and eleven wrongful deaths. Added to that were the two suicides and possibly two or three accidental deaths, or some such combination of misery and misfortune. The death toll arising from the two cases stretched back nearly thirty years if, as they strongly suspected, Annabelle Gryce had been murdered by her husband. The ACC was beside himself at the prospect of such a monumental success story for the Lancashire force, entirely missing the point that all but three of the deaths arose from the actions of ex DCI Andy Bithell, a bent copper. Yvie decided that before briefing anyone she first needed to run through the details one more time, just to get her own thoughts in order. One of Autumn's presentations would have helped but, in her absence, James, as ever, gave it his best shot.

"If I understand it correctly," he began. "The first person to die, and we believe she was murdered by her husband Victor Gryce, was Annabelle Gryce."

"Yes," Yvie agreed and, judging by the gummy smile he gave her as she bounced him on her knee, so did Conor. "She didn't leave her children after all, I'd say it's odds on that he killed her, but we'll probably never know for sure."

"Seven years later, Amy Gryce took her own life after becoming pregnant by their father, the aforesaid Victor Gryce. Her twin brother Edwin then murdered him, took his body up to their holiday home near Arnside, then buried him in the same garden as the mother."

"Yes, the burial site is a bit of a coincidence, which I'm not entirely comfortable with," Yvie agreed, "but Anne and Bill both heard him confess to his father's murder."

"Next death was Anthony Daniels, but again, we'll never know for sure if he jumped, as Bithell claimed, or if he was pushed."

"Okay." Yvie was quickly making more notes as James summarised what was rapidly becoming a catalogue of horror.

"Williams and Stansfield were both beheaded by Edwin Gryce, not Eric Gryce as previously believed."

"Yeah, he confessed to both of them as well, told Anne that he killed them to make amends to his brother, whatever that may mean."

"Do we accept that the death of Bill's fiancé, Julie, was an accident?"

"I think we have to, but it occurred in the line of duty and is certainly connected to the case. Eric Gryce was trying to evade capture, a direct result of Bithell's actions."

"Okay. Eric Gryce was next, and we're fairly sure he was killed by Edwin.

"I believe it's likely that he went to the house, armed with their father's pistol, with the sole intention of stopping his brother." Yvie shook her head, sadly. "It almost makes me wish we hadn't got in the way."

"Okay, after Eric Gryce's death, we jump forward twenty odd years, which means that Sophie Elletson was next. Possibly an accident, but with her body being placed in a freezer…?" James queried.

"I know? In her diary, Lucy confessed to murdering both of the Bithells, would she lie about her mother's death?"

"Oliver Bithell, although she called him Anthony, was intentionally run down and killed by Lucy Elletson. Then, one week later on Easter Saturday, she murdered Andy Bithell at the re-enactment."

"God, this is getting complicated." Yvie complained. "He was possibly the most significant victim, given what he was responsible for."

"Next, we have Brandwood and Garmond, they were both beheaded by Edwin Gryce."

"Okay," Yvie was still putting names into different columns and adding her own shorthand symbols.

"Lucy Elletson took her own life and," James sighed deeply, "finally, we have Edwin Gryce who died in the river." They were both silent for a few moments, even Conor sat still, content to play with the buttons on Yvie's old rugby shirt. "It's like a Shakespearian tragedy, bodies everywhere, and we're sat here discussing it as though it was something we'd watched on TV. All those lives lost, all that misery. I have to be honest Yvie, I'm struggling with this. I know it's what you do, but this is too awful for words."

"It is, you're right. Victor Gryce, we believe, killed his wife and abused all three of his children over several years. He was the reason his fifteen-year-old daughter took her own life, and he caused untold mental trauma to his sons." Yvie again shook her head sadly. "Bithell took the child from the Old Vicarage, simply because his wife was desperate for a baby. That one action has led directly, or indirectly to at least eleven deaths, twelve including Edwin Gryce."

"So, who is the bigger monster?" James asked. Yvie didn't reply, she didn't have an answer, she just closed her notebook.

What she needed right now was some time with her son and the man she loved, the dead would have to wait.

Having insisted that Joe take the day off, she knew that saving Anne had taken more out of him than he'd ever admit, and with Anne and Bill still at the hospital, Yvie travelled to Hutton by herself to take the briefing. Tom had offered to join her, more for moral support than anything else, but she decided he was best placed with Cathy and Autumn who were tackling the mountain of paperwork generated by the multiple wrongful deaths. The drive gave her some much needed time to focus on herself for once, she'd allowed herself to drift in the past and was determined never to make that same mistake again. On arrival at HQ she was ushered straight through to the Chief Constable's office, but her heart sank when she saw that he, and the ACC, were sat the small conference table with the Head of Media and Engagement, and Fran, the Senior Press Officer.

"Yvie, thank you for coming in so promptly." The smile, the greeting, and in particular the use of her first name by the ACC, something he'd never done before, immediately made her wary. "Particularly after your adventures yesterday evening. I believe you already know Phil and Fran." He waved towards the media team who managed to drag their attention away from Fran's laptop for about half a millisecond. She accepted a coffee from the ACC, yet another first, and then took a seat at the table.

"Well done Yvie, an excellent result by you and the team." The Chief Constable began. "In fact, numerous excellent results by all accounts."

"Thank you, sir. Chief Superintendent Atkinson, and Sergeant Bill Thomlinson, also deserve recognition for their contribution to the entire investigation, sir."

"Indeed so. I understand that Anne will be released from hospital later today?"

"Yes sir, I spoke to her earlier this morning."

"Excellent news," the ACC chipped in, wanting to move things on. "Now, we've been working on a rough draught of the media release and, ideally, we'd like to have it finalised in time for the one o'clock news." He slipped a slim tablet in front of Yvie while the media team looked on. "First impressions?" Fortunately, as she read through the 'draft' media release, Yvie was able to hold back her first impressions, and her second ones as well, although it wasn't easy. In front of her was a sensational success story, how a major operation had come together to solve a host of murders past and present. It was a complete and utter whitewash without so much as a passing nod in the direction of the underlying truth, or any reference to the investigation having been closed down prematurely. What was being proposed was a glossy account of how a case from ex DCI Andy Bithell's past, one where he and his deeply committed team had selflessly taken on a deranged killer from an abusive and murderous family, had come back to haunt them years later. How his son, other officers involved in the investigation, and even a journalist, had all been targeted and brutally slain. No mention of the child he stole, the lives he ruined, the misery he caused. No mention of the failures to support a deeply damaged Lucy, or the injustices heaped upon her mother. Not even a mention of the entirely blameless victims of domestic abuse, suicide and suspected murder, Amy and Annabelle Gryce. Before her was a fairy tale where good eventually prevailed over evil. Didn't we do well! Never mind the details, never mind the human cost and consequences. Yvie was utterly appalled.

"I notice you're not in your dress uniform DCI Gray." If the smugly smiling ACC had been able to read her thoughts Yvie would have been sacked on the spot and escorted from the building.

"No sir, it didn't occur to me that I would need to be." Yvie lied, still seething at the words on the screen.

"Never mind, I'll do the media briefings myself. What time will the film crew be here Phil?"

"Eleven-thirty, sir, as you requested. They're bringing your usual hair and make-up assistant."

"Your thoughts on the media release DCI Gray?" The Chief Constable asked, watching her closely while the others were seemingly taking it as a done deal. Yvie had the distinct impression that he was no more impressed by it than she was. The man had come up the hard way, he'd been a copper himself, long before the role of politician was forced upon him.

"It's fine sir," Yvie looked at the faces around the table, this was a game she no longer had any stomach for, "just fine."

Epilogue

The team debrief, the one that really mattered, was held over until 10:00am the following morning. With the Chief Super out of hospital and, at least according to her, fully recovered, she'd asked them to meet up at the Great Eccleston house. With mugs of tea all round, and a huge lemon drizzle cake Val had sent over with Joe, it was finally time to put the case to bed. Autumn had prepared one of her presentations which, along with contributions from everyone involved, made the whole sorry affair significantly easier to understand, at least in terms of the who, the what, and the when. Many of the 'whys' were likely to remain topics to be argued over by the psychologists.

"I'm still struggling to identify all the victims here." Cathy said when Autumn shut down the presentation.

"Yeah, I know what you mean." Tom added. "Even Eric Gryce was framed for a crime he didn't commit, is he just as much a victim?"

"Maybe, but he was still directly responsible for Julie's death, accident or not." Bill added. "I'll never forgive that."

"No, you're right. I'm sorry mate." Tom apologised.

Joe's concerns at possibly missing lunch were allayed when Iron Annie announced that fish and chips, with mushy peas, curry sauce and a selection of pies and pickles, would be arriving shortly, by way of a thank you for pulling her out of the river.

"You didn't need to do that, lass," he seemed genuinely touched. "You didn't forget to ask for vinegar, did you?"

"You still haven't told us how you managed to find her, Joe." Bill said. "She could have been anywhere in the estuary, and it was going dark?"

"When we were kids, me and our Martin used to spend our summers racing inner tubes, home-made rafts, anything that would float, down the river there. I knew exactly where she'd wash up." Joe smiled at the memory of some of the terrifying things he and his brother had got up to.

"Less of the washed up, if you don't mind Joe Penswick!" Iron Annie laughed. "That's twice I've been pulled out of that bloody river, I'm never going near it again."

"Sorry Ma'am." Joe turned to Bill. "I meant to say, that was clever, keeping Gryce standing in one place like that. Anyone who's spent any time around the estuary should have known about the sinking sand."

"Aye, he should have done, but I'm glad he didn't. Anyway, at least he died with his boots on." Bill said grimly, the touch of black humour indicating he was back to his usual self. "Actually Joe, Anne and I have got a proper gift for you, it's a thank you from the pair of us for..., well, you know what for."

"Oh come on, that really wasn't necessary," Joe began, but was cut short by Iron Annie as she passed him a large, flat cardboard box.

"Maybe it wasn't necessary for you Joe, but it was for me and Bill. Especially when Yvie told us what you'd done with your old one." They all watched as Joe removed a brand-new Barbour waxed jacket from its packaging and then, rather stiffly, put it on.

"Thank you, Ma'am, Bill." The big man paused, clearly touched by the gesture. "It's a good fit, give it another twenty years or so and it'll feel just about right!"

With work completed for the day, the fish and chips now no more than a sharp tang of vinegar in the air, the team were settled with fresh mugs of tea and chatting about anything and everything, so long as it didn't include murder and death. Yvie took in the room, the people around her, friends who had become more like family than workmates. Certainly the bonds were much stronger than she could ever have imagined possible when she moved up to Lancashire. She thought of James and Conor, new love, new life, new family, and new decisions. Shaking her head, she stood up and reached for her jacket.

"Come on you lot, get yourselves off home. I think we all deserve an early finish for once." Yvie announced, and immediately received a chorus of hearty cheers.

"Oh Yvie," the Chief Super beckoned to her as the others were saying their goodbyes, "this will keep until next week, but I've been asked to take a look at what may be a rather strange double murder. Do you want to stop by my office on Monday morning, see what you think?"

"About that Ma'am, we need to talk."

ACKNOWLEDGEMENTS

Firstly, my thanks to you the reader for taking a chance on the unknown. It really is appreciated, especially by those of us who are non-minted, non-celebrity authors without the backing of a publisher or a huge advertising budget.

I sincerely hope that you enjoyed the book and, if you did, please tell your friends or, better still, leave a rating and/or a review – it makes a huge difference.

Special thanks to my beautiful wife Yvonne, without whose ongoing encouragement and support I'd still be dithering over my first book.

Also, thank you once again to my daughter Sarah for spotting all the typos and errors that I was convinced I'd already got rid of. Any that remain are ones that I thought I knew best about!

Thank You All,

JD Benn

Printed in Great Britain
by Amazon